THE TREASURE

OF THE

VISIGOTHS

Volume 3, The Languedoc Trilogy

AMR (Adventure, Mystery, Romance) Series No 9

Michael Hillier

The right of Michael Hillier to be identified as the Author of this Work has been asserted by him in accordance with the Copyright, Designs and Patents Act 1998.

To my late wife Sue.

Inspiration, researcher, critic, editor and best friend

Author's Introductory Note

For those to whom Visigoth is just a name, I provide the following brief history of the race as far as it is known :-

Until the late fourth century the Visigoths were one of a number of migrant Arian tribes in Central Europe. However, when they were united under their elected new king, Alaric I, they soon became a force to be reckoned with. In fact, in the next few years they invaded Northern Italy, Southern Gaul (the name of Roman France) and a part of the Balkans – all areas abandoned by the Roman legions as the Empire fell apart. In 410AD they reached Rome itself and, after a long siege, sacked the city and carried off the wealth stored there. This included the Jewish state treasure which the Romans had brought back after they destroyed the Temple in Jerusalem.

The Visigoths then continued their progress westwards into Southern Gaul and ultimately to Spain. In about 414AD it is believed they settled one of their headquarters in the city of Rhedae in the Languedoc on the northern side of the Pyrenees, near to the Mediterranean. The town had been founded by the Romans, but was quite small until the Visigoths settled the area. The site was easily defended, being the highest point on a rough sloping plateau, whose steep surrounding hillsides dropped down to the rivers of the Aude and the Sals. It is recorded that, in the following decades, the population expanded to nearly 20,000 inhabitants who lived in and around the new walled city, making it almost certainly the largest urban area in France at that time. They fortified the highest part of the mountain in a similar way to the Old City at nearby Carcassonne and it is likely that they kept their most valuable possessions inside the stone walls. The modern village of Rennes-le-Chateau occupies what was once the ancient fortress of Rhedae.

Meanwhile, the Franks were gradually taking over most of the rest of Gaul and the Low Countries. In 508AD their king, Clovis I, captured Toulouse and laid siege to Carcassonne, although Rhedae, only about 20 miles to the south, appears not to have been attacked at that time. The Visigoths gradually extended their occupation south into Spain. They established a new capital in Toledo in 567AD. The uneasy truce between the Visigoths and the Franks in Southern Gaul appeared to hold until 711AD, when the Muslim invasion of Southern Europe began. This spread rapidly across Spain and into France, taking over the areas previously controlled by the Visigoths, who ceased to exist as a separate nation.

The Moors were finally halted by Charles Martel at Poitiers in 732AD and retreated into Spain where they remained for more than seven centuries. In 800AD, Charlemagne, the great king of the Franks was elected Holy Roman Emperor. In 1067AD Rhedae was sold to the newly formed state of Barcelona, and the town gradually decayed. It was later sacked by warrior bands and was reduced to the few buildings one sees today. That was before the domain was created by the priest, Bérenger Saunière, who found a local source of great wealth in the 1880´s. It is the hidden secret of where those riches came from, which has fascinated historians and travellers ever since.

The main characters in this novel are the same as in the two previous books in the Languedoc Trilogy – **The Secret of the Cathars** and **The Legacy of the Templars**. Philip Sinclair is the English descendant of one of the Cathar *parfaits* who escaped from the mountain stronghold of Montségur in 1244AD just before the Cathars were wiped out. His fiancée, archaeologist Jaqueline Blontard, is heavily involved in the preparation of her new series about the Cathars. Jeanette Picard, the voluptuous Paris *poule* thinks this gives her the opportunity to entice Philip away from her. Armand Séjour is now employed by Jackie to help with her excavations at le Bézu and Jean Luc Lerenard is still recovering in hospital from his near-death experiences. Candice Ambré is about to take on the work that she has been trained for. The atmosphere is tense.

1

Paris was sweltering under a blanket of early summer heat when Philip Sinclair arrived. He hadn't seen his fiancée, Jacqueline Blontard, the darling archaeologist of the French television screens, for three weeks, since she rushed off to the studios of TV France to start on the writing and filming of her new series *The Destruction of the Cathars.* The series was due to go out in the autumn, and work on its preparation had been delayed nearly for two months, as a result of the adventures she and Philip had been involved in, around the ruined fortress of le Bézu and in the village of Rennes-le-Chateau. This was exacerbated by the programmes being delayed by the *Vendredi Treize* organisation. Now she was working sixteen hours a day, seven days a week to try and make up the lost time.

Jackie had rung him on Thursday evening. "I'm sorry, darling, there's no way I can get back to Rennes this weekend. There's too much to do up here."

"That's the third weekend in a row you've promised to spend a couple of days with me, and then you've cried off," he complained. "I'll soon forget what you look like."

"Well, you could always come to Paris to see *me*. You ought to be able to spare the time."

"Jackie, you know I don't like Paris in the summer. It's too hot and dusty." He thought about it for a moment. "In any case, would I even be able to find you when I got there?"

"I've told you I'm at the Saint Michel in Rue Gambrienne. It's just round the corner from the studios and you know how to get *there*."

"All right, I'll think about it. It seems as though it's the only way I'll ever get to see you. And it's important, Jackie, we've got a lot we need to talk about. After all, we *were* planning to get married in the near future."

"We never set any dates, Philip." She sounded a bit cross. "I can't even talk about that until October. I hope the series will all be in the can by then."

He sighed. "OK. I suppose I´m going to have to wait for that. But will you be able to spare some time when the series is finished? Or will you be rushing of to cope with all the other demands on your time – cataloguing the Templar treasure, translating their accounting records, sorting out this secret organisation which has made you their president, all the other things."

"I know. There´s so much to do. I don´t know when I´ll have a minute to call my own." She took a breath. "In fact, I must rush off now. I see the director´s beckoning me. He obviously wants to do another re-take. Goodbye darling."

"Goodbye." He sighed and switched off.

Philip had a sleepless night. Jackie´s comments had set him thinking. Of course, she was right. Since she was so busy, he decided *he* would have to go to Paris to see *her* - and he would do it straight away. When he thought about it, he knew he could easily leave the builders on their own for a few days to continue the restoration work on the house across the yard from the chateau, which he and Jackie had purchased as their home while they were restoring the chateau. So, as early as he felt he decently could, he rang the hotel Saint Michel and left a message for Jackie telling her to expect him that evening.

As soon as the men arrived, he gave the foreman, Albert, his instructions in his slowly improving French.

"You and Gaston can continue with forming these new window openings looking out onto the yard. When do you think you will finish that?"

"Oh monsieur, not until the end of next week."

"OK. I will be back well before then. We can decide on the next priority when I return. I´ll delay getting the carpentry and the frames till after that."

Two hours later he was on his way.

Arriving in Paris in the early evening, he was able to park in the basement of the hotel. He couldn´t help thinking that the charge they made for it was extortionate. It was taking him some time to adjust to the fact that he was now a rich man, and didn´t need to worry about little matters like that. He carried his bag up to reception. The place was very busy, so he leaned across the counter and called to the young man trying to deal with the crowd.

"*Chambre cinq cents treize, s'il vous plaît.*"

The receptionist broke off without question, to take the card out of its slot and hand it to him, before he returned to dealing with the latest group of young Japanese women who were booking in.

"*Merci.*"

Philip went up to the fifth floor and along the corridor until he found room 513. He didn't have any expectation that Jackie would be there waiting to greet him. She might not even have got his message yet. He grinned to himself, as he thought about the surprise she would get when she came in. He dropped the card into the slot, pressed down on the handle, and went into the room.

The curtains were closed, which was a surprise, because it was a sunny day outside. Philip crossed to the window and pulled them back. He turned to look round the bedroom. It was a large room with a big double bed against the side wall. The bed was disarranged and there was a sort of heap in the middle.

Then the heap sat up and said, "Is that you, Jackie?"

"Who the hell are you?"

The man stretched and blinked. "I might ask you the same question."

"This is the room of Mademoiselle Blontard. What the hell are you doing in her bed?"

"Oh. Are you this guy Philip, who she's taken up with?"

"If you mean, am I Jackie's fiancé from the Languedoc? Yes, I am." Philip tried to control his fury. "And now can you tell *me* exactly who you are and how you came to be sleeping in this room?"

"Yes, well." The man swivelled out of the sheet which covered him and lowered his feet to the floor. He was dressed only in a T-shirt and underpants. "It's not what you might think. I'm one of the engineers on the set. I was working all last night and most of this morning to get the equipment ready for today's recording session, and I was knackered. They've said they want me to do the same thing tonight, so Jackie said I could use her bed instead of going to my home, which is the other side of Paris. This hotel is just round the corner from the studios."

The man sounded genuine, but Philip wasn't going to let him get back into bed now. "OK. You've had your rest. You'd better get on your way."

"Yes. Yes, of course." He picked up his trousers which had been lying on the floor beside the bed and pulled them on. His jacket was hanging behind the door. Philip watched him in silence.

The man indicated the bathroom door. "Mind if I pee and wash my face?"

"Go ahead."

When he came out of the bathroom, he made straight for the door. As he went out, he turned back and asked, "Shall I tell Jackie you've arrived?"

"Yes."

As the door shut, Philip lifted the bedside phone and asked for the maid to come and change the bed.

2

Jackie didn't turn up until nearly ten o'clock that evening. By the time she arrived, Philip had taken a brief sleep himself and followed that with something to eat in the hotel bar, along with a couple of glasses of *vin rouge*. He returned to the bedroom and turned on the television, struggling to understand the rapid French which was being spoken by the characters in the drama.

When she came into the room, she dropped her bag just inside the door. "*Mon dieu.* I am absolutely exhausted."

He jumped up and went over and took her in his arms. "Jackie, it's good to see you."

She allowed him to kiss her, before she disengaged herself. "I'm desperate to go to the toilet."

"Of course. Would you like me to order some food, or shall we go out?"

"No. I've had something to eat on the set. They've arranged caterers to be there permanently to save time."

She disappeared into the bathroom and shut the door behind her, leaving Philip wondering about her attitude. She hadn't seemed exactly pleased to see him. She hadn't hugged him back or responded to his kiss in the way she would have done a few weeks ago.

When she came out, she said, "Well, it's a surprise seeing you here. I gather you frightened poor Charles half to death,"

"It was you who suggested I came to Paris." He tried to smile engagingly. "So I thought – why not?"

"But I hadn't expected you to take up my invitation quite so soon." She smiled at last. "You're looking well, Philip. Working out in the sun seems to do you good."

Her comment made him look at *her* more carefully for the first time. Jackie certainly didn't look at her best. Her face was pale, and her lovely eyes were dim. Her hair was unbrushed. She was wearing a shapeless sweater, jeans and flat shoes. Even when she had been excavating at le Bézu, she had always looked tidy and very feminine.

"It's the first time I've seen you without any make-up on in the day-time."

"Oh, I've been caked with the stuff all afternoon to make me look glamorous under the cameras, all the way down to my cleavage."

"Do you have to wear revealing clothing while you're on the set?"

"Of course. This is France, Philip. They expect their women to look sexy when they're on TV."

He smiled at her. "I'd like to see some of the filming while I'm here. Do you mind me watching while you perform?"

"I'll see if I can get you a pass." She put her head on one side. "I warn you though, they may not let you in. They're very strict about admitting the public. They're always afraid somebody may talk to the newspapers about what we're doing."

"Why? Is it secret?"

"They want to control the advance publicity, to maximise interest just before the series begins in the autumn."

"Oh, I understand that," he agreed. "Of course, you can rely on me not to say anything."

"They'll probably insist you sign a declaration to that effect, before they'll let you in." She sighed. "We'll see."

"It'll be a change for me from the rustic life I've been leading recently."

"How is the work going on the house?"

"Well, it's early days, but we're making progress."

He told her of the details of the improvements he was making to the old building across the yard from the chateau, where they were going to live while the renovation of the castle building itself was in progress. The big project hadn't started yet and would take several years. However, he hoped to have the house habitable by the autumn. It was necessary to do this building first, because the negotiations with *Vendredi Treize* and the historic buildings authorities were going to take a long time before work could be started on the chateau.

Jackie was now the new president of *Vendredi Treize,* the owners of the castle since the extinction of the *Hautpoul de Blanchefort* family in the French Revolution. Having discovered what they believed to be part of the archives of the Order of the Knights Templar in the basement of the chateau, she and Philip were in the process of buying the place as their future home, together with its contents. They had paid a deposit to secure their ownership. But, of course, being a building which formed part of the French national heritage, obtaining the necessary consents to carry out the restoration of the building was a long and complicated affair.

"I'm worried about those Templar documents," she said. "They are terribly exposed where they are."

"But Jackie, they've been there for centuries. Surely another year or two won't matter so much."

"It's not the atmospheric conditions they are in. I agree those are dry and well ventilated. I don't think there is a danger of their quality deteriorating." She shook her head. "No. I'm more worried about their security. If word gets out about what we found, all sorts of people will be interested. That will make their value climb astronomically. And they are hidden in a half-ruined old building which a clever criminal could easily get into."

"Do you want us to move them? I presume your friends at *Vendredi Treize* could find somewhere secure to put them."

"Yes, but if we do move them, it must be done properly. We need a person skilled in handling old documents to check through them and catalogue them so that they can be accessed correctly in the future."

Philip smiled apologetically. "I don't think I'm the right person to do that sort of thing."

"Certainly not," she agreed. "You haven't had any suitable training. No, it's something I must think very carefully about. I need to talk to the right people. The trouble is, I just haven't had the time recently to do that." She took a breath, "Meanwhile, Philip, can you see that the chateau is locked up tight and make sure nobody is allowed to look round the place?"

"OK. I'll keep it permanently locked when I get back." He moved close to her. "Now, can we forget about that for a while, and have a chat about *us*? We haven't done that for a long time."

"Oh, I don't think so, Philip. I feel so tired, I don't know that I'd say the right things at the moment. All I want to do is go to bed."

"Well," he said cheerfully, "you know I've never objected to that."

"But no sex tonight, please. I really don't feel up to it."

So, when they climbed into bed, she turned her back on him. He cuddled her from behind, but she didn't respond. For half an hour she was restless, until he moved away from her. Then she seemed to fall into a deep, impenetrable sleep. Possibly as a result of his short sleep earlier in the evening, Philip found it difficult to drop off. He lay awake for hours, turning over in his mind the way in which the deep love affair, which they had enjoyed through the spring, had now seemed to fade. Was this the way their married life would work out – short sessions of intense loving time together, followed by long periods when they didn't see much of each other and shared little affection?

If so, would this sort of life to be satisfactory to him? He couldn't help feeling that Jackie's career and the fascinating archaeological explorations she carried out, were going to prove to be more important to her than her family life. That meant he would be sidelined most of the time. If he was occasionally admitted to the professional side of her life on some occasions, he would probably be an embarrassment to her – something to be explained away and left out of future discussions.

Then what about children? He still liked the idea of having a family – something denied him in his earlier marriage to Madeline. Would Jackie be willing to spare the time for such a thing? And, if she did, would she simply want to leave them at home and employ a nanny to look after them, while she was away carrying on her professional life?

Philip was beginning to realise that he was going to have to make a decision. Did he want his life to develop in this way? And what was the alternative? He and Jackie were now deeply involved together in what was going to happen in Rennes-le-Chateau. He couldn't just turn his back on it, even if he decided it was going to be necessary. What was he going to do? He had no answer to that question.

He sighed. His brain was exhausted by turning the questions over and over in his mind. So he fell into a restless sleep, haunted by unsatisfactory spectres of which he couldn't recall the details when he woke next morning.

3

They set off for the studio soon after eight. Philip had been allowed to have a quick breakfast. Jackie wasn't interested. She was in a hurry to get there and wasn't in a talking mood. Philip felt that he was already excluded from this part of her life, which at present seemed to be all-consuming as far as she was concerned.

It was only a five-minute walk. The front door of the building was open, but the reception desk was unmanned. Jackie ignored it and led him up to the first floor. They went through a pair of double doors and turned left along a corridor. After a short distance they turned right and immediately came to a desk built against the wall. A large, bald-headed man sat behind it. To Philip he looked like a night-club bouncer.

"*Bonjour mademoiselle.*"

"Hello Harri." She paused and turned to indicate Philip. "This – er – this is my friend. Can he come in with me?"

"Does he have a pass?"

"No. I haven't had time to get him one."

The man shook his head. "I am sorry, mademoiselle. You know I am not allowed to let anybody through without a pass."

"Mademoiselle Blontard hasn't got a pass," Philip pointed out.

"I have it somewhere in my bag."

"Mademoiselle doesn't need a pass. Everybody knows Mademoiselle Blontard. She is the star of the series. Without her there will be no recording."

"Can't you make an exception for this gentleman who is with me, Harri?" she asked. "I will vouch for his good behaviour."

He shook his head again. "I have been told there are to be no exceptions. In any case, mademoiselle, you can't be with him all the time. You will be on the set, in front of the cameras. What will happen then?"

"So what can I do?" asked Philip.

"You must go to reception and the girl will arrange for you to be interviewed by the studio manager."

"There is no girl there. The reception is unmanned."

"She will be in at nine o'clock. She will be able to put you in touch with the right man."

"But that's going to be an hour away."

He gave a Gallic shrug. "I am sorry, but that is the way you will have to do it."

"God!" cursed Philip, "These French and their bloody rules."

Jackie turned to face him. "I'm sorry, Philip. Harri's only doing what he's been told to do. *He* can't change the rules. Now I'm going to have to go and prepare for recording. It starts promptly at nine."

"How long is this rigmarole of getting a pass going to take?"

She shook her head. "I don't know. If you tell them you're involved with me, perhaps they'll hurry it through."

"So I don't know when I'll actually see you then?"

"I'm sorry. I've got to go."

She turned away and hurried down the corridor. She went without even kissing him goodbye, so completely absorbed was she in preparing for her day's work on the set.

The guard looked apologetically at him. "I'm sorry, sir. Perhaps you'll go down and wait in the entrance hall. There are chairs down there."

As requested, Philip returned to reception. There was still nobody about. He soon got fed up with sitting, waiting for the receptionist to turn up. He decided he was damned if he was going to sit around for the best part of an hour. So he went into the street outside. It was like a narrow canyon between the five-storey buildings which lined both sides. It was starting to fill with a haze of diesel fumes from the slow-moving traffic. Philip thought Paris was dreadful at this time of year. There was no relieving breeze, no sense of early morning freshness in the air. He set out to walk to the riverbank where he might pass the time looking at the *bookinistes*.

When he returned soon after nine, there was a smart young lady in reception. Otherwise, the place was deserted. He went up to her.

"I am the fiancé of Mademoiselle Jacqueline Blontard." He said in his prepared French. "I am visiting her for a couple of days and apparently I need a pass to go and watch her during the recording. Can you arrange for me to see the manager who can give me the pass?"

"Oh." She looked startled as though he was asking for something unexpected. "Wait a minute please."

She lifted the phone on her desk and pressed a button. There was a short interval before she started to talk. Philip found his French was inadequate to follow what she was saying. After a couple of minutes, she rang off and looked up at him.

"I am sorry, monsieur. The man who authorises the visitor passes is the studio manager, and he is not here this morning."

"When do you expect him to come in?"

"Not until Monday. He is spending the weekend with his family."

"What? – while there is recording taking place?"

"Yes. He is not directly involved in Mademoiselle Blontard's archaeological series."

"Is there nobody else who can give me a pass? I am only here for the weekend."

"No. He is the only one who can do it. The company is very careful about issuing passes. Much of the recording work is confidential until it has been approved for transmission."

Philip took a deep breath. "Can he be contacted at home? He could speak to Mademoiselle Blontard who would be able to reassure him about me."

She shook her head. "I am sorry. I am not allowed to do that."

Then Philip had a brainwave. "What about Alain Gisours? He is the director in charge of programming, and he knows me personally. I'm sure he would authorise me to go into the studio."

"All right. I will ask." Once again, she lifted the phone and was soon talking to her manager, but that alternative was no more successful.

She put the phone down and looked up at him. "I'm afraid the director is at present in the USA." She did manage to look disappointed.

It was then that Philip discovered he had run out of enthusiasm anyway and had lost interest in watching Jackie performing in front of the cameras. He thanked the woman and left the building. He had the whole day ahead of him. Paris had some of the most beautiful parks in Europe around its centre. He would explore *them.* He set off up the street, keeping to the shady side because the heat was already starting to build up.

4

Two hours later, Philip was feeling exhausted and very overheated. Paris might be a lovely place to visit in the spring, but by the end of June it was hot and dusty and very tiring. He found himself a pavement café, where he could sit under a sunshade and buy an ice-cold beer. Then he leaned back in his seat and surveyed the motley crowd as it passed along the pavement.

Suddenly his attention was taken by a spectacular woman walking towards him. She looked like the personification of summer. Her blonde hair was fluffed up around her head but partly covered by a large straw hat; her face was made up softly with just the faintest colouring of the full lips; her bronzed shoulders were projecting from a white almost see-through blouse with a draw-string neck that rested on her prominent boobs; her short, multi-coloured skirt swirled round her brown thighs; her feet were in white, strappy, half-heeled sandals. She looked a picture of summer excitement. And, despite the dark glasses which obscured her eyes, Philip realised he knew her.

"Jeanette," he gasped.

She heard him. After only the slightest hesitation she ran to his table. "Philip, is it really you?"

"It certainly is."

"Is this the café where I found you last time? Oh Philip, we've got to stop meeting like this."

"Well, I promise you I'm not as drunk as I was the last time."

"Oh, I didn't mind that."

"I know you didn't, but I did." He feasted his eyes on her ripe body. "I must say, Jeanette, you look absolutely gorgeous."

"Thank you." She swivelled her hips for him. "But what are you doing in Paris? Oh, let me guess. You've come to see Jacqueline recording her new series."

"That's why I came, but they won't let me in. Apparently, I need an official pass, and the guy who hands them out has gone off with his family for the weekend."

"But didn't Jackie arrange something for you?" She put her head on one side. "Surely she could have sorted that out before you got here."

"Well," he confessed, "I did make a sudden decision to come on Thursday night. I sent her a message yesterday morning, but she was so busy that she didn't get it before I arrived yesterday evening." He chuckled. "In fact, when I went up to her room at the hotel, I found some engineer-bloke sleeping in her bed."

"What!"

"Oh, Jackie wasn't in there with him. In fact, he explained it satisfactorily. Apparently, he was working over-night and was absolutely knackered, and he was going to have to do the same again last night, so she said he could catch up on his sleep in her room while she was working, rather than go to his own home the other side of Paris."

"And you believed him?"

"Of course I did. I have no doubts about Jackie's fidelity while we're apart."

"Oh, Philip you're such an innocent."

"I am *not*." He switched the subject. "Would you like a drink?"

"I certainly would. I've been waiting for your invitation." She took off her hat and sat down beside him.

Philip realised he very much wanted to be able to talk to Jeanette, with her rather flirtatious way of chatting. She cheered him up. He needed someone who was interested in talking to him personally, without spending all her time thinking about other things. The waiter arrived, no doubt attracted by the lovely new arrival at his café.

"What will you have, mademoiselle?"

"I'd like a white-wine spritzer with ice."

"Good idea." Philip turned to the very attentive waiter. "And I'll have another ice-cold beer." Reluctantly the young man departed.

"So, Jeanette, what have you been doing since you left Quillan?"

She wrinkled her nose. "Nothing really. Armand paid me enough to mean I didn't have to earn a living for quite a few months."

Philip knew what she meant by that comment. "What, no men? A gorgeous lady like you?"

She removed her glasses and looked straight into his eyes. "You've ruined me for other men."

"Don't be silly." He hadn't noticed before how dark her pupils were. It gave him a strange feeling in the pit of his stomach. "There must be hundreds of them queuing up to get in your bed."

"But not you, eh?"

The drinks came at that moment to save his embarrassment.

Not put off, she continued after she had taken a deep drink, "Philip, you and I could have had a great thing going if you had been willing to forget your English reserve." She almost snorted. "*I* wouldn't have cleared off to record a television series, leaving you all alone. Not like Jackie."

"Jeanette, I should to have known all the time that this sort of thing was going to happen. If I'd thought about it, I'd have realised that there would be periods when we would be kept apart by her job. TV series are very demanding. I can't expect Jackie to spend most of her time keeping *me* happy."

"Why not? If I was her, and knowing what I do about you, I would have insisted that the recording programme left me some time to spend with you. They couldn't have refused her. After all, they wouldn't have been able to find anyone else to put in her place." She laid a hand on his arm. "Tell me this – did you both have a wonderful night last night, making up for the weeks you'd been apart?"

He smiled weakly. "Well, she *was* very tired."

"I thought so. And did she hug and kiss you and hold you tight and tell you she wanted you to be with her every night when she came back from her recording sessions?"

"Of course not."

"Well, I would have done." She poked him in the ribs. "Let me tell you, Philip Sinclair, that when I really give myself to a man, he knows that he will come first in everything I do."

He was silent in the face of her forthright comments. He had never before heard her speak so strongly.

"Do you realise, Philip, that this is what the rest of your life is going to be like? You will always be playing second fiddle to some television series which has to be out by a certain date, or else her first priority will be investigating some new collection of treasures or ancient artefacts. You will have to get on with your life and your happiness on your own. Next time she forgets you, you will think of me, and of what you rejected."

"Jeanette." He gripped her hand hard. "No more, please. It's been a difficult time for me. I've got to learn to cope with this stuff on my own."

"Why, for God's sake? Why don't you ask someone else to help you, someone to stand up for you before she wrecks your happiness?"

"You for instance?" He tried to grin.

"Yes, me." She took a breath. "I know I'm only a cheap little trollope to you, but I can be caring and loving and, more than anything else, I would make you feel like the most important person in our lives. I will prove it."

She moved towards him, removed her glasses again, then reached forward and kissed him softly and tenderly on the lips. It was a lovely, welcoming kiss and, for a second, he teetered on the brink of the slippery slope of surrendering to her. With a desperate jerk, he broke away.

"Jeanette, I certainly don't think of you as a cheap trollope. I have never seen you looking so lovely or so desirable. For a moment, I almost persuaded myself that I wanted you more than anything else. I know that I would enjoy nothing more than to go back to your flat and undress you and make love to you in your soft, welcoming bed. But that would be the easy way out." He shook his head. "I must sort this out with Jackie first. If that leads us to agreeing to go our separate ways, then I promise I will contact you to see if you are still interested in me."

She sighed and sat back in her chair. Her hair was a little disarranged and there was a slight smear on her lipstick. But otherwise, she was in careful control of herself.

"All right, Philip. I will let you do as you say." She sighed. "But I think you will need me sooner than you expect. If that happens, you always know where I am."

"Yes." He took a deep breath. "Now let us talk about everyday things."

So he told her about his progress with restoring the house opposite the chateau at Rennes. He said how he hoped to have a two-bedroom section of the building ready for occupation by the end of the summer. Meanwhile he had rented a little terrace cottage just round the corner.

"What do you do for meals and laundry and things like that?"

"Oh, various local ladies help out when I need it. They seem to have accepted me in the village. Of course, that is probably because I'm giving their husbands well-paid work. You've no idea how many local skills I've unearthed – carpenters, masons – all I need now is a good plumber."

She smiled at him. "I think you're going to make a big success of this, Philip. You're the sort of person people like to work for."

"I don't know about that, but I am enjoying having a real project to work on. It gives me satisfaction when I complete each stage of the work. Of course, I know it's going to take several years before the whole project is completed. But I can accept that."

They continued to chat for another hour or so, then they parted, and Philip set off to walk back to the lonely hotel bedroom. But in a way he was feeling happier. The experience of talking to the warm, desirable Jeanette had cheered him up. And the memory of that soft kiss lingered with him.

5

Heinrich Hitler (née Winkelhofer) was standing with his back to the empty hearth. His six-foot-two, eighteen-stone frame was squeezed into semi-military clothing. This included a broad black belt which attempted to restrain a stomach that seemed to have expanded rather too much in recent years. Perhaps the matching diagonal strap across his swelling chest would raise the eye from his bulging waistline. The leather boots into which his trousers were tucked were also black but were showing signs of wear. Unfortunately, funds didn't run to replacing them at the moment. Nevertheless, he hoped he presented a figure of sufficient stature to impress the young woman whom Anna Sondheim had just ushered into the room.

"This is Gretel Skorzeny," she announced. "This is the girl I told you about."

Heinrich nodded to the young woman. She could hardly be called a girl. In fact, she was strikingly beautiful, in a not quite Aryan way. She had long almost white hair and full lips and bright blue, luminous eyes. It was the lips and especially the contempt in those eyes which destroyed the Aryan impression. Her body was slim but shapely and she carried herself, in her tight, V-necked sweater and jeans, with an upright self-confidence. The thought occurred to him that she might make a very suitable consort in the future Fourth Reich, if only something could be done about those eyes – tinted contact lenses perhaps?

In her turn, Gretel was looking him up and down, but with none of the respect that should be shown to the leader of Fasces45. Heinrich had the uncomfortable feeling that she was visually assessing him and finding him less than inspiring.

He shook off the thought and addressed her. "You are the grand-daughter of Otto Skorzeny?"

"The *great* grand-daughter." Her German was carefully correct, indicating an education in a private school in the south of the country.

"Er, yes." He found the directness of her gaze was quite off-putting. "And you have information about your – er – your great grandfather's archaeological surveys which he carried out in the south of France?"

"I do. My mother recently gave me his notes which she had stored away and hadn't told the rest of the family anything about." She paused, increasing the tension. "They reveal that in 1944 he had developed a new technique of seismic surveying of buildings and areas of land, which had been demonstrated to the Fuehrer. Our leader agreed that it showed signs of potential success."

"Oh, the Fuehrer. Yes. And what exactly did this – er – this seismic survey set out to achieve?"

"Are you aware of the modern science of seismology?" Was there a hint of scorn in the smile she gave him?

"You tell me about it."

"Well briefly, the technique is that recording devices are set up at intervals around a location, an explosion is set off and shock waves travel through the ground and reflect off the various strata in different ways, revealing the nature and the depth and thickness of the strata. In my great-grandfather's day of course the results were crude and inaccurate. They were still learning and building up a library of records for comparison. However, they were able to tell, for example, if a body of dense materials had been buried in a certain area. Do you understand?"

He drew himself up to his full exasperated height. "Of course I do. Please continue."

"Very well. The Fuehrer required my great-grandfather to demonstrate the science in action. So he selected an old building and placed a substantial amount of gold bullion in a hole dug beneath the cellar. You will appreciate that gold is one of the densest materials on the planet. Then he set up the recording devices, which he had designed, in locations around the building. When they were ready, he dug shallow holes in three places around the building and detonated quite small quantities of dynamite in each. These were done at intervals. Readings were taken from each device as the explosions were set off." She paused, waiting for his interested comment.

All he could think of, was to ask, "So what happened then?"

"He had to go away with the figures and map out the readings on a plan of the building. You will understand that where the pressure graphs coincided, that would be the most likely position of the gold."

"So what did they do once they had found the gold?"

Her face took on an infuriatingly self-satisfied smile. "It was very simple. They demolished the building and excavated in the marked spot."

"And they found the gold?"

"Apparently the first two tests were unsuccessful. One was a complete miss, and the other was five metres out. However, my great-grandfather was improving the technique all the time and the third one was a success. It was correct to within one metre in finding gold which had been buried five metres underground. It was that which convinced the Fuehrer."

"So what did he decide?"

"Well, he was of course aware of the ancient writings left by our forebears, the Visigoths, recording that they had hidden the treasures which they had taken from Rome somewhere in the Pyrenees in Southern France. So he sent my great grandfather to Occitania to see if he could find anything."

Heinrich could feel the excitement beginning to build up in his chest. "And what *did* he find?"

"He was posted with the Second Panzer Division to the Languedoc. Their temporary headquarters were in Carcassonne. They had been sent there to regroup after their experiences on the Russian front. My great-grandfather was able to go out on expeditions into the surrounding mountains. He had to have a large escort because the local French were not friendly, and the *Résistance* was strong in the region. But my great-grandfather's notes recorded, that by asking lots of questions, he finally ended up in an area near a place called Rennes-le-Chateau. Apparently, fifty years before, the village priest had suddenly become very wealthy, and everybody seemed to think he must have found gold in his church when he was carrying out renovations."

She paused for breath and Heinrich urged her, "Go on. Go on."

"My great-grandfather's notes say he set up his equipment all round the church and set off several explosions but, when he checked the results, there was no sign of a hoard of gold anywhere in the church. In fact, he found the opposite. There seemed to be an open void underneath the nave – that is the main hall of the church. Of course, he wanted to go into the void, but nobody seemed to know a way in. So he was disappointed.

"Is that all?" Heinrich felt deflated.

"Oh, no. That was just the start. He went back a second time and began to check the area all round the village. That was because there was a story going round that the priest and his woman used to go out into the country nearby, digging up places and coming back in the evening with baskets full of what looked like rocks." She shook her head. "But he had no luck there either, despite making several surveys. All they found were a few small, dense objects. When they dug them up they usually proved to be old agricultural tools. They did find one small cache with a dozen or so gold Napoleons – those were French coins – but there was nothing of real value."

"So it was all a waste of time."

She raised a finger. "That is what they thought, but on the last visit – I believe it was their seventh - when everyone, including my great grandfather, had almost given up – he decided to have another go near the church." She paused dramatically.

"Yes. Go on. What did he find?"

"This time he decided to try outside the church, at the east end. His notes make it clear that he was actually trying to find a way into the void under the church. Some villagers had told him they thought there might be a way in from the churchyard. However, when he checked through the results from the sensors, he couldn't see any other voids, but there did seem to be something dense further to the east. So he went back to Carcassonne that night with the intention of returning as soon as possible to check the piece of land between the church and the near-by chateau."

She sighed. "Unfortunately, when he got back to Division Headquarters, they told him that the whole Panzer group had been ordered to march north immediately to help repel the Americans who had landed in Normandy. The division was packing up and would leave in the morning."

"Couldn't your great-grandfather have stayed for a couple of days to complete the survey?"

"If they had left just two or three men to protect him, they would all have been in danger from the local *Résistance*. The village people had been brutally questioned about the treasure and there was a lot of hatred for the Germans. So he didn't dare stay on without a well-armed company of infantry to protect him. He asked for this, but the general refused to let him have that many men. So, reluctantly, he gave up the idea of further searches until another opportunity might come along. In his notes he promised to go back later, but he never got the chance."

"But *you* might be able to continue where he left off?"

"That is correct. Of course, I don't have any seismic equipment and, in any case, the authorities wouldn't allow me to set off explosives to help with the search. But I have his notes and I have been back to Rennes-le-Chateau and I know my way round the area."

"Do you think you could find the treasure if it's still there?"

She smiled broadly for the first time. "Well, I can try. Using the identity documents that Fasces45 made for me, I have been able to get close to Jacqueline Blontard, the famous French archaeologist who has been excavating in the area. I will suggest to her that she should send me to Rennes to start cataloguing the Templar archives which she recently found in the village."

"Do you think she would do that?"

"Why not? She is busy on her television series about the Cathars at present, and she will want work to be started on the cataloguing as soon as possible, to avoid any risk of the papers deteriorating or being stolen. Her English fiancé, who is presently living near the chateau, knows nothing about archaeology, so *he* can't help her. I have the right qualifications. Therefore, when I put it to her, I think she will see the sense of sending me. Once I am accepted there, I should be able to do whatever I wish."

Heinrich had to admit that her suggestion was a good one and might lead to finding some of the funds his organisation so desperately needed to establish itself as a potent political force, in the changing German national situation. Maybe this was the message from the Almighty which he had been waiting for. He nodded to her.

"Very well. You go with my support. I will send Anna to make contact with you two or three weeks after you have settled in. She will act as a go-between so as to give me information about your progress."

The woman smiled briefly. "Thank you – er – sir. I hope to give you some good news in the not-too-distant future."

She turned promptly on her heel and left. Heinrich Winkelhofer was wondering whether it was he who had authorised her future activities, or the reverse.

6

Philip got back to Rennes-le-Chateau on the Sunday afternoon. His parting from Jackie had been less than satisfactory. Once again, she had been late getting back to the hotel from the recording studios the previous evening. Then the news she had given him had been disappointing.

"I'm sorry darling, but we're leaving Paris in the morning. We've got to go and do some filming on location."

"Does that mean you'll be going to le Bézu?"

"I don't know yet. The director will tell us what the programme is when we get on the coach at nine o'clock tomorrow."

Did he detect a slight hesitation in her speech, as though she was holding something back?

"OK." He smiled weakly. "You'll ring me to let me know where you'll be, won't you? That's especially if you're near Rennes. Then we'll be able to meet up, if only for an hour or two."

"Of course I will. But I don't know when that might be. The programme is going to be very demanding." She took a breath. "Now I've got to get on with my packing. I won't have time to do it in the morning."

"Do you want any help?"

"No. You go and get something to eat." She reached up to lower her case from the top of the wardrobe. "You can stay on here after I've gone if you wish. The room's reserved for the filming of the whole series."

When he got back from having a snack in the bar, she was already in bed. Once again, she was too tired to make love, and Philip couldn't help reflecting how much better his night would have been, if he'd taken up Jeanette's suggestion of an offer.

Once Jackie had left, Philip decided there was no point in staying on in Paris alone. He'd had enough of the hot, dusty city. Jackie had gone already. So he set out for Rennes after breakfast. The roads were crowded with Sunday motorists – inexperienced drivers who trundled along, taking their families on trips to the countryside or visits to friends – so his journey was slow and frustrating. As a consequence, it was a relief to pull into the yard in front of the chateau late in the afternoon and to get out and stretch his legs and inspect progress.

Of course, it being a Sunday, nobody was working. He noticed that very little more had been done to the house, but he reminded himself that it had only been two days since he had left the men on their own. Had they used any more of the loose stone from the castle ruins? He wandered over to the double full-height gates which led into the courtyard of the chateau. When he tried it, he found the little personnel door in the right-hand gate was unlocked.

"That's annoying," he said to himself. "I must tell Albert to be more careful in future when he finishes work for the day and leaves the site."

Now he got out his spare key and locked the door. Then he dropped off his bag in the little cottage just round the corner which he was renting until he could move into the restored house. Feeling thirsty he went up the road to the local bar for a drink. Who should he see in there but Albert? He wandered over to where the man was sitting with a couple of his mates.

"Albert," he challenged in his best French, "you forgot to lock the door to the chateau courtyard when you finished work yesterday evening."

"No. Monsieur. I certainly locked up everywhere before I left the site."

"Well, how do you explain that it was unlocked when I tried it just now?"

"I do not know, monsieur. I am sure I locked it."

Philip suddenly thought about burglars. "Was there anybody hanging round when you were finishing last night?"

"There was no-one last night, monsieur. But I did see two men earlier in the day."

"Two men – anyone you knew?"

"No, monsieur. They were not from the village or anywhere nearby. They might have been from Couiza, but I don't think so."

"Do you mean they were foreigners?"

Albert thought carefully. "I don't believe they were French. I don't know why." He thought a little more. "Perhaps it was the way they dressed, or because they didn't seem to know exactly where they were going."

"What were they doing?"

"I do not know, monsieur, but Jacques said he saw someone later walking along the path down the hillside as if they were going round to Magdalen Tower."

"Really? That's strange."

Philip was aware of a footpath that was cut into the bank that went round the north side of the steep hill on which Rennes-le-Chateau was built. It passed about thirty feet below the foot of the castle walls and several of the window openings looked down on it. In fact, it had been through one of those openings that Philip, supported by his friend, Jean-Luc, had climbed in to rescue Jackie when she was imprisoned in the basement of the chateau, where she had discovered the Templar archives. The windows were out of reach of ordinary passers-by and in any case few visitors chose to take that path which only led to the other side of the village. Furthermore, they would have to get very long ladders to reach the lowest opening. So he wasn't too worried about people getting in that way. Nevertheless, it gave some added urgency to Jackie's request that the papers should be stored somewhere more secure.

He returned to questioning Albert. "What sort of men were they?"

"Well," the fellow shrugged. "They were just men."

"But they weren't tourists? What were they like? I mean, were they tough-looking?"

Albert raised his eyebrows. "What is tough-looking?"

"Well, did they look as though they were sizing the place up – perhaps thinking about a break-in?"

He poked his lips out, considering the idea. "It is possible they might have been. They certainly walked all round the walls, as far as they could. And then as I said, they might have gone along the path below the chateau. Jacques said he saw them going along there but I did not see them down there."

Philip shook his head in frustration. He bore in mind that the men might have been sent by *Vendredi Treize* to look the place over, before they signed the contract of sale.

"Did they look as though they might have been surveying the place? How were they dressed? Would you say they looked like surveyors?"

"Oh, no." Albert was definite on that point. "They were not surveyors."

"How can you tell?"

"Well, they had no surveyor's boards, no paper for notes. They weren't studying the shape of the walls. They were just looking."

"Was there anything about them that would make you remember them?"

Albert put his head on one side. "Well, one of them had a short beard."

"Were they young or old?"

"Oh – er – not young, but not old either. I would have said they were in their late thirties or early forties. Perhaps the man with one arm was a bit older."

"One arm! Why didn't you tell me that before."

He shrugged again. "I've told you now, haven't I? Why? Do you know a man without an arm?"

Philip felt a sudden surge of interest. He somehow thought that if he went to see César, the daughter of the former *capo* of *La Force Marseillaise*, there was a good chance she would be able to tell him who the one-armed man was.

"Which arm had the man lost?"

"Um," Albert thought carefully. "I think it was this one – the right one. It had been taken off at the shoulder. His shirt sleeve was fixed across his chest."

"Was he the bearded one?"

"No, he was clean-shaven. I would say he was the boss of the other one, even though he had lost his arm."

Now that he had realised the information might be important, Albert was warming to his theme. He started coming out with a rush of largely irrelevant speculation.

"I bet he has trouble blowing his nose. I always use my right hand for that. And I wonder what he does if someone offers to shake his hand. Perhaps he could have an artificial arm fitted to do what the original arm used to do. It's wonderful what they can do nowadays. But would an artificial hand be able to blow his nose . . ."

Philip thanked Albert and asked his foreman to let him know if he saw either of the men again. Then he excused himself and went back to unpack his bag and spend the night in his lonely bed.

7

Next morning Philip woke up with a new objective for the day. Since they had started negotiations with *Vendredi Treize* to buy the chateau and he had been given the keys, he hadn't really set out to explore the place. He had only ventured through the main entrance gates into the central courtyard where there were substantial heaps of rubble resulting from the partial collapse of the building. They had been given permission to mine it for suitable pieces of stone to help them in the restoration of the house across the yard. That was where he and Jackie were going to live while they were restoring and converting the castle, possibly into a hotel.

Recent comments she had made had raised worries in his mind about the security of the Templar archives which they had found in the cellars a few weeks ago. The only way out for them on that occasion had been through a partially blocked window high above the footpath cut into the hillside to the north of the building. It was true that it was running through the wooded slopes and was seldom used. However, Philip reasoned that there must be a way into the cellars from the ground floor of the chateau.

This report from Albert that a couple of men had been seen walking round the area, apparently looking at the castle, had suddenly made it more urgent in his mind that a secure access to the ancient documents should be found and the possible way in from the outside through the window should be blocked up, even though it was unlikely that anyone would seek to use it. So he set out to make his first complete exploration of all the parts of the building to which he could gain access.

That was not as easy as it might sound. About a quarter of the chateau on the north and east sides of the building had collapsed from the roof virtually down to ground level, leaving the large heaps of rubble where the buildings used to be, and various other detritus scattered across the courtyard. The perimeter buildings on three sides of the chateau had been built strongly enough to withstand any further collapse, and it was only a part of the north side, the area which had later been punctuated by more and larger windows, that was partly ruinous. Unfortunately, the collapsed part of the building was above where he suspected the cellars were located.

Nevertheless, Philip decided to investigate the unruined part of the building first to find out more about the structure. Generally speaking, the castle plan was an approximate square of rooms, three storeys high round a central courtyard, with the entrance in the middle of the east side through an arched doorway. This was currently closed by two wooden, full-height doors with a small personnel door let into the right-hand one. A large, square tower projected from the building on the south-east corner which was a storey higher than the rest of the structure. On the south-west corner was a circular tower of the same height. Both towers had tiled roofs rising to a central apex. The walls of the buildings around the perimeter had sloping roofs which drained into the central courtyard.

The castle could not be called a beautiful building. Its surrounding walls were plain with very little decoration. They were punctuated almost haphazardly with simple, small windows which had obviously been added later. There were no cornices or castellations round the top of the building and even the main gateway lacked a portico. In fact, the place had more the look of a fortress than the usual French chateau.

Philip went first to the square corner tower where he already knew a staircase ascended to the upper floors. From here he was able to walk round the corridors at the two upper levels. Modest rooms opened off both sides of the corridors which extended round most of three sides of the chateau, and it showed how suitable the place was for conversion to a hotel after it had been restored. On the north side, above the steep hillside, the partially collapsed building made the corridors impassable. There were a few extra rooms on the top floor of both towers.

When he explored the ground floor, he found the rooms were larger, with higher ceilings, and these extended across the full width of the building, with no central corridor. There were often double doors in the centre linking them to the next large room. Throughout the ground floor, on the three sides he could get to, there was no sign of any access to the basement. In fact, he doubted if cellars existed under most of the building, because he suspected the chateau had been built straight off the rocky top of the mountain, which was near the surface in this part of the village. He guessed the cellars only existed under the north side of the building, where the hillside fell away, making it necessary to dig deeper to find suitable foundations for the north wall. That meant the most likely location for the staircase down to the basement would be somewhere under the rubble.

With a certain amount of trepidation, Philip approached this area. He was aware that he and Jackie were not yet owners of the chateau and, strictly speaking, they should get permission from *Vendredi Treize* before he started digging out any of the fallen debris from the ruined part of the building. Furthermore, he had no intention of risking any additional collapse of the structure, which might happen if he removed a large amount of material without the advice of a professional engineer. On the other hand, they had been given permission to make use of the rubble masonry strewn across the courtyard to carry out repairs to the adjacent house. So, in a way, anything he moved could be regarded as a minor extension of that permission.

At the same time, a lot of hard work and a certain amount of danger was going to be experienced in clearing a way into this part of the chateau. He stood back and surveyed it. What seemed to have happened was that the inner perimeter wall between the building and the courtyard had collapsed into the central area and this had provided most of the stone lying about. He suspected that villagers had been robbing suitable pieces of masonry for centuries to carry out repairs or alterations to their own dwellings and for other uses. In fact, Bérenger Saunière had probably been one of the main robbers when he was building his domain.

The collapse of the inner wall had been followed by the roof and internal floors subsiding, partly into the courtyard, but mainly within the building, and this had been followed by the partial collapse of the outer wall. Most of it seemed to have fallen inwards but some had probably tumbled down the forested hillside and been overgrown in the following centuries. Whatever had happened, Philip thought it must have been a spectacular sight when it occurred. Now it looked as though a bomb had been set off inside the building.

He started to climb the rubble very carefully. He chose a location nearest to the part of the castle which was still standing, mainly undamaged. However, he had made little progress before he decided he wasn't suitably clad or equipped to do this kind of work. He realised he needed leather gloves, stout boots and a hard hat before he ventured far into the destroyed part of the building. So he retreated and went back to the little cottage he was renting, in order to get the things he needed.

As he went round the corner of the chateau and crossed the road, he was astonished to see there was a lady standing outside the door of the cottage, surrounded by suitcases and bags. She was dressed in a light loose, sweater, which totally failed to disguise her substantial bosom. Very short shorts and strappy sandals showed off her curvy legs. Her shock of blonde hair blew about in the breeze. No doubt the matrons of the village were already discussing her surprise arrival.

"Jeanette!" Philip gasped, "What are you doing here?"

She pouted. "You've locked your door and I can't get in to take my bags off the street. I have been waiting nearly two hours for you to turn up."

"But how did you get here?"

"Armand brought me. He was in Paris at the weekend but was told to return to le Bézu to prepare for the filming which is starting there later today." She grimaced. "We had to leave at five o'clock this morning. I am already tired out."

"Why did he drop you here?" But Philip already knew the answer to that before she replied with a toss of her head.

"I decided that you needed someone to look after you. I can do your shopping and cooking and cleaning and laundry. That will give you more time to get on with your work of repairing the building." She looked at him defiantly. "I will even help you with your building work when you need me to."

Philip was amused at the idea of this soft, scented creature doing housework and physical labouring. "Jeanette, that's not why you're really here, is it?"

"Yes it is. Of course, if you want me to serve you in other ways that is up to you, but whatever you ask me to do, I shall expect you to pay me at least three hundred euros a week." She frowned at him. "Now, will you please unlock this door and help me carry my things up to my room."

"To your room?"

"That's right. You told me this place has two bedrooms. Is anyone else using the second bedroom?"

"No, of course not, but . . ."

"Has it got a bed in it?"

"Yes."

"Very well, I will soon make it habitable. I won´t be able to help you with your work today but, in any case, you will probably want to go to le Bézu to see your fiancée." She gave him a self-satisfied little smile.

It finally filtered through to Philip that Armand must have been preparing the site for filming for a couple of weeks. Of course, that meant Jackie would be coming to do the archaeological site work for the series. And she hadn´t even admitted to him that she was going to be here. It was obvious that she didn´t want him around while she was recording. He became aware that Jeanette was watching him silently as he worked it out.

"Are you telling me that Miss Blontard is at le Bézu now?"

She looked at him with a smug expression. "Yes. The cast and the director drove down yesterday and they´re staying in Quillan. That is why Armand had to be here as early as possible this morning. They are going to start filming this afternoon."

"I must go over to see her."

"You won´t be welcome. You´ll be interrupting the filming."

"Nevertheless, I need to talk to her. I will try to meet her before she starts."

"Very well." She shrugged. "Help me take my things inside and I will see you when you come back this evening."

He opened the door, picked up two of her numerous bags and took them upstairs and deposited them on the unmade bed in the back room. She followed him and gazed around. He went back to get the last two cases and brought them up.

"It´s not very big, is it?" she complained.

"I´m sorry, Jeanette. It´s the best I can do at the moment. Maybe I can get part of the house that we´re restoring ready in a few weeks." He patted her arm. "I´m sure you can make it much more homely with a bit of effort. Now I want to have a quick shower before I go over to le Bézu."

He left her to get on with it.

8

Philip reached le Bézu soon after lunchtime. The road below what remained of the castle was cluttered with the television recording company's equipment vehicles, making it difficult to get through. He had to drive past and pull half up the grass bank beyond, to find somewhere to leave the MG out of the traffic. The steep path up to the chateau bore signs of the cumbersome equipment which had been dragged up it by Armand's team in the last few weeks.

Philip hurried up to the site. The first person he saw when he got through the entrance gateway was Armand. The young Frenchman shook him warmly by the hand.

"They're just about to start filming down on the stone floor," he told him. "They have put me here to stop anybody interrupting."

"You mean the area that you and I uncovered a few weeks ago?"

"That's right."

"Well, I know how to get down there without making a noise."

"Philip, I am told I must stop everybody from going further unless they are authorised." He made as if he was going to block the young man's path.

"Armand, you know that I am Jackie's fiancé. I must be allowed to see her. I promise I will not interrupt the filming in any way."

The fellow shrugged and stepped aside. "Well, I suppose *you* may go, but no-one else."

"Don't worry. I'm on my own."

He stepped past the slightly reluctant young Frenchman and started across the site. As he took the steep, rough track down to the stone floor, where they had done a lot of the excavating, he noticed that it had been widened and cut back on both sides. Steps had been cut to ease the carrying down of heavy equipment and it was now quite easy to negotiate. This was obviously part of the preparatory work that Armand had been carrying out over the last few weeks. As he approached the stone slab, he could see that several fixed camera locations had been erected, including one on top of a small scaffold tower which looked down on the hollow in the rock wall where they had discovered the back way into the treasure room.

However, what most held his attention was his fiancée. Jackie was standing just to one side of the hollow in the wall. She was looking very glamorous. Her beautiful titian hair was tumbling about her shoulders, gleaming in the sun. She was made up so that her face and chest glowed with summer warmth. Her eyes were darkened, and her lips made fuller. She was wearing a white, long-sleeved silk blouse with no fastenings down the front. It was open to her cleavage, revealing just a hint of black bra beneath. The blouse was tucked into gold, skin-tight, trousers with a broad black belt at the waist and matching high-heeled ankle boots on her feet. To Philip she looked absolutely gorgeous.

A young man, presumably the director, was standing with her on the wide stone slab. Now he stepped towards her.

"You've got to look your best here, darling," he said. "Lean a bit more towards the rock – that's right. I think we'll have your right hand resting on your hip and your left hand just loosely indicating the cave. And I think we'll show a bit more of your bra." He reached inside her blouse, cupped his hand under her left breast and lifted it so that the black lace could be seen more clearly. "That'll have them drooling in front of their TV screens."

Philip was astonished, particularly at the way Jackie smiled back at the director without any embarrassment. Clearly, they were used to working together in this way.

The man stepped away. "Right. Cameras roll."

Jackie started her speech.

"Just here was where we made the most exciting discovery. Believe it or not this small cave had been filled across the front by a stone wall. Just imagine it." She indicated the hollow. "The wall had been built so cleverly that, at first sight, it appeared that this almost vertical rock face continued straight down to the stone slab on which I am standing. However, a document had come into my possession that described how one of the *parfaits* of the Cathar faith had walled up their greatest treasure in just such a shallow cave as this." She stood erect again with her chest thrown out but with her blouse pulled wide and still displaying the top of the black bra holding up her swelling breasts. "So we decided to carry out a little investigation. We began to remove the stones which had been so tightly built into the wall and little by little this secret cave was discovered. When the wall was half demolished, I could no longer resist peering into the cave. What would I find in there? Would I even find *anything*?"

There was a pregnant pause as she half-turned back towards the wall, revealing her magnificent profile. "Well, let me tell you that was a scary moment. You can see how shallow the cave is. It's not much more than a hollow. I had to turn my head sideways to see anything behind what was left of the wall, and the light in there was gloomy to say the least." She shook her head. "I couldn't be sure, but I thought there was something down at the bottom – was it a stick? It was certainly stick-shaped. I tried reaching down to see if I could touch it but I couldn't reach past the rough backs of the stones. Then suddenly the whole wall gave way with a rush and disappeared into the chasm below. It almost took me with it. But much more important than that, was the fact that we might have lost a priceless artefact. What on earth were we going to do?" She advanced on the camera, giving the viewer a full frontal again.

She shook her head. "Well, it wasn't very professional, but I wasn't going to let a possible piece of evidence escape me. One of the lads volunteered to go down into the hole where the wall had disappeared, dangling on a rope. It was a brave act and potentially disastrous. It might have resulted in the damaging or even destruction of the artefact. And what did he find? That is what you'll discover in the next episode." She raised her head and took a deep breath.

"OK," said the director, "everybody stop recording. Jo, can you bring your camera down here and we'll see what you've got."

A relaxed chatter broke out as he spoke. That was when Jackie raised her head and saw Philip. A look of vexation crossed her face.

"Louis, I want to go and speak to my friend. I won't be a minute."

"OK." He turned to the approaching cameraman.

Jackie picked her way across the rough ground to confront Philip. She did not appear to be pleased to see him. Close up, he could see she had a thick coating of make-up applied to her face. There seemed to be none of her usual scent.

"What are you doing here?"

"I've come to see you of course. What else would I be doing? Why didn't you let me know you were going to be here for a few days?"

She tossed the thick locks of her hair back. "Well, I can't talk to you now. I'm in the middle of a recording session."

"That's all right. I'm quite happy to stay here and watch for a while."

"I don't want you watching me, Philip. It will put me off. I'll be aware all the time that I'm speaking, that you're standing here, and I'll find it difficult to concentrate on the script."

He almost said, "You mean you don't want me to see the other bloke handling your private parts without you objecting." But he had the sense to keep quiet about that. Instead, he said, "OK. But I think it's important that we have a chat when you can spare the time, now that I'm here."

"All right – but not here, not in front of the cameras."

"Where then?"

"Is your car down on the road by the vans? Go back to it and I'll come and talk to you when we've finished for the day. But I warn you, you're likely to be waiting for several hours."

Philip was on the point of suggesting they met at the hotel in Quillan later in the evening. But he decided that it was important that they talked on their own as soon as possible in, order to try to clear the air.

"OK. I'll be waiting for you."

He turned and left.

It was nearly three hours later, and Philip had dropped off to sleep, when Jackie turned up. She had wrapped a big shapeless cardigan over her revealing blouse, although her legs were still squeezed into her skin-tight trousers. She opened the passenger door and climbed into the car.

"What do you want to talk about?" She leaned back against the door, creating a no-trespassing space between them. He noticed that most of her make-up had been removed.

Philip had been turning over and over in his mind what he should say to her before he fell asleep. Now, suddenly awakened, he had nothing prepared. "Well, it's obvious, isn't it?"

"What is obvious?"

"Only a few weeks ago we discovered we had fallen in love and wanted to get married as soon as possible. We spent a lot of time planning what we were going to do for the rest of our lives. But, for the last month, you seem to have forgotten all that and cleared off to Paris to do this series. I think you've been deliberately avoiding me, and I want to know why."

"I haven't been avoiding you. I've just been very busy"

"What do you call coming to le Bézu – only a few miles from Rennes-le-Chateau – and not even letting me know that you're here?"

"Philip, you don't seem to have noticed that producing a television series is a very demanding occupation. We're having to pack five or six months' work into less than three. It leaves very little time for a personal life."

"You mean you're so busy that you can't even spare a couple of days for me. I realised after a while that you were never going to come to Rennes. So I searched you out in Paris, and even then you were too tired to let me make love to you."

"Well," she avoided his gaze, "I'm sorry, but when I'm concentrating on my work, it becomes the only thing on my mind, and it takes up all my time and all my energy. You just have to accept that I'm that sort of a person."

"So is this what our marriage would be like? Are there going to be long periods when we have no contact with each other?"

She tossed her head, shaking out her lovely hair. "You knew all about me when we got together, Philip. You knew that these television series were an important part of my life. I'm a career woman and I have to keep delivering to my public, to make sure they keep following me."

"Perhaps I didn't understand how much personal contact you were prepared to spread around in order to further your career."

"I see." She shot a glance at him. "I realise you didn't like Louis pulling my shirt open to show my bra to the cameras."

"He seemed to do rather more than that."

"Oh, you English are such prudes. I suppose it's perfectly all right for you to maul me when you fancy it, but no other man's allowed to so much as *touch* me." Now she was furious. "Well, I can tell you that such things are an everyday occurrence in the film and TV worlds. Louis is the director. He knows what the French public wants and he's not afraid to titillate their appetites to get them to follow the series." She jabbed a finger at him. "And *he's* a success. What he does with his hands means nothing to him or to me. I know he's doing it to achieve the best results for the series."

Philip was shocked into silence by her tirade. It took him a few moments to summon up a response. "Well, I understand I'm not welcome in your television world. Does that mean I'm not going to see you again until the series is over?"

"Maybe not even then. Alain is trying to sell the series to the Americans. We may have to go over there to re-record it in English."

"Oh, my God. That's it then."

"It may not happen like that. I don't know anything more about it at the moment. I'll tell you when I know."

"So that's what I have to accept if I want to share your life."

She placed her hand briefly over his, the first small sign of affection he had received for a long time.

"I'm sorry, Philip, but I must follow my star." She sighed. "If you want something different, you'll have to find another girl."

He smiled weakly. "OK, I'll wait to hear from you when you're ready."

"That's right. I can't offer you more than that at the moment." She opened the door and climbed out. "Goodbye."

"Cheerio."

He watched her in the rear-view mirror as she went down the road towards the personnel bus. She didn't look back. With a heavy heart, he started the car and carried out the complex manoeuvring to head back to Rennes-le-Chateau.

9

As he drove back to Rennes, Philip felt he had some important decisions to make. Jackie had made it clear that he was going to see nothing more of her for at least three months. If the American plans came to fruition, it was likely to be much longer than that. From the way that she was speaking, it seemed their relationship was to be put on ice, at the very least, until the Cathar series was finished.

As far as he was concerned, he had no wish to be famous or to have the public interested in his personal life, nor did he wish to be the husband of a star. He was now a rich man as a result of the discoveries he and Jackie had made, but he had no wish to use his wealth as a stepping-stone to celebrity status. He wanted to do something useful with his money. So the idea of purchasing the chateau at Rennes, and restoring it to the condition it had been in two hundred years ago, was an attractive one. However, it wasn´t something he really wanted to do on his own. His personal life was important to him.

Jackie had made it pretty clear that, if he wanted female companionship, she expected him to look elsewhere. What did that mean for him? He was aware that Jeanette was waiting for him back in the cottage round the corner from the chateau, and he had little doubt that she would be happy to take Jackie´s place. He liked the bubbly, sexy lady a lot and it was a tempting prospect to take her into his bed. But what would that mean for the future?

Whether Jackie had considered it or not, they had entered into an agreement together to buy the chateau and restore it to its former condition. There was also the question of what was to be done with the Templar archives in the basement. He was certain, that once she had finished the television series, Jackie would be expecting to turn her attention to the reading and cataloguing of the chests full of papers which she had found. She would probably want to do it down in the cellars of the chateau. She had often told him, that the context in which something was found, was almost as important as the actual discovery. So how would that work out, if she found he had installed Jeanette as his live-in housekeeper when she came back to the village?

He still found Jackie very desirable, especially when she was dressed to kill, as she had been today. But it looked as though he was going to have to give her up, at least for part of the time, to her large, possibly international, TV audience. And what might happen when she was away filming and promoting the series? He was only too well aware of the high divorce rate among film stars. Did he want to be involved in that sort of life? As a result of his meditation, he was feeling depressed when he got back to the little, hill-top village.

The sun was starting to sink into the west when he parked the car in the yard opposite the chateau and wandered disconsolately back to his rented cottage. He felt in his pocket for the key and, finding it missing, tried the door. It was unlocked. Of course – he remembered now that he'd left it with Jeanette who had arrived this morning. Without consciously willing it, he found his depression beginning to lift.

He went in and looked around. Was it his imagination, or had the place been tidied up? Was she up in the second bedroom he had allocated to her? He went upstairs to check. He discovered her cases were lying opened and empty on the unmade bed, but she wasn't there. Her clothes were not hanging in the small wardrobe in the corner. The little set of drawers under the window proved to be empty. However, when he checked in the bathroom, she seemed to have completely taken the room over. There was a small table which he hadn't noticed before. It was installed beside the washbasin. It was completely covered with body and face-creams, with make-up and other female items.

Slightly puzzled, he went into his own bedroom. This was the larger one at the front. The double bed, which he'd left unmade that morning when he rushed out to explore the chateau, had been neatly made. In fact. it looked as though clean sheets had been put on it. The ironed pillowslips were tidily placed against the bedhead. On the right-hand one a skimpy night-dress had been neatly placed. That made him check the hook behind the door where he found the diaphanous negligee which she had worn at the Hotel du Chateau a few weeks ago, when she was trying to seduce him, because she thought Jackie had disappeared.

He crossed to the wardrobe and opened the doors. His own few hangers had been pushed to one end, and a variety of summer dresses and other clothes had now filled the rest of it to bursting. It was a similar situation in the chest of drawers where she had taken over the top two and filled them with various frothy under-clothes and other items and had relegated his clothes to the two lower drawers. It looked as though she was taking over.

It was obvious that she wasn't upstairs, so he returned to the ground floor, but she wasn't there either. Had she gone out, leaving the place unlocked? He went into the kitchen. Everything there was neat and clean – not at all like he had left it. He was getting the impression that Jeanette intended to be very thorough in carrying out the house-keeping duties she had volunteered for upon payment of three hundred euros a week. Perhaps he would feel grateful to her, when they had sorted out the question of the bedrooms. At that moment the back door opened, and she stood there, covered in a large butcher's apron.

"Ah, you're back." She smiled. "You've timed it perfectly. I was just about to put the food on the barbecue in the back yard."

"Barbecue? I didn't know there was a barbecue."

"It was in the shed in the corner. There are all sorts of things in there. The barbecue was a bit mucky and rusty, but I've cleaned it and it will do very well now."

"What about charcoal?"

"I borrowed some from the woman down the street. She also gave me some chicken legs and two pieces of steak." She frowned at him. "Your fridge was almost empty. I'll take your car tomorrow and stock up in Limoux. You'll have to give me a hundred euros."

"What did you say to the lady down the street?"

"Of course, I told her I was your new housekeeper. She and I agreed that all men without wives need a housekeeper to look after them." She turned back to the door. "Come on. I need you to blow on the fire to keep the charcoal burning."

She preceded him into the yard. That was when he became aware that she had nothing on underneath the huge apron except a bikini. Speechless, he followed her plump, gyrating buttocks out to the barbecue. He supposed it was lucky that it was a warm evening.

Outside everything had been organised. There was a long table in front of a bench on which Jeanette had managed to provide cushions. The barbecue was already well alight and he didn´t think it would need any blowing on from him. He also noticed that a bottle of wine and two glasses stood on the table. He picked up the bottle and read the label.

"Where did you find this wine? It´s a good one. I didn´t know I had any wine."

"You didn't. I got it from the bar."

"Did you also tell them in the bar that you were my housekeeper?"

"Of course. That is why they were willing to give me two bottles of a good one. I told them you would pay tomorrow."

"Did you wear your bikini when you went to the bar?"

"Of course not. The bikini is only for you, my darling. I was still in the same clothes I had on this morning when I arrived."

Philip recalled the outfit with her substantial boobs thrusting through the loose sweater and the long, bare, curvaceous legs. He could see he was going to be the object of many humorous comments when he next went into the bar for a drink.

"Can you go and get the salad out of the fridge?" she asked. "I was on my way to do that when you arrived, and your lovely face drove it out of my mind. Now - I´ve only got two chicken-legs, so that´s one each. Would you like the large piece of steak?"

Watching her as she bent over the glowing barbecue, Philip realised he was quite hungry. "Yes, I can manage that," he said.

"That´s my man. You can´t perform properly without a good meal inside you."

He forbore to respond to that comment as he went to get the salad. When he returned, the meat was sizzling, and the wine had been poured out. She handed him a glass.

"I think the English say ´cheers´."

They clinked glasses and drank deeply. Philip thought that it was truly a good wine.

"I see you have put a lot of your things in my bedroom," he observed.

"No. The front bedroom will have to be mine. The back room is unsuitable for a woman. It is too small. There isn´t enough light. There is no mirror and the little *comptoire* is too small to take all my clothes." She smiled smugly at him. "You will have to decide whether you wish to share my bed in the front room or sleep on your own in the back. The sheets and blankets are there, so you can make up the bed quite quickly. You can put my cases in the corner."

"Jeanette," he chuckled, "you seem to have everything sorted out."

He took another deep draught of the wine and felt happier than he had for some time. He sat on the bench and watched Jeanette's shrouded but obviously voluptuous body as she expertly cooked the meat. In no time at all she was serving it on the plates she had ready. His glass was nearly empty, and she drained the bottle into it, after topping up her own.

"I have done you one of my sauces," she said. "It's on the side. I will get it."

When she returned with the sauce and the second bottle of wine, Philip saw she had removed the butcher's apron and was now clad only in her bikini, which was a white cotton fabric. It was very skimpy and exposed a lot of her attractive body and left little to the imagination. He tore his gaze away and took another substantial swig of his wine. She sat close beside him, and he could feel the warmth of her flesh against his bare arm.

"Try some of this sauce." She poured it over the meat, her right breast rubbing against him as she did it. How much more could a man stand?

He sampled a chunk of steak covered in the sauce. "It's delicious, Jeanette. It seems to turn the steak tender and juicy. How do you make it?"

"Ah, that is my secret recipe." She lifted her empty glass to him. "Can you fill me up please?"

"Now that *will* be a real pleasure."

They both laughed at the innuendo.

"So," she asked him, with the glass to her lips, "how was your meeting with Jackie?"

He shook his head. "Not very good. She doesn't want to know me while she is doing this series. She told me to go off and do my own thing until that was finished in three months' time. Then we would meet up and decide what we were going to do next."

"That is what I hoped would happen." She snuggled up against him. "So you will have three months with nobody to share your bed except me."

He no longer tried to pretend that he didn't want to accept what she offered. First, he concentrated on finishing his food and the second bottle of the very good wine. Then he pushed the plates away and leaned back to watch the dying embers of the barbecue. It was now nearly dark. Jeanette was leaning close against him, and he liked the feel of her soft, warm flesh against his. He lifted his arm and rested it across her shoulders.

She suddenly shivered. "I'm feeling cold. I must go and get my gown."

"I'll come with you," he said. "These plates and things can be cleared up in the morning."

They got up and went into the house. As they entered the kitchen he slipped his hand off her shoulders and undid the top strap of her bikini. On the stairs they paused to undo his shirt and throw it aside. By the bedroom door their shoes were kicked off and he started to slide his trousers down his legs. At the bedside the rest of their clothes were left on the floor. Her scrap of a night-dress was ignored.

"Oh, Philip," she complained, "why can I only get you to make love to me when you're half drunk?"

"That's going to change from now on," he promised.

He felt as though he had crossed a desert and was drinking at the first oasis he had reached. But when they had reached a climax and he had collapsed across her soft, welcoming body, the picture which swam across his mind was of the director lifting Jackie's lace-clad breast to show it off to the viewers.

10

Philip slept late the next morning. Some time during the night he had rolled off Jeanette's voluptuous body, so it was she who woke first and went downstairs to tidy up. She returned with a jug of coffee and two mugs which she placed on the bedside table.

She shook him awake. "Come on, You've got to get up and start clearing the rubble away to try to find that staircase down to the cellars."

"Oh, dear," he groaned. "I think I must have drunk too much last night."

"Don't tell me, that once again you can't remember what happened."

"Oh, no. I can remember that all right. It was great. It was the first step into my new French lifestyle." He recalled Jackie's accusation. "There isn't going to be any more English prudery round here."

"Good." She leaned forward and Philip became aware she was wearing nothing but the see-through negligee which had been hanging behind the door. "Because I had to answer the door when Albert called for his instructions."

"What!" Philip was suddenly wide awake. "Did you talk to him?"

"Of course I talked to him. I told him you weren't capable of giving him any instructions for a little while." She put her head on one side. "He wanted to know what you had planned for him to do this morning. I asked if he'd finished what he was working on yesterday and he said `no'. So I told him to carry on doing the same thing and you would go down and see him later if you wanted anything different."

"And what were you wearing – just that thin thing that shows everything you've got?"

"I only opened the door half-way."

"So he only saw half of what you've got."

"Yes. But he didn't seem to mind. He just grinned, and said I was to make sure you didn't hurry. Then he went off with his mate, who was waiting across the road."

Philip shook his head. "By now it will be all round the village that you're a lot more than simply my housekeeper."

"Does that matter? They would be saying that anyway."

"Well," he said, "I might as well enjoy what the rumour-mongers will be telling each other." He grabbed her wrist and dragged her unceremoniously back into bed

"I do like this new French-style lover," she murmured a few minutes later before they parted.

Philip was now fully awake. After a few minutes he rolled over and sat on the edge of the bed. The coffee was cold when he poured it out, but he nevertheless had a good drink of it before he went into the bathroom for a shower. After a search he found his soap and flannel among the bottles and potions which his new housekeeper seemed to find essential for her continued existence. It reminded him briefly of his life back in England with the errant Madeline.

By the time he got downstairs there were eggs and toast waiting for him, prepared by Jeanette in a loose dress that was wrapped round her and fastened at the waist. He noticed it was almost hiding her bra but left her bare legs largely uncovered, except for the flat slippers.

"Where did you get the eggs and bread?" he asked. He knew he didn't have such things in his kitchen cupboards.

"Oh, I promised the lady across the road that I'd give them back when I've done the shopping."

He looked at her suspiciously. "You didn't go out dressed like that."

"Why not!" She pulled the dress more modestly over her bare parts. "I didn't have time to put on anything more complicated." She smirked. "I decided it was more important you had your breakfast after your activities in the night."

Philip shook his head. It was clearly a waste of time to expect Jeanette not to make it obvious to the whole of Rennes-le-Chateau that she was sharing his bed. For now, he pushed to the back of his mind the need to make a decision about how he would deal with their relationship when Jackie returned in three months time.

He changed the subject. "You said you wanted to go shopping today for supplies."

"That's right."

"Well, I've decided I'll come with you. I've already lost quite a big chunk of today's worktime, so I might as well start looking for the way into the chateau cellars tomorrow. I promised Jean-Luc Lerenard that I would call in to see him in hospital some time this week to check up on how his recovery is going. So I'll take you in to the hypermarket in Carcassonne, if you wish, and visit him while you are shopping. Would that suit you?"

"It certainly would." She held herself upright with a beatific smile in her face, "It will be just like going shopping with my husband."

"Hmm. I don't know about that. However, if I'm to accompany you, I insist you dress more modestly and display less bare flesh to the world."

"Of course I will." She tried to look suitably chastened. "While you are eating your breakfast I will go and shower and change."

"There's no great hurry. I also want to go and have a chat with Albert. So you have at least half an hour."

She scurried off upstairs.

They actually set off nearly an hour later. Jeanette was sitting upright beside him with a broad grin on her face. As instructed, she had put on a summer dress which, although it was very pretty, exposed much less of her cleavage than her earlier outfit. In the little sports car she lifted her knees so that the skirt fell away to expose most of her thighs, but only Philip could see that.

It took them less than an hour to reach the outskirts of Carcassonne where he dropped her, making arrangements to meet her in the coffee hall an hour or so later. Then he went to the convalescent wing of the city hospital where his friend had a private room. This was to ease his recovery from the surgery necessary to re-inflate his collapsed lung. It was a week since Philip had last seen Lerenard, and the big man was looking much better. He was dressed and sitting in an easy chair near the open window through which came the jumbled sounds of the hospital activities and of traffic beyond the walls.

Philip bent forward to clasp his hand. "Jean-Luc, I *am* pleased to see that you are looking so much better. Thank God you're recovering so well. I felt terrible about being the cause of you almost dying."

Lerenard had been hit by three bullets from a machine pistol after Philip had pushed a large upright chest on top of the criminal holding the gun. The man had inadvertently fired the entire magazine, killing the head of *La Force Marseillaise* and himself in the process. But three rounds had passed through *le Compte's* body and hit Jean-Luc, who was standing just behind him. Two had only caused flesh wounds, but the third had entered his chest cavity and it had resulted in the collapse of his left lung, needing urgent surgery.

The big man patted his arm. "You should not feel any blame for what you did. Your quick thinking saved all three of us from certain death. And now you can see that it was only a temporary problem for me."

"So when will they let you out of hospital?"

"They say I can go in about a week. That will be a relief, let me tell you. I am becoming very bored." He shook his head. "The only problem is, that they say I must go to a place where I will have somebody to look after me, and that is difficult. I don't have any relatives or close friends."

Philip had a bright idea. "In that case you must come to Rennes-le-Chateau. You know it's on top of a mountain with clean, fresh air. There are quite a few tourists around during the day, but they leave us alone. And I have – er – a housekeeper who will look after you wonderfully."

"A housekeeper? You surely don't mean Mademoiselle Blontard."

"Oh, no. Jackie's spending all her time in Paris, making this new series about the Cathars. But you do know the lady. It's Jeanette Picard."

"Jeanette?" Lerenard regarded him with a knowing grin. "Wasn't that the little lady who was anxious to get into your bed?"

Philip nodded shame-facedly. "Yes, it was. And you might say that she has succeeded." He sighed. "What happened was that Jackie told me it was going to be at least three months before we will be able to decide whether we want to marry or not. She said I should forget her and make my own life until then. So, when I got back from our meeting, I was feeling pretty depressed, and there was Jeanette, cooking me a barbecue in her bikini and she'd got two bottles of a very nice wine and – well – I decided that since

Jackie was obviously not interested – and – Jeanette very clearly was – so, I thought, why not?" He came to a mumbling conclusion.

Now Jean-Luc had a broad grin on his face. "My dear Philip, these women seem to be able to wind you round their little fingers – isn't that what you English call it?"

"I know. I do seem to find French women rather irresistible."

"Well, there is obviously something about you that they like as well. But what are you going to do in three months' time when Mademoiselle Blontard finishes her TV series and comes back, expecting to take up your relationship where she broke it off?"

Philip shook his head. "This only happened yesterday, Jean-Luc. I haven't had a chance to work that out in my mind. All I can say is that I'd be very grateful if you would come to Rennes for a while to give my life a little stability."

"How can I refuse when you put it like that?" The big man was now laughing heartily.

Philip had never seen him so amused. They agreed that he would make arrangements for Jean-Luc to be put up somewhere in the village.

"I don't want to stay in the same house as you two and spoil the pretty domestic scene," he said.

"All right. In fact, I think I might be able to complete one of the rooms in the house we're restoring by next week. We could make that comfortable for you. And you could still join us for meals."

"OK. But you'll have to sort out your sex life for yourself. Don't expect me to help you with that."

So it was agreed that Philip would collect him from hospital a week later and they parted with that agreement.

11

César Renoir was suspicious when she heard the knock at the front door of her cottage. Visitors were rare in this back road near Rennes-les-Bains. In fact, this was the first time she had received a call from anybody without them previously phoning to tell her they were coming. There was no knocker on the door, and this was a firm rap of the knuckles on the wood, as though the caller did not intend to be refused entry. Although she thought the threat to her life, which had existed until *le Compte* had been killed, had now receded, she was still very cautious about opening the door to strangers.

The knocking came again. She went to the door and hesitated. Unfortunately, there was no vision panel and no restraining chain if she opened the door a few centimetres to view the visitor.

"Who is it?" she called loudly.

"My name is Gérard Vauclus. You won´t know me but I am a friend – er – was a friend of Alain Hébert. Can I come in?"

She noticed the voice was quite cultured. Perhaps it was that which persuaded her to open the door. The man facing her was tall and clean-shaven and dressed casually but well, in a light sweater and slacks. However, what struck her immediately was that he only had one arm. The other was missing at the shoulder.

"You´d better come in." She led the way into the front room and turned to face him. "You say you are a friend of Alain´s, but he never mentioned you to me. What do you want, Monsieur Vauclus?"

He didn´t answer her question directly. "How long have you known Alain?"

"Long enough to feel I knew him well." The memory of her special friend was still raw. It gave her a jab in her emotions when she talked about him.

"How close was your relationship?"

"It was close." She wasn´t going to tell him they had been lovers even if he had the cheek to ask.

"I understand you had only known each other for a few weeks."

"Er – that´s correct."

"But you lived here together."

She paused before answering. "I didn't live here. Sometimes I spent the night here."

"Quite often, I think."

That was enough. "Monsieur Vauclus, what right have you to come probing into my relationship with Alain. Are you a policeman?"

"No." He smiled infuriatingly. "I am not a policeman."

"So how do you know so much about me and my friendship with Alain?"

"Later." He took a breath. "This is his house – no?"

"He had rented it for the summer." Was that why the man was here – collecting the rent? "Alain gave me to understand that he had paid the rent and all the other costs for the place in advance. But if there is rent due, I am quite willing to pay it."

She didn't want to be evicted before she was ready to leave, and that was not yet.

"No. No, I have no interest in the rent or anything else connected with this place. As far as I am concerned, you can stay here as long as you like." He paused. "No - I am interested in other matters."

"What other matters?"

"Do you know anything about Alain's past life before he came here? Do you know what he did before he – er – shall we say before he retired?"

"We talked very little about his earlier life. I believe he worked in some capacity for the government in Paris."

"Did he tell you anything about an organisation called the Clemenceau Unit?"

She shook her head. "Alain never mentioned that name."

"No? Well, I suppose he wouldn't." Vauclus walked over to the window and gazed out. He was quiet for a time. César had the feeling he was considering what he should say next. Then he turned back to face her.

"Well, your friend Alain worked for the Clemenceau Unit. It is not a government organisation, although there are rumours that the French government provides it with financial support and information. The organisation was set up in 1919 to represent the special interests of France at the Peace Conference in Paris by the

Prime Minister at the time – Georges Clemenceau. You have surely heard of him."

"Of course."

"However, the Clemenceau Unit was not closed down after the Treaty of Versailles in 1920. It continued to campaign secretly for the weakening of the alliance between Germany and what remained of the Holy Roman Empire. That carried on through the Second World War. Even now it is still attempting to neutralise the effectiveness of the Habsbourg dynasty."

César was regarding him closely. "Are you telling me that Alain was involved in some kind of underground activity?"

"Not only involved, but he was remarkably successful in his involvement. In fact, it is believed that he had obtained certain documents which might be extremely embarrassing to the Vatican and the central European powers if they were released." Vauclus took a breath. "That is why I have come to see you, to try and make sure these documents reach the correct recipients."

She felt a sinking feeling in the stomach. She guessed the documents he was referring to were probably among those contained in the bag with the double-headed eagle crest on the side which she had so lightly handed to Philip a few weeks earlier. However, she wasn't about to admit it to this man.

"Monsieur Vauclus, I know nothing about you. You don't have any kind of introduction which might give me confidence in your good faith. Tell me why I should hand over to you any documents which might have originated from Alain."

The man jutted out his jaw. "I think I have been extremely open with you, Mademoiselle Renoir, about my purpose in coming here. I have not tried to mislead you about my intentions." He paused. "What I must tell you now, is that it would be extremely dangerous for you if you failed to hand over these documents to me. I am not exaggerating when I tell you that there are men who would kill to obtain them. So I strongly advise you to get rid of them straight away, both for your own safety and that of any others who may be involved."

There was something about the man that made César believe him. But she also didn't quite trust him. She doubted whether he had ever been a friend of Alain's as he claimed, but she agreed that it would be a good idea to let him have whatever documents he was interested in. She realised she must get in touch with

Philip and find out what he had done with Alain's bag, which she had so willingly handed over to him.

She took a deep breath. "Well, Monsieur Vauclus, I can tell you that I no longer have any of Alain's papers here in this house. There were some papers in a bag which I passed on to another person, who wanted some of them for what I am sure was a different purpose from the one you have described."

"My God! Who is this person? You may have put him in serious danger."

"Well, I'm sorry about that, but I think I must keep his identity secret until he authorises me to give it to you. I will contact him as soon as possible and tell him what you have told me, and I will enquire whether he can let me have the bag back. Obviously, that will take me a few days."

"I hope to God, that he hasn't found this vital document, and especially that he hasn't passed it on to anyone else. He might be signing his own death warrant."

"Very well," she said. "I will emphasise to him how dangerous this is. That should encourage him to let me have the bag back as a matter of urgency. As soon as I have it, I will contact you. How will I do that?"

"I will call here in three days at the same time in the morning. And I must again impress upon you and this other person, that this is a matter of life and death. If he obstructs you in any way, you must let me know about it when I come. If he is not willing to return the bag to you, you must tell him I will be contacting him direct. I will see you on Friday."

He turned on his heel and left, shutting the front door behind him as he went out.

César was left wondering whether this was really a serious problem, or whether the man was a dissembler. Of one thing she was certain – she must ring Philip and discuss it with him.

12

As he had expected, Jeanette was not enthusiastic when Philip told her he had invited Jean-Luc Lerenard to stay in Rennes-le-Chateau during his convalescence.

"Oh," she complained, "I thought we were going to have three months alone together before your fiancée came back to spoil the end of the summer."

Philip thought that comment was interesting. It seemed to suggest that she had accepted that their relationship was only temporary, and it relieved him of one worry. He had been wondering exactly how to tell Jeanette that she would not be sharing his bed on a permanent basis. However, he realised that now was not the time to discuss the future.

"Jeanette, he won't be living in the cottage with us. In fact, he insisted that I must find him somewhere else to stay. He will only be around during the day, and of course he will share our meals. I have no doubt there will be some cleaning and laundry to do for him when he needs it, but he won't make many demands on your time, and he certainly won't be around at night."

She pouted a bit, but gave in fairly easily. "All right, but I shall expect my weekly wages to be increased to five hundred euros."

Her mercenary attitude made Philip laugh. "An increase of two hundred euros for just doing the laundry and cooking for Jean-Luc. I will have to tell him how expensive he is. I expect he'll demand alternate nights in your bed if he has to pay so much."

Jeanette also laughed this time, in spite of the fact that she knew they were going to have to share a part of their lives with Lerenard. "But seriously, Philip, where are you going to put him?"

"I think I can finish off a bedroom and a bathroom during the next week in the house we are renovating. His arrival next week will make me push on with getting the place ready."

"So are you going to abandon your attempt to find a way down into the cellars of the chateau?"

"Just for the week while we're getting the rooms ready for Jean-Luc."

However, that discussion was forgotten when they got back to Rennes and Philip found César Renoir waiting for him.

"César," he greeted her. "How are you feeling now? I have been intending to visit you to see how you are doing, but things have been a bit hectic here in the last few weeks."

She smiled. "That's all right, Philip. I've been taking plenty of rest since you removed the threat to my life. I haven't previously thanked you for that."

"Don't worry about it." He grasped her hand. "I must say you look as though you have recovered well."

Only a few weeks ago she also had been near to bleeding to death after one of the criminals from *La Force Marseillaise* had thrown a knife at her which had penetrated six inches into her stomach, However, surgeons had been able to save her life.

"Are you still a lady of leisure?"

She shook her head. "I am planning to go back into journalism again, and there is still that series about the Cathar castles which I was working on."

"When Jackie's series comes out in the autumn, I expect there will be a lot of public interest generated in the Cathars. That will be good time to publish your work."

"Good idea. I'd better get on with it." She took a breath. "But that's not why I've come to see you. There's a serious business I have to talk to you about."

"OK. Let's go into the chateau. We won't be interrupted there."

Leaving Jeanette to put away the shopping, he led César round the corner to the front of the chateau and unlocked the gate. They entered the courtyard where it was private and quiet.

"What did you want to talk about?" he asked.

"Do you still have that bag of Alain's which I gave you - the one with the double-headed eagle crest on the side?"

He clapped his hand to his mouth. "César, I don't know where it is. When Hector Ramise said he no longer wanted to have the contents, we sort of lost interest in it. I think it was put up on top of the wardrobe in our room at the Castle Hotel. Jackie wanted to go through the list of treasures which we found in it. She thought it was possibly a list of the stuff we had found at le Bézu. But I don't think she'd had a chance to really work through it. I'm sorry. I forgot all about the bag, what with everything else that was going on. I don't know what happened to it after that."

"You didn't bring it to Rennes with you?"

"I'm sure I didn't. It isn't with my stuff in the cottage. Why? Do you want it back?"

"*I* don't, but it appears that there may be something in the bag, which means that whoever has it may have been put in danger."

"What on earth do you mean?"

She smiled grimly. "I'd better tell you the whole story. I had a visit this morning from a man calling himself Gérard Vauclus. Something about him frightened me. He said he was a friend of Alain's but I think that was a lie. Alain had certainly never mentioned him to me. But it's what this guy told me that disturbed me most."

César proceeded to describe her discussion with Vauclus and the veiled threat he had made to her. She concluded, "I don't like this man at all. There is something about him which I find quite frightening."

"You don't think he came from *La Force Marseillaise*?"

"Oh no. I wouldn't say he was a criminal. I am used to those sorts of guys, and *they* don't worry me. I would say he is more serious than that."

Philip knew César had been through a lot in the last few months with the murder of both her father and her lover by members of *La Force* and with her own near-death experience. But he also knew that she was a tough individual and wasn't easily frightened. He was impressed by the fact that she had taken the trouble to travel to Rennes soon after she had met the man, and hadn't relied on a telephone call to tell him about their meeting.

"Well, I'm sorry, César, but I'm sure the bag isn't here. I can only think that Jackie must have taken it with her belongings when we checked out of the hotel."

"And she isn't here at the moment?"

"No. She's in Paris doing this damned Cathar series. She's told me she is not going to concentrate on anything else until that is finished. And that's going to take about three months."

"Would she have taken the bag to Paris with her?"

He shook his head. "I would hardly think so. I expect that everything she didn't immediately need would have been sent to her home in Béziers."

"Béziers?"

"That's right. I suppose I could phone her aunt Charlotte who lives there in her flat, and ask the lady to see if she can find it among Jackie's stuff." He paused, thinking. "But César, I don't think we should send this bloke to Béziers. If he strikes you as frightening, I hate to think what it would be like for Charlotte to meet him. She is quite a gentle old lady."

"Oh no," she agreed. "All I ask you to do, Philip, is to see if you can locate the bag and let me know when you've done that, preferably not by phone. He says he is coming back in three days, and I want to be able to tell him that I'm doing my best to try to find it for him."

"Of course I will. I'll let you know as soon as I find out where it is."

With that promise, César left him, and he concentrated his efforts on preparing the room in the house for Jean-Luc's occupation.

13

By Thursday the recording team was working back in the studios in Paris. Louis had decided that he had got all the location shots that he needed. Armand had been told that he could pack everything up at le Bézu. He was to fill in the excavated areas and return the site of the ancient castle to the semi-wilderness state that had existed before the archaeologists turned up a couple of months ago. No doubt, once the series came out, the ruins would no longer enjoy the peace which had settled on them over the last few centuries. But that was the way of modern life.

Jackie was pleased to get away from the place. While they were there, the fear lurked in the back of her mind that Philip would turn up again and demand some sort of decision from her. She still regarded herself as being committed to them as a couple, but she wasn't quite sure what the relationship was going to be like in the future. At the moment all her thoughts and energy had to be concentrated on the series. After all, she wasn't merely the presenter on the screen. She also had to write all the scripts and work out with Louis how they should plan each episode of the twelve-part series. Philip didn't seem to understand how great were the demands that had been put upon her time and energy.

She accepted, that once this series was completed, she would have to think very seriously about the direction which her life should take. She didn't deny, that if she continued her television career, it would be bound to have a huge effect on her private life. In addition, there was her professional archaeological career, which seemed to offer such a rich future. She would have to make some serious decisions about where she should concentrate her efforts in the future. And, most important of all, was how her personal life should be fitted in with all these other demands.

She sighed. When the series was completed and she and Philip were together again, they would have to decide how these other parts of her life would fit in with their relationship. She knew that he wouldn't allow a repeat of what was happening this summer. In fact, she suspected he would demand that their life together would have to receive priority when she made her future plans. She realised there would have to be a decision on whether life with Philip was more important to her than some aspects of her career.

There was no doubt in her mind that she still loved Philip and wanted to spend the rest of her life with him. She thought he was good-looking and a wonderful lover. He also possessed a sensitive and humorous personality. She thought it was that quality which had especially attracted her when she first met him. The question she had to face was whether she was willing to give up at least a part of her bright professional future to concentrate on marriage and raising a family, which she appreciated were bound to be priorities for him.

She returned to the same hotel suite that she had occupied before they went to le Bézu. As she unpacked her suitcases, she thought again about the man who had committed himself to her. Less than a week ago, a frustrated, angry Philip had come here to share it with her. She realised she hadn't treated him very well. That was foolish of her. She really ought to have made the effort to give him a little of the affection and enthusiasm for their relationship which would probably have been enough to send him back to Rennes-le-Chateau in a happy frame of mind. She really shouldn't have been so overwhelmed by all the other demands on her time and energy, that she hadn't been able to find the little bit of the personal love for him that he needed.

Once she had finished putting away her clothes, she decided she should go down and have something to eat before having an early night. It would be important for her to be up first thing in the morning and functioning fully for tomorrow's filming. Emerging from the lift into the entrance foyer, she was hailed by one of the girls on reception. "Hello, Mademoiselle Blontard, I have a message for you." She waved a white hotel envelope at her.

"Thank you." Jackie took it with her as she went into the dining room.

Having ordered food and a modest glass of wine, she opened the envelope. Her heart sank when she saw it was from Philip and dated two days ago. Wasn't he going to leave her alone even when she returned to Paris?

She started to read. The message was simply addressed to "Jackie". There were no endearments, no messages of affection. But why should she expect any?

César came round this morning. She wants the bag back – the one with the double-headed eagle crest on the side. Apparently, she's been told there was something important in the bag – possibly even dangerous. I haven't got it, so I presume it was taken to your place in Béziers when we left Quillan. I've tried ringing Charlotte several times but there's no reply. Can you tell me how I can get the bag? César wants it by Friday. – Philip.

Again, he didn't end with a promise of love. He was obviously still upset with her. She moodily munched her way through the meal without really tasting it, as she read the note again. It sounded as though it was fairly urgent that he should return the bag to César. He had probably tried to ring her, but she had switched off her phone for the last few days to avoid any interruptions to her schedule.

To be fair to Philip, he had obviously tried Aunt Charlotte first. Of course, he wouldn't have known that she and Hector were taking a fortnight's holiday to celebrate the professor's retirement. She also couldn't remember what exactly had happened to the bag, but he was probably correct in assuming it had been sent back to Béziers. Quite possibly it would now be residing in the office at her home.

Since he had said César wanted it by Friday (that was now tomorrow) she supposed she ought to ring him. But she shrank from what might turn into an unpleasant phone call. In any case that wouldn't provide him with the key which he would obviously need to get into the flat in Béziers. While Charlotte was away the only ones were in her handbag upstairs. She assumed he wouldn't be enthusiastic about driving all the way to Paris and back under the present circumstances. It was also important that the list of Cathar treasures should not be returned with the bag. Was the list still in the bag or had she put it in one of her own files, preparatory to checking it against the items in the *Vendredi Treize* vaults. There was no way that she could spare the time to go to Béziers herself to find out.

While she had been reading back through Philip's message and chewing over what to do, she suddenly became aware that she was not alone. She looked up to find a strikingly attractive young lady standing by the table. She was smartly dressed in a mauve silk suit and matching high heels, with her long, pale blonde hair curling over her shoulders. As Jackie took in the vision in front of her, the woman pulled out a chair and sat down beside her.

"Mademoiselle Blontard, I don't know if you remember me."

The girl did indeed look familiar. "Wait a minute. Didn't I see you with Armand Séjour a few weeks ago?"

"That's correct, mademoiselle. He and I are both employees of *Vendredi Treize*. My name is Candice Ambré."

"So it is." Jackie took a breath. "To what do I owe this visit? Is it on business?"

"Well, it is for me, mademoiselle. I have come to ask if I might help you, particularly with the cataloguing of the Templar archives which you found at Rennes-le-Chateau."

"Really? How did you know about those?"

"I was present in Quillan when you were discussing them with Armand and your friend Philip."

"I don't remember that." Jackie wondered whether all the pressure she was under at the moment, was driving things out of her mind that she would normally have easily remembered.

"It was on the occasion in the reception area of the Castle Hotel, when you were told that you had been selected to be the next president of *Vendredi Treize*."

"Goodness gracious!" She shook her head. "It must have been the shock which made me give away secrets like that."

"Well, mademoiselle, I remember you saying you would like the archives to be catalogued as soon as possible, before the winter damp got at them again and I wondered if I might be suitable to help. I have been employed recently by Marcus Heilberg as an investigator, but he has nothing for me to investigate at present."

"Are you qualified to carry out this sort of work?"

Candice opened her handbag and produced a sheaf of papers which she handed over. "I took a degree in history with archaeology at Lyons University. The course also included Mediaeval Latin. You can see I was awarded a first class honours."

"Well," agreed Jackie as she glanced at the document, "that appears to be very suitable. Are you already on the payroll of *Vendredi Treize?*"

"No, ma'am, they have been employing me as a contractor at two hundred euros a day but that has now stopped."

"Oh, I can easily afford that."

Candice appeared very anxious to please, and now it occurred to Jackie that this girl would be a very good way of solving the problem of César's bag.

"When are you available?"

"Straight away, mademoiselle."

"Could you travel down to Languedoc tomorrow morning?"

"If it is urgent, I'm willing to go tonight."

"No. Early tomorrow would be good enough." Jackie paused. "I want to send a message and a key to – er – to my friend, Philip. Can you make sure he gets it as early as possible?"

"Certainly."

"I must also write an authority for you, so that he will let you have access to the archives. Before you start work on them, you will need to get suitable storage cases which you should label by date and source location. Do you understand me?"

"Yes, mademoiselle."

"There is a place in Carcassonne where you can get things like that. I will give you their address. Now, can you go to reception and get several sheets of headed paper and a couple of envelopes. I want to give you the notes now and then you can set off as soon as you like."

As the girl hurried off, Jackie relaxed back in her chair. How convenient it was that the problem raised by Philip had now been solved for her.

14

The period after César's visit was a busy one. Philip dutifully tried to contact both Charlotte and Jackie, but neither answered their phones, so he had to content himself with leaving a message for his fiancée at her hotel. Then he plunged into the preparation of the house for the arrival of Jean-Luc.

He already had a plumber lined up, and Albert was sent with a message that it was urgent the man should turn up at the weekend at the latest. The shower, toilet and wash basin, with their associated bits and pieces, had been obtained from a *bricolage* in Limoux. The electricity supply was already connected to the house and a few hours work by a local electrician would provide the light and power which the big man would need.

The upstairs rooms had been plastered some time ago, and the floors had been laid. Philip borrowed a pick-up vehicle from a friend of Albert, noting that he must get one for his own use in the near future. In this he collected the windows, doors and frames and sundry fittings. He also selected suitable tiles and decorating materials. He reckoned he knew enough from his own do-it-yourself experience to do those trades himself. With Jeanette employed as a painter, he was hopeful that the work could be finished within a week.

He was interrupted by a phone call from César on the Friday morning. Until then the consequences of her visit on the Tuesday had slipped his memory.

"Philip," she enquired, "Have you had any luck with locating that bag of Alain's?"

"Oh, César, I'm sorry. Neither Aunt Charlotte nor Jackie answered my phone calls. So I left a message for Jackie but I haven't had a reply. I must chase her up again."

"Well, I've got this man, Gérard Vauclus, with me at the moment. He's very anxious about the bag. He wants to talk to you."

"OK. Put him on."

"No, I mean he wants to come over to your place and discuss where it is with you. Are you willing to let me tell him how to find you?"

Philip detected a note of anxiety in her voice. The man had obviously got César worried. He felt he should relieve her if he could.

"Of course I am. You can tell him how to get to Rennes-le-Chateau. Does the bloke want to come over now?"

She broke off to consult Vauclus and came back to him. "Yes. He'll drive straight over in the next half hour."

"OK. Tell him I'm working on the house opposite the entrance to the chateau." He paused and had a quick thought. "Oh, and César . . ."

"Yes?"

"I take it you don't mind me giving the bag and its contents to this guy when I do manage to find it?"

"No. I just want to get him and the bag off my back."

"OK. I'll let you know when I've sorted it out."

"Thank you."

She hung up and Philip returned the phone to his pocket more thoughtfully. There must be something about the bag or its contents which were pretty important to this man.

He'd hardly turned back to his work when he heard a car drive into the yard, and looked up to see a small white Peugeot pull into the area in front of the chateau. As he watched, a young woman got out and looked around. She was wearing a white shirt above rather tight jeans that revealed a slim but shapely figure. Her long, pale blonde hair was tied back in a pony tail. He judged that, despite her flat shoes, she was only a couple of inches shorter than he was. Then he realised that he knew her.

"Hello, Candice." He advanced to meet her, wiping off the sawdust from his hand as he held it out to shake hers.

"Good morning, Philip." Her English was almost accent-less. Her attitude was professional. "It hasn't taken me long to get here from Paris, has it?"

"All the way from Paris this morning? You must have left early."

She smiled briefly. "Before five o'clock. Luckily the roads were clear at that time. I was anxious to take up my new post."

"What post is that?"

"I have two letters for you." She leaned sideways into the car which resulted in the front of her shirt falling open and revealing her small but shapely bra-supported breasts for his appreciative eyes. She emerged a couple of seconds later, leaning back slightly. The challenging look on her face showed she had noticed his interest in her body. No doubt a woman like that was always aware of the effect she had on men.

She held out the two envelopes to him. "They are from Mademoiselle Blontard. The top one explains why I am here. The second one is a reply to the message you left at the hotel for her earlier in the week."

Of course Philip was more interested in the second one. It was heavier than expected and, when he opened it, a key fell out. He picked it up and put it in his pocket. He was particularly anxious to read the contents of the note. He saw there were no endearments when he read it.

Philip, I didn't get back to the hotel until tonight (Thursday) so I have been unable to reply to your message before. Although I don't remember seeing what happened to the bag, I agree it is likely that it will have been sent to Béziers, and Charlotte has probably put it in my office. She and Hector are on holiday for a fortnight, so I have enclosed one of my own keys to the flat. Please take care of it and let me have it back when we next meet. You have my permission to go into the flat and recover the bag if it is there. Please remove the list of Cathar treasures, if it is still in the bag, before you give it back to César. I would also like you to check through the contents to see if there are any other items which I might be interested in. Thanks, Jackie.

Philip shrugged as he folded the note and tucked it in his back trouser pocket. He supposed he shouldn't expect anything more affectionate from her, since his own message had been factual. He raised his eyes to see that Candice was watching him closely. Her head was thrown back so that her long hair hung down her back and her chest was thrust out. Her legs were astride in a way that suggested she was in control of events and was here to stay. The idea was interesting.

"The other note explains why I am here," she said.

He opened it. The explanation was brief.

Philip, I am employing Candice Ambré to start cataloguing the Templar archives. Please can you arrange some accommodation for her? Other than that, she should be able to work on her own and cause you minimum trouble. Jackie.

He looked back at the girl. "Did Mademoiselle Blontard tell you how you were going to reach the archives?"

She shook her head wordlessly.

"How good are you at climbing ladders?"

"All right, I think."

"Well, Candice, the only way into the Templar archives at the moment would be up a very long, very steep ladder, and then in through a window opening that has been partly blocked by the floor inside collapsing more than half-way across it." He smiled bleakly. "I think you may have a problem starting your new duties."

She drew herself up to her full height. "I would like to look at this window you describe, if you please."

"OK, come with me. You can leave your car where it is."

He led the way out of the yard, down the road to the start of the footpath, and round the hill until they were below the ruined part of the chateau. He pointed up at the window that he and Jackie had escaped through several weeks ago.

"That is the only way into the archives at present."

She looked up at the opening high above her but said nothing. He guessed she was just beginning to see the problem she was taking on.

"When I climbed back in through that window to rescue Mademoiselle Blontard," he said conversationally, "we had to erect a three-section ladder to its fullest extent, and it reached to about two feet – er – half a metre below the sill. Then I had four men holding it steady while I inched up it one rung at a time because it was so steep. When I got to the top, I had to hug myself against the wall until I could reach the bottom of the window opening. Then I had to pull myself up and over the sill into the room. It was very unpleasant. I certainly wouldn't want to do it every day."

"What about scaffolding?"

"I suppose we could have a company come in and erect a staircase tower. However, I´m not very happy about that idea, and I don´t think Jackie would be very keen on it either."

"Why not?"

"Scaffolding isn´t very secure. It would be impossible to prevent anybody who was seriously interested in looking into the castle cellars, from using it when we weren´t there. And I don´t think it would be practical to take on a watchman to guard the place all night."

"Is there no other way into the place where the archives are at present?"

Philip had no intention of telling her how they had found their way into the cellars from the crypt of the church. Only he and Jackie knew about that, and it was quite impractical at present anyway.

"I think there are probably steps down to the cellars from the ground floor, but I haven´t been able to find them yet. I guess they must be buried somewhere under the rubble from the ruined part of the chateau."

She turned to face him. "I will help you look for the steps."

"Not wearing those clothes, you won´t. You will need overalls and boots and leather gloves and all the safety equipment. And it may be necessary to shore up parts of the ruined building to prevent any further collapse as we dig down. I warn you, getting down into the cellars is not going to be easy."

"All right. I will get those things this afternoon. Can we start looking for this staircase when I get back?"

Philip shook his head. "I´m sorry. I have other priorities. It will be the end of next week before I can start to look for the staircase."

"What are those priorities?"

"First I must finish preparing the house for Jean-Luc Lerenard to come to start his convalescence. Then I have to find this bag of César´s. It will mean a trip to Béziers at least, and that will take a day out of my time."

"You can employ some other men to look for the staircase."

"What´s the urgency, Candice? Those archives have been there for centuries. Another week or two this summer won´t hurt them."

"But what am I going to do while I am waiting to get into the cellars?"

"I don't know. You can help Jeanette with the painting while we are getting the house ready."

She tossed her hair back. "Painting – hah! I will phone Mademoiselle Blontard and get her permission to hire some men to look for the staircase."

She turned and stormed back up the path. Philip followed her more slowly. This woman obviously had a temper. He had a feeling she was going to cause him trouble in the future.

But that was all forgotten when he reached the castle yard, for he saw there was a large black car parked beside Candice's little white one and leaning against it was a man with only one arm.

15

The one-armed man came to meet him as he walked into the yard. He was tall and muscular, perhaps in his late forties or early fifties. Except for his missing arm, he appeared to be fit and athletic in build. His hair was short, and he was clean-shaven. His dark, deep-set eyes seemed to glower as he talked.

"I am Gérard Vauclus." He spoke in English with a clipped continental accent. "Mademoiselle Renoir told you about me." He did not offer to shake hands.

"I believe you came here a few days ago," said Philip. "Why did you come here?"

"Who told you that I was here?"

"My foreman saw you with another man. And one of the villagers saw you walking along the footpath below the chateau. I repeat, why were you looking round this place?"

"There is no mystery, Monsieur Sinclair, I was told that you had been meeting Mademoiselle Renoir and that you were here. The natural thing was to check if the woman was still here with you."

"She has never been here. Who told you she had?"

"That is information I will not disclose."

Philip took a breath. "I understand you are interested in the bag that she gave me."

"She should not have given it to you. It was not her property to give away."

"Well, Monsieur Vauclus, I understand it belonged to her close friend who had recently been killed. There was nothing in or on the bag to say it was anybody else's property. Why should she not dispose of it as she wished?"

He could already feel a sense of confrontation with this upright, serious man. His bearing suggested he could have been a policeman or some sort of military person. His arrival certainly had to be treated as important.

"Mademoiselle Renoir had no right to the possession of the bag. Neither, in fact, did her friend, Monsieur Hébert. He had received the bag from a person who was not authorised to give it to him."

"What are you talking about? It's only a bag. People are giving bags to each other every day."

"Not this bag. Surely you saw the crest on the side. That clearly tells you who owns it."

"I don't know about that. You tell me who is the mysterious owner of this so-important bag?" Philip took a step closer to the fellow. "And who exactly are *you*, Monsieur Vauclus? Where is your authority to demand we hand the bag back to you?"

For a moment Philip had the uncomfortable feeling that Vauclus might be considering resorting to violence, but the man controlled himself. "I am employed by the owners of the bag to recover it on their behalf. They have given me sufficient authority to demand its return."

"Do you have that authority in writing?"

"I certainly do."

"I would like to see it."

"Very well." Vauclus went back to his car and Philip accompanied him. He reached inside and picked up a briefcase. He riffled through the papers contained in it and emerged holding a sheet which he passed to Philip. The piece of paper was headed in the centre by the same double-headed eagle crest which he had seen on the side of the bag and on the blazer pocket of Professor Hector Ramise. There was a single paragraph in two languages on the sheet of paper - in German and in French. Philip's French was just about good enough by now to translate.

Monsieur Gérard Vauclus is authorised by me to take whatever action is necessary to recover the letter dated 21st July 1871 signed by Marie, Marquise de Hautpoul de Blanchefort.

It was signed by a scrawl and underneath was: *On behalf of the Holy Roman Emperor* and a recent date.

Philip returned the piece of paper to the other man. "What is so important about this letter it refers to, that you need to recover it?"

"Ah." Vauclus shook his head. "That I do not know, and I do not wish to know. You also would be wise to ask no more about it. Now – can you tell me where the bag is that contains this letter?"

"I think I might know where it is."

"Please tell me where I can go to pick it up."

"Hmm." Philip scratched his head. "I'm afraid I am not prepared to do that at the moment."

"Why not? Haven't I explained the importance of recovering the bag? It is vital that it is not lying around for any casual person to look into it."

"There is no danger of that. If it's where I think it is, the location is a private house some way from here. It has probably been deposited with a pile of other luggage in an unused room. It is quite safe there. Nobody is occupying that address at the moment, so no-one will look at the bag or its contents. However, I am not prepared to let you enter somebody else's private property without their agreement. Your authority certainly doesn't entitle you to do that either."

Vauclus' voice took on a dangerous tone. "Monsieur Sinclair, you should not attempt to play with me. I have been given this job to carry out and I do not intend to fail. Anyone who gets in my way is likely to regret it."

"There is no point in threatening me," said Philip. "That will almost certainly result in your losing the bag. I am prepared to get it for you, but I will do it in my own way and at a time to suit me."

"I want to get it as soon as possible, so that I can complete my job. I can run you to the place and accompany you when you pick up the bag."

Philip shook his head. "No. That wouldn't be a good idea. I must go alone, so that the owners of the place will let me go into the room where I believe the bag is. They will want to come with me so that they can satisfy themselves that I have taken nothing else. The contents of the room belong to a third party."

He was all too well aware of Jackie's request that he also remove the list of treasure which clearly had nothing to do with the letter that Vauclus' authority referred to.

The man seemed to have been considering Philip's comments. Now he said, "Very well. When will you have the bag here for me to collect?"

"Er – not until later next week. The owners of the property are on holiday at present, and I don't want to break into their house when they are away. In any case, I have some other jobs which I must complete before I take a day off to collect the bag."

Vauclus was looking at him searchingly. "I hope you do not think that, by winning yourself some extra time, you will make a lot of money for yourself by showing the bag to someone who will pay you for it. Because, if you do, I must warn you that I would make sure that you seriously regretted doing that."

His threat sent a shiver down Philip's spine. "I can assure you, Monsieur Vauclus, that I have no intention of preventing you getting the bag. I am English. I have no interest in anything to do with France or the Holy Roman Empire – if that still exists. And I have plenty of money, so I will not offer it to anyone else to get myself some more."

"OK." Vauclus suddenly gave up. "So when will I be able to collect this bag?"

"Shall we say a week from today? Leave me your phone number and, if I can't get the bag for you by next Friday, I will ring you and explain why."

"Very well. I have been trying to track down this letter down for months. I can wait another week."

He reached into the car again and brought out a wallet from which he extracted a visiting card and handed it over. "You will be able to get me on that number any time, day or night."

Then he climbed into the big black car and backed out of the yard without a further word or gesture.

16

Candice carried out her threat of phoning Jackie while Philip was talking to Vauclus. She came across to him as soon as the black car had driven out of the yard.

"I can't get through to Mademoiselle Blontard."

"Neither can I. I think she has switched her phone off. She won't want to talk to you while she is in the studio."

She tossed away her ponytail from where it had become looped over her shoulder and took a deep breath to swell her chest. "I will have to speak to her tonight. Meanwhile I think it is important that I find a way down to the cellars."

"OK. You go ahead and do that if you want to, but make sure you get the right clothes and equipment before you start. I don't want to have to carry you off to hospital because you've damaged yourself in some way."

"I – er – I don't have much money."

"Didn't Jackie give you any? Surely she would have known you would have expenses in getting set up down here."

"Well." She looked at him defiantly. "I didn't ask her for anything. I assumed you would see that I was all right."

Philip smiled ironically. "It seems to me, Candice, that you and Jackie have been assuming rather a lot between you. Apparently, I've got to find accommodation for you, arrange how to get you into the cellars to work on the archives, and now I'm supposed to finance you as well. I think I'd better start running up an account."

He turned back towards the house, anxious to get on with his work, but Candice wasn't willing to let him get away that easily.

"You must make all the arrangements for me before you go back to your work."

Philip let out a sigh. "I suppose you're right. Come on, I'll take you round to meet my housekeeper. She'll have to sort out your accommodation. While we're there, I'll give you a couple of hundred euros so that you can go and get your equipment. You can leave your car here until she's found you somewhere to stay."

He set off for the house with Candice trailing behind him. When they got there, Jeanette was upstairs making the bed. Philip led the way up to talk to her.

"Jeanette, this is Candice Ambré. Jackie has sent her down from Paris to start cataloguing the Templar archives. She asks us to find accommodation for her. Can you do that please?"

The housekeeper threw her arms wide. "What – find somewhere for her to stay just like that? This is a small village. Who on earth would be willing to take her in?"

"She could always go in the back bedroom and I´ll camp out in one of thre bedrooms in the house."

"Oh no. That´ll be much too small for her with all her smart clothes and things. She wouldn´t be able to fit in there."

"I´m willing to go anywhere for a while," Candice said.

Jeanette turned on her. "That room is quite impossible. You have a car. You can book into a hotel down in the valley. It is only a short drive from there up to the village."

Philip didn´t want to waste time on arguments. "Well, you sort out something between you." He took two hundred euros out of his wallet on the bedside table and handed the money to Candice. "There you are. When you´ve booked in to where you´re staying, you can go and get your work clothes and I´ll see you later."

He left them to sort out the accommodation problem and went back to the restoration of the house. He had already wasted a couple of hours that he could ill-afford on unnecessary banter.

It was the middle of the afternoon before Candice reappeared. The back seat of her car was piled high with bags and boxes. She came across to where Philip was fixing the window frame on Jean-Luc´s bedroom and looked up at him.

"Have you found some accommodation?" he asked.

"I have booked myself into a *chambre d´hote* in Cuiza. Your housekeeper told me there was nothing in Rennes."

"Well, Cuiza isn´t far. It´s only four kilometres down the road."

"I would have been quite happy with the back bedroom in your house," said Candice. "But Jeanette said that was your room."

Philip couldn´t help grinning. He knew why Jeanette didn´t want anyone else in the cottage. She didn´t fancy having another attractive woman around the place all the time and overhearing their far from silent love-making at night.

"I think she was lying." The girl's expression was acid. "I looked into the room and the bed wasn't even made. "I don't think she is just your housekeeper. I think you share her bed."

Philip shrugged. "Never mind. At least you've found yourself some suitable accommodation."

"I had to spend your money on the deposit. So I have used my card to buy the clothes you told me to get. I have brought the receipts so that you can reimburse me."

"OK. Let me have them before you go. Now you can start work once you have changed into your work clothes."

"What work do you expect me to do?"

"You said you wanted to find a way into the cellars. Well, to start with, you should begin by removing all the loose rubble from round the edge of the collapsed part of the building. You'll find a wheelbarrow and a shovel in the courtyard. You can dump the rubble you remove in the corner of the space over there." He pointed to the end of the outside wall of the chateau. "On your own, I think that would keep you going for several weeks, but we'll join you before you've finished."

"Several weeks!"

"There's an awful lot of rubble there, Candice. Oh - and make sure you don't remove anything which might be supporting any part of the walls or the roof. That could cause further collapse. Leave anything you're doubtful about until I join you."

"Are you expecting me to do all this on my own?"

"I told you, Albert and Gaston and I should be able to join you towards the end of next week. Until then, you'll have to cope on your own."

"I didn't come here expecting to be used as a labourer. I've come here to do a professional job."

"Well, you can't start doing your professional work until you can get down into the cellars, can you?" He shrugged. "Of course, you can clear off back to Paris and I'll send a message to Jackie, telling her that you can come back, when we've found a way down to the cellars. But I don't know how long that will be."

"Oh, you're infuriating," she shouted at him, brandishing her fists. "I turn up to work for you and I have to find my own accommodation. Then I'm sent off to get my own clothing and equipment. And finally, I'm expected to carry out this hard and perhaps dangerous work all on my own. I am nothing but a labourer as far as you're concerned."

Philip was startled by her outburst. He had the feeling, that if he hadn't been ten feet above her, she might have physically attacked him.

"Of course," she complained, "I can't expect any sort of gentlemanly consideration from an Englishman."

"Now steady on," he reproved her, "*I* didn't ask you to come here, so don't expect me to run round looking after you. If you think the job's too much for you, I suggest you go back to Paris. You can tell Mademoiselle Blontard that she's asked you to do something that's impossible until a way has been found to get to the archives. If she wants to get a contractor in to clear the rubble and shore up the collapsed parts of the building, she will have to discuss it with me."

"You know that's not the answer. It was you who told me she was too busy to think about anything except her damned television series. She'd just tell me to come back and do the best I can." She glowered at him. "But I'm sure she would expect you to give me a bit of help."

"And so I will, when I've finished preparing this place." He tried to smile consolingly at her. "You must just accept that you can't do it all by tomorrow. Look around. It's a lovely summer day. Find somewhere to stretch out and relax and enjoy the sunshine. You can start work next week when we are ready."

"Oh!" She stamped her foot. "I'm obviously going to have to do it all on my own."

She went back to her car, pulling off her shirt as she went. She opened the car door, undid and pushed down her jeans, then sat on the side of the driver's seat while she kicked off her shoes and pulled her jeans over her feet. Then, standing up in nothing but her bra and pants, she reached into the back of the car and searched around for her work clothes, pulled them out and started to put them on.

They consisted of overalls the colour of army fatigues. However, the material they were made of appeared to be very thin and to cling to her body, almost like a second skin. As a result, the shape of her underclothes could be clearly seen through the fabric. She did up the zip at the front to just above the start of her cleavage. One didn't need a strong imagination to see what she would be like naked. Only the boots, the gloves and the helmet seemed to be for protection.

Philip could hear the appreciative comments from Albert and Gaston downstairs, whose interest had obviously been aroused when they heard the argument going on.

With a grin, Philip turned back and tried to concentrate on fixing the timber window frame into the prepared stonework surround.

17

By six o'clock Philip decided he was finished for the day. He had fixed the door frames and hung the doors and cut in the locks and handles. Both windows had been fixed and primed and they were ready for glazing. He had sent Albert down to Cuiza with the dimensions for the glass. The man said he could have it cut by a mate of his and delivered in the morning. Albert seemed to have mates everywhere.

Jeanette came to ask him what time he wanted dinner.

"Have you included Candice in your plans?" he asked.

"Of course not. She will go back to her *chambre d'hôte*. They will give her dinner or tell her where she can go to get food."

"She's been working hard this afternoon, Jeanette. I think we ought to offer her food if she wants it."

He suddenly realised that, although the girl had been coming out of the chateau gates with a barrow of rubble every few minutes and depositing it on the heap which he had indicated for most of the afternoon, he hadn't actually seen her do that for some time. What had happened to stop her for the last hour or so? Suddenly he was concerned for her safety.

"I'll go and check if she wants to join us," he told Jeanette. "After that I'll come back for a shower and let you know. Then we can sit and have a drink together before we eat. Let's plan dinner for seven o'clock."

"OK." She gave him a half-smile as she went.

Philip packed away his tools and tidied up. Then he went across to the chateau. As he crossed the internal courtyard, he noticed that Candice had cleared a sort of recess into the rubble beside a half-standing wall. She obviously wasn't frightened of hard work. The barrow stood close by. It was nearly full, and the shovel was lying on the ground a few feet from it, but there was no sign of the girl.

"Candice," he called, but there was no reply.

He stepped over the shovel and got close to the area where she had been digging. The side of the heap was very steep here and he judged there was a real risk of a fall occurring in this area. He must tell her not to dig here any more without putting up some protective planking to make sure a collapse didn't occur. Looking down he saw what looked like a step leading down, close against the partly ruined wall. Perhaps she had found the start of a staircase, but it was only one step. The rubble filled the area below the step. Philip surveyed the area carefully. This looked like newly fallen material. He began to get an unpleasant picture of what might have happened. It looked as though Candice, while clearing the rubble, had uncovered the start of the staircase. Maybe she had been able to get down the steps close to the wall, at least part of the way. But while she was down there, the heap of rubble above had collapsed and imprisoned her, or maybe even covered her. With his heart in his mouth, he realised she might have been killed.

"Candice!" he yelled as loudly as he could. "Candice, can you hear me?"

"Yes." The voice was faint but at least she was alive. He thought it came from under the rubble. "Oh, Philip, thank God you're here."

"What condition are you in?" he called.

"I found the staircase to the cellars. Then I got trapped."

"But what about you? Are you hurt?"

"I have a beam across my middle. It fell on me, and it is too heavy for me to move because a lot of rubble fell on top of it and on my legs. I can't get them out."

"Have you broken any bones?"

"I don't think so. I can still wiggle my toes."

"That's good. Are you in pain?"

"Not really. The rubble is up to my chest, but I can still breathe all right."

"OK. Now listen, Candice. I'm going to go and get Jeanette to round up some of the villagers to help dig you out. I also need some equipment and some planking to prevent any more rubble falling on top of you. I'll be back in a short while and we'll start to get you out. Just keep still and be strong."

"Please don't leave me for too long, Philip. It seems as though I've been here for hours. I've been shouting my head off but – but nobody seemed to hear me."

Philip thought it sounded as though she was near the end of her tether. "Don't worry, Candice. I'm here now, and I'll get you out as soon as possible. Just rest as much as you can and keep still. I don't want any more rubble to fall on you."

He rushed off, but nearly ten minutes had passed before he got back. Albert had just returned from Cuiza, and he told him what had happened. The man went off to get as many of his mates as he could to help with the rescue. Meanwhile Philip put on his safety boots, leather gloves and hard hat.

He told Jeanette about Candice's plight, "When Albert and his mates get back, tell them to find as many stout planks as they can for strutting, to prevent further collapse of the rubble while we're digging down in the staircase."

"OK. Give me a kiss before you go down the hole."

He did so. "Oh, in about half an hour it would be a good idea to bring down some refreshment for the workers."

He set off, taking a pickaxe with him. He collected a plank, which he knew was in the back yard, and took it with him. When he got back to the start of the staircase, he let the girl know he was there. Then he spent a few minutes working out how to lean the planks diagonally against wall to form a sort of sloping bridge over the steps. It was necessary to dig footings for them so that they wouldn't get pushed aside by any further collapse of the rubble. Within a few minutes men were starting to turn up. Through Albert, he told them how he wanted to protect the staircase from falling debris, and they set to with a will, collecting planks and driving them into the rubble.

As soon as enough planks had been put up to stop further rubble falling down the stairs, they started to dig down. There were six men including Albert and himself and they organised themselves into pairs – one pair digging out the rubble into buckets, two men carrying the buckets up to the barrows (there were now three of those), and the other two barrowing the stuff to the spoil heap in the yard. They changed roles every fifteen minutes. If they came across large stones it sometimes required three or four of the men to lift them out. He told Candice what they were doing from time to time, to try to keep her spirits up.

Jeanette brought flasks of coffee to them and said that apparently several of the village women were helping her with preparing refreshments. Later they brought torches to light the area as the evening darkened. Philip was impressed with the way the locals were rallying round and helping.

They had been digging for nearly two hours, and Philip and Albert were working in what had now become quite a deep hole seven steps down, when they hit the end of a large timber beam in the middle of the rubble. It seemed to be sloping diagonally across the staircase. They cleared the area as best they could and exposed a large length of wood nearly a foot square in section.

"There's no way we're going to be able to move that," said Albert.

"I'm pleased we've reached this."

The beam told Philip they may be getting close to the girl. It was this beam which had probably prevented her head from being completely covered by rubble. That might have asphyxiated her. He called out, "Candice, you say you have a beam across your middle. Is it thick – say about eight inches by twelve inches - er – about twenty by thirty centimetres?"

The answer came back, "Yes. I think so."

"I believe we're close to breaking through to you," he told her. "Make sure you cover your face in case we cause some of the rubble to fall on you."

Now he was very careful as he levered the pickaxe into little gaps in the rubble close to the wall, pulling it back for Albert to load into the buckets. Suddenly the point of the pick broke through into a space and a hole opened up.

"I can see light," Candice gasped. "Oh, thank God."

There was a cheer from the men above him in the yard. Philip dropped the pick and pulled away the rubble with his gloved hands, trying to make sure that none of it fell through into the void. Soon he had an opening six inches across and Candice's dirty white face appeared in it, still wearing her yellow safety helmet.

"Oh, thank you. Thank you," she murmured and burst into tears.

"Don't be upset Candice. We'll soon have you out now."

During the next half-hour, he removed all the rubble around the beam. However, it must have been a long one, because they still couldn't move it, even when three of them tried together in the restricted space available. Reaching down, he cleared the stuff from above her overalls and then she was able to move her feet and even bend her knees a little, but she couldn't get the lower half of her body out from under that huge length of timber.

"What has happened," Philip explained to her, "is that the end of the beam is resting on the step above where your body is trapped. Actually you're very lucky. If it had landed on *you*, instead of the step above, you would undoubtedly have been crushed."

"I don't feel very lucky," she grumbled tearfully. "How am I going to get out of here?"

He noticed that close to the wall there was a void below where Candice was lying. "I'm going to wriggle through over the top of your body into that space below you," he said. "Then I'll dig away the rubble underneath you, and I hope that will let me pull you out sideways from underneath the beam."

"Let me do that," said Albert. "You must be very tired by now."

Philip shook his head. "You're too big to get through that hole. Besides you're just as tired as me."

He didn't add that the thought of Albert easing his big, rough body over the top of delicate Candice filled him with disgust.

"Now," he told her, "I'm going to have to come over the top of you, feet first and face down, so move your head to one side to make sure I don't hurt you."

He tried not to rest his booted feet or his knees too hard on her soft chest as he wriggled through the hole. She bent her head and kissed him as he passed.

"Thank you so much, Philip."

"Don't be too grateful," he warned her. "You're going to get a right telling off when we've finally got you out of this little prison of yours."

He started digging under her body with his gloved hands. Albert passed him a trowel someone had found which proved to be a big help. Within a short time, he had filled up the void around his feet, so they passed him small containers to fill with the excavated material. It was desperately slow and constricted work. It was also very hot down here, and soon sweat was breaking out all over his body and soaking his clothes. But gradually he was winning. After a while he had cleared the area around her legs, and she was able to bend her knees fully and flex her feet.

However, the problem was her pelvis. One buttock was almost free, but the other was immovably held between the heavy beam and the stone step. Philip thought it was amazing that none of her bones had apparently been broken, but he presumed she must have a young, flexible frame.

"Can you twist away from me?" he asked. "I'll put a hand under your waist and we'll see if I can pull you clear."

"Ah – ow," she protested as they tried it.

"Does that hurt?"

"It does when you pull my body like that."

He rubbed the back of his hand across his greasy forehead. "I can see now that your overalls are trapped under the beam on the step above your body. How on earth it trapped your clothes without smashing your hip is quite amazing."

"The beam did hit me very hard," she remembered.

"Well, you must have popped out from under it somehow."

"What if I undid my overalls?" she asked. "Do you think you could pull me out then?"

"He grinned. "We could try. The men above would enjoy watching that."

"Well, if it's the only way, let the dirty buggers enjoy it."

"Albert," Philip called up to him, "The girl's clothes are trapped underneath the beam. I'm going to have to cut them away and then we'll see if we can slide her out of them. I need a knife. And can somebody go and ask Jeanette to bring a blanket to wrap her in when we get her out."

Once he was handed the knife, he soon had Candice's overalls undone to the waist. Philip helped her struggle out of the arms so that her top half was bare except for her bra. She was bathed in dirty perspiration. Next, he carefully cut away the lower part of her clothing and removed her boots. Albert told him that Jeanette had arrived with a blanket from the spare bed. They were ready for the pull.

"Hold your hands up to Albert," he told her. "Now, Albert, can you pull her up steadily but gently. For God's sake stop, if she shouts that it's too painful."

Philip put one hand underneath her waist and the other in her crotch to pull her sideways from under the beam.

"Are you ready?" he called, and Albert nodded. "Right. Away we go."

They both pulled together. Candice howled as they hauled on her angled body.

"Do you want us to stop?"

"No!" she gasped. "Go on."

Philip could feel movement. Then suddenly, like a cork from a bottle, her body came away from the trapping beam and she was lifted out through the hole. As she went, gasping and crying, he could see a great livid bruise on her right hip. If that was the worst that her body had suffered, she was very lucky. Wrapped in the blanket, she was carried off somewhere by the women. Then Albert helped Philip slowly extract himself from the hole.

18

By the time Philip and Albert had emerged, everyone else had disappeared. It seemed that they had all got together to carry Candice away, wrapped in her blanket, to some unknown destination. That was fine as far as Philip was concerned. He was feeling dirty and sweaty and dog-tired. All he wanted was a shower and to fall into bed.

He took a look around. It was nearly dark, and all the torches had been taken by the others when they departed. As far as he could see, the barrows and the buckets and the excavating tools had been left where the blokes had put them down, but that wasn't a problem.

"I think we'll leave everything here just as it is," he told Albert. "There's nothing that can't be left until the morning."

They trudged across the courtyard and through the open gates. They dragged them closed. The key was still in the keyhole, so he locked up and put the key in his pocket. Then he trailed across the yard behind Albert. They turned the corner and suddenly found themselves in the middle of a crowd spread across the road. It looked as though the whole village was having a party to celebrate the rescue of the girl. Philip and Albert were welcomed into their midst and their backs were slapped by all and sundry until Philip, for one, felt quite sore.

Down the road came the bar-owner carrying a small barrel of the local wine. His wife followed behind with a tray of glasses. Somebody brought out a table to stand the barrel on, and the next minute glasses of wine were being handed round to the company. Philip usually thought this local tipple was too sour to be pleasant, but this evening it tasted like nectar to him. He downed his glass in about five gulps, only to have it replaced by another. Everyone was over-filled with joyfulness. Then he became aware that Jeanette was standing beside him, and she seemed to be the only person who wasn't enjoying herself. He offered her a slurp of his wine, but she refused.

"They've put that girl in our bed," she complained. "They brought her back to our cottage and carried her upstairs. When they took the blanket off her, she started shivering uncontrollably and her teeth were actually chattering. One of the women said it was the result of exposure, so she was put in our bed, even though she was so dirty." She took a breath. "Because they think she might be suffering from hypothermia, they've sent someone to get the doctor. But I think you ought to come and look at her."

"OK." Philip sighed and handed his half-full glass back to the bar-owner with an apology. He followed Jeanette into the cottage and upstairs to the front bedroom. Two of the women from the village were there. He vaguely recognised them, but he didn't know their names. Candice was lying in the bed with just the top of her white face sticking out of the blankets. He went over to look at her.

"What's the matter, Candice? Are you feeling ill?"

"I'm so cold, Philip. I can't stop shivering. Can you come into the bed and warm me up?"

The women were prattling behind him, and Jeanette translated. "They say it is the shock and something called exposure. She's been trapped in the ground for so long. This shivering is a reaction."

"Well, you've sent for the doctor. What can we do while we're waiting for him to come?"

There was another round of argument.

"They say you shouldn't wait for the doctor. Somebody needs to get into the bed with her to warm her up. She can be helped by someone else's body warmth."

Philip looked at Jeanette. "Will you do that for her?"

"Not me." She shook her head violently. "She is so dirty and smelly. You must do it yourself. You're dirty, just like her."

Candice intervened. "Please, Philip, I feel so cold."

"I ought to have a shower first."

"There is no time for that. You must take off your clothes and get in with her now."

He looked round. The other women seemed to be urging him to do as Jeanette instructed.

"OK." He stripped off his clothes, except for his underpants, and climbed in and lay close against the girl's back. She was still trembling violently and her back felt icy cold as he hugged his warm, sweaty body against it. She wriggled her hips to press her buttocks into his groin.

"Oh you're so warm," she cooed. "Please put your arm round me and rub my front. That's right – all the way down to my knees and right up to my neck. I want you to rub me all over."

"So he did as she asked, trying to ignore the effect this had on his own body. And indeed her shivering did seem to moderate considerably, apart from occasional short, violent shakings. Soon even those died away.

"Well, it seems to be working," he told the women. But when he looked around, he saw they had been left alone. Candice was lying quietly in his arms and even the noise outside in the street seemed to have reduced considerably. He soon dropped off to sleep.

He was woken by the arrival of the doctor, accompanied this time by just one of the village women. There was no sign of Jeanette. Everything seemed to have gone very quiet outside. Suddenly, embarrassed by being found in bed with Candice, Philip tried to pull away from her, but she clung to him. And the doctor didn't seem the least put out by Philip's presence, as he carried out his inspection of the girl. It was quite brief. She had to stick her tongue out and have it inspected. He lifted her eyelids and shone a torch into her eyes. He reached inside the sheets and felt her body in several places. He took her temperature and grunted his approval when the thermometer was removed. Then he stood up and delivered his verdict, which Philip of course didn't understand. He noticed the village woman had disappeared while the doctor was inspecting the girl.

Candice translated for him. "I have mild concussion and he would like me to stay in bed for a day. He says that my husband's warmth has prevented hypothermia, which would have been dangerous, but that you should remain in bed with me for the next six hours. She smiled at him. I think he believes you have saved my life."

"What's this about your husband?"

"He means you."

"But I'm not your husband."

"He knows that, of course. He is only being polite. He also says I have to drink some warm milk. Ugh!" She pulled a face. "I hate milk, so he says it can be laced with brandy. Perhaps that will make it acceptable."

"Do I need to get that for you?"

"No. You stay here. Madame Schmidt is getting it. She will bring you a drink too."

The doctor finished his instructions and Candice said "*Merci, monsieur.*" And Philip echoed her comment. The man put a small packet of pills on the bedside table before he left.

"Those are to make me sleep," she said as she turned to cuddle her front against him. "Well, husband, you must stay in bed with me for six hours. My back has been well done, so now you can do my front."

Despite their dirty, sweaty bodies and his tired, aching muscles, Philip decided he could survive six hours of holding this beautiful young girl tight against him. So he put his arm round her waist and hugged her willing body.

Some time later, the woman brought them two mugs of hot milk and brandy and they propped themselves up and drank the stuff. Then she left them alone and they returned to their medical embrace.

Candice kissed his grubby cheek. "This is my compensation for the hours of suffering you put me through in that hole in the ground," she murmured.

Philip was rendered speechless by her impudence.

The brandy had the effect of putting them back to sleep again and it was some hours before he woke. He found he was lying on his back. Candice's head was resting on his shoulder, cushioned by the skein of her hair. Her left arm was stretched across his chest and her bent leg was lying heavily on his stomach. He urgently needed to urinate. As gently as possible he pushed her arm and leg off his body. He pulled the pillow close and transferred her head to it from his shoulder. Then he slid out of bed and made for the bathroom.

As he came out, he was confronted by Jeanette. He saw, by the light in the back bedroom, that she had made her bed in there for the night.

"What is happening?" she asked.

"The doctor said I am to remain with Candice for six hours to ensure she doesn't suffer from hypothermia."

"What about my hypothermia?"

He grinned. "That will have to be treated tomorrow night."

"Not in the same way, I hope."

"No. Not in the same way."

He returned to the warm bed with Candice, who immediately reclaimed him with her limbs. However, he was now wide awake. He didn´t get back to sleep until the first light of dawn came filtering through the curtains.

19

In the morning, Philip woke early. His first priority was a shower, to wash the dirt and the sweat off his body and out of his hair. When he returned to the bedroom to dress, Candice was awake.

"Are you coming back to bed?"

"Of course not. I have a lot to do." He decided now was not the time to tell her off for the trouble she had caused yesterday evening.

"I want a shower as well."

"Go ahead. But, as the doctor said, you must go back to bed for the rest of the day after you've had it, to avoid problems with your concussion."

"I don't want to stay in bed on my own. This bed is damp and dirty."

"Well, it's your own dirt and sweat."

"And yours."

"Yes, and that's because I was told to get into bed with you to prevent you from suffering from hypothermia. You should thank me for that."

"Well, thank you. It's the first time I've spent the night with a man I hadn't invited into my bed." She smiled dreamily. "It was quite good."

For some reason her comment annoyed him. "If you hadn't got yourself into trouble by doing what I told you not to, none of this would have been necessary."

"What did I do wrong?"

"You know that I specifically told you to be careful how you cleared the rubble, so as to prevent any further collapse. And then of course, you saw the first step in what you assumed was the staircase down to the cellars, and you went digging away without thinking. That's what brought about the collapse." He wagged a finger at her. "You might have been killed."

"Would that have upset you?"

"Of course it would. What would Jackie have said about the death of one of her helpers? And there would have been all sorts of questions to be answered with the police. It would have

96

messed up my work here considerably. It would have caused a load of trouble."

She stuck her chin out. "That's all you're worried about – whether I'm going to cause you trouble. Well, I wasn't killed, and you must admit I've found a way down to the cellars."

"Yes, and now you've filled it up again with tons of rubble. Let me tell you, my girl, that once I have made sure the area is safe for you to work in, it's you who will have to dig it all out again. That should take you a good few weeks before you're able to get through to start your work on the archives."

Suddenly she burst into tears. "Oh, you're such a sod," she gasped and buried her face in the pillow.

"I'm sorry, Candice." Immediately regretting his harsh tone, he went across and laid a hand on her heaving shoulder. "What you've got to learn, is that you can't have everything just the way you like it, as soon as you want it."

She ignored his softer tone and continued to cry silently.

Philip thought to himself. "Why am I saying this? I'm a soft bugger – a few tears and I keel over and let her have her way." So, after a while, he left her alone and started to put on clean working clothes. When he had finished, he gathered up the dirty clothing strewn around the floor and took it downstairs to put in the washing machine. Jeanette was in the kitchen, and she was not in a good mood.

"What's going to happen about this woman?" she wanted to know. "I need to change the bed and clear up all the mess from last night. When is she going to leave?"

"The doctor says she has mild concussion and must stay in bed for today."

"Well, she can't stay here. She'd better get on back to her *chambre d'hôte* in Cuiza and give somebody else some trouble. Her stupid behaviour has mucked everything up. Have you seen the state of the road outside? There's all sorts of litter and half-eaten food and empty glasses everywhere. She's the cause of it all. It's been nothing but chaos since she arrived."

"Come off it, Jeanette. It's not as bad as all that. The whole village was celebrating her rescue last night."

"Yes, and where was *she*? Shacked up in my bed with you cuddling her like a fool."

"She was shivering violently, Jeanette. It was a reaction to what she'd been through. You were one of the women who told me I had to get in with her to warm her up."

"Humph," she snorted. "Well, I think it's time she cleared off and left us alone."

"Don't worry about me," said Candice from the doorway. "I know when I'm not welcome. I'll just have a shower and wash my hair and then I'll be gone."

The girl was wrapped in a blanket with her bare legs protruding. Despite her grubby face and greasy hair, somehow she still managed to look beautiful.

Philip went over to her. "Go back upstairs. You're supposed to be lying down and resting. You know what the doctor said."

"Well, I can't rest here, can I? You heard what your woman said about me."

"You can go in the back bedroom," Jeanette offered. "That will let me clear up in the front room."

"No thank you. I'll take myself back to Cuiza as you suggested. I won't be working today, Philip. I'll start again tomorrow."

She rushed back upstairs, and he followed more slowly. When he got there, he saw she had already thrown off the blanket and was in the process of removing her bra, revealing the bare body which he had been cuddling all night.

"Are you sure you're well enough to drive yourself back to Cuiza?" he asked. "You could stay here for today until the risk of problems from your concussion have gone away."

"I don't want to spend any more time in that dirty bed." She looked at him a shade wistfully. "We had a whole night together in it, and it shows."

Candice indicated the disarranged heap of bedclothes. Philip didn't know how he should reply to that.

"I'll just clean myself up and I'll be on my way."

"Well," he agreed. "I suppose it isn't very far for you to drive."

"Oh," she said, as she pushed down her pants. "Of course, I will need my clean clothes. They are in a bag on the back seat of the car. Will you get them for me?"

"OK. And I'll also get you a towel."

"Can I have two towels please? One is for my hair."

He nodded and turned and made his way downstairs. Jeanette was waiting in the kitchen. He told her about the arrangements.

She nodded. "Good. She'll be much better in her own clean bed."

"I hope she'll be all right – driving down that winding road with mild concussion."

"Of course she will. It's only four kilometres. Now you go and get her stuff and I'll take her towels up and strip the bed."

Full of thought, Philip went out to Candice's little white car to get her bag of clothes. Although he could see the sense of Jeanette's comments, he felt a little guilty about kicking the girl out.

In fact, Candice had seen enough down in her hole by the side of the staircase to convince her that she had found the way to get into the cellars of the chateau. As soon as she started exploring the cellars, female logic told her that she would discover clues that would lead her to the ancient treasure left by her Aryan ancestors.

Philip would doubtless have been less considerate about her feelings if he'd known that her intention was to phone Heinrich with a progress report once she got back to her *chambre d'hôte* in Cuiza. It was a report that led the boss of Fasces45 to send his personal assistant, Anna Sondheim, to stay in the area as a contact who could call in the heavies as soon as they would be needed.

20

Saturday was a productive day for Philip. Albert and Gaston weren't working over the weekend and Candice had gone to her *chambre d'hôte* in Cuiza to rest. So he was able to make good progress without any interruptions. Jeanette soon regained her cheerful attitude to life, and she had a smile on her face when she brought him his lunch. He showed her how well he was getting on.

"The glazing is complete, and the windows and doors work properly. I've levelled out the floor in the bathroom and I'll start tiling it this afternoon. It's not a very big area, so I'm confident I'll finish that today. Then I'll be able to start on the walls tomorrow."

She patted his arm. "Do you know, I think you really enjoy doing this sort of manual work. It seems to make you happy and fulfilled."

"Yes. It is so satisfying to see the end product of your work." He gave her a hug. "When I was working at the university, I found the work very interesting, but it was all theoretical. There was nothing to see at the end of the day, so you couldn't look at something and tell yourself, 'I've done that today.'"

After a quick meal, he got down on his knees and started tiling. In fact, he had almost finished when Candice turned up in the late afternoon to spoil the day for him. She stood in the doorway, once again groomed and immaculate. She was wearing one of the sets of overalls she had recently purchased which showed off her figure to perfection.

"You ought to be in bed," he reproved her.

She scowled at him. "I can't stay in bed any longer. I was very good and went straight off to sleep when I got into my room at the *chambre d'hôte*. I slept for two or three hours. Then I woke up. I was feeling hungry, so I went out and got myself something to eat. When I returned, I did climb back into bed again, but I just couldn't get off to sleep this time. I think I'd had too much sleep by then. So, after tossing and turning for half an hour, I gave up and decided to come and talk to you."

"Didn't the doctor give you some pills that were supposed to make you sleep?"

"Yes, but I don't like taking pills. And really, I do feel quite all right. Lying in bed started me thinking about how to get down that staircase and finding out what was beyond it. I couldn't remember exactly how everything looked." She smiled suggestively. "So I came back to check up."

"Candice," said Philip firmly, "You are not going back into that chateau on your own without someone to look after you."

"I don't want to actually do anything. I just want to look."

"Well, you can't look now. I won't let you go back in there unless I'm with you. And I can't spare the time to go in there now, because I want to finish this floor."

She put her head on one side. "The floor can wait half an hour. If you take a break now, we can have a look at the area and work out what needs to be done next, and then I'll help you finish the floor to make up for the time you've lost."

"I said 'No', Candice. I don't need your help to finish the floor. It's a one-man job and I certainly don't need *you* to help me. In any case, bending down and straightening up again is the last thing you should be doing when you're suffering from concussion."

"I haven't got concussion any longer. I feel completely recovered."

"Nevertheless, you are not going to do any work today. So go away and let me get on with *my* work." He got down on his knees again and continued with the floor.

Disappointed, Candice watched him for a few minutes. Then she gave up and left him alone.

However, while he was working, his mind was worrying about what he ought to do with her. Damn the woman. He knew she wouldn't let up until he had gone back into the chateau with her to plan some sort of campaign for clearing the staircase and getting into the cellars. Slowly he came up with a possible solution – at least for the short term.

The plumber had said he would be coming tomorrow. The man had told Albert that Sunday was the only day he could spare from his other work. Philip had intended to give the guy any help he needed with collecting materials or tools so that he could finish the work as quickly as possible. That would also make sure everything was located just where he wanted. But he wouldn't be able to do any work himself while the plumbing was going on.

So he decided, after a certain amount of thought, that he would mark out exactly where he wanted everything to go on the walls and the floor this evening. He would take Jeanette with him, and explain it all to her, then she could answer any queries the man might have when he turned up in the morning.

Meanwhile he was almost certain that Candice would come back again tomorrow, demanding to get into the chateau. So he decided he would use his wasted day to go to Béziers to locate and collect the bag from Jackie's flat. He would take the girl with him, to keep her away from exploring the staircase. In fact, he decided they would go in her car, which would be more comfortable for such a long journey than his noisy, draughty sports car.

He reminded himself, as he planned the trip, that he had decided he would have to replace the MG with a pick-up type of vehicle which would be more useful. However, he hadn't got around to it yet. He must do something about that on Monday.

The trip to Béziers would remove Candice from Rennes for the day and solve his worries about her finding a way into the chateau, when he wasn't there to keep her under control. Also, he told himself, he would be driving and that would give her a nice restful day to make sure she was fully recovered from her mild concussion. After that she could be kept quiet, until Jean-Luc arrived, by helping with the painting and cleaning up after the building work had been completed.

Satisfied with his plan, Philip finished off the floor and wiped it over to ensure it was smooth. He neatly put away his tools and went back to the cottage to get some chalk to do his marking-up for the plumber. Going out into the yard, he saw Candice's little car was still parked there and the window in the driver's door was open. He crossed to check and saw she had reclined the driving seat and was stretched out on it and snoring gently. So much, he thought, for her claiming she had had too much sleep. As if his peering in had disturbed her, she suddenly awoke and gazed up at him with her dark eyes.

"You were out like a light," he informed her and grinned. "You obviously needed more sleep than you thought."

"I was only resting my eyes while you finished your work, before we went to inspect the steps."

"That'll have to wait a few days. I've got other plans for you."

"What's that?" She sat upright.

"I've decided that tomorrow we're going to drive to Béziers in your car and find the bag that this guy Vauclus is so desperate to get hold of. Of course, you'll come with me, but I will drive. That means you'll have a nice, restful day, and enjoy the views as we drive along."

"How do you know I'll agree to that?"

"If you don't, I'll borrow your car anyway and leave you in Cuiza to have your restful day there."

She thought for a minute. "All right. I'll agree, as long as we go and have a quick look at the staircase now."

It was Philip's turn to consider the options. In the end he nodded. "I can spare you half an hour. Come on. I've got the key in my pocket."

She opened the door and jumped out of the car. He had to admit that she showed no sign of the threatened concussion. She took his arm as they crossed the yard and let themselves into the chateau. Her mood was happy and excited. It was as if they were going out together for the evening. He felt his own spirit lifting.

Inside, everything was in a mess, but they ignored that as they made their way to the site of yesterday's disaster. He stopped her from going closer than the top step as they gazed down into the depths. They could see the partly exposed beam that had trapped her. Beyond it was the terribly small hole that he had climbed into to release her body from the entrapping rubble. Otherwise, the staircase was impassable.

"I could see down several more steps before the stuff collapsed," she told him. "If the guys were allowed to concentrate on it, I think it would only take a couple of days to dig enough out to get past the blockage."

He shook his head. "First of all, we'll have to dig away a lot of the rubble above the stairs so that we can put a row of planks in to stop more of the debris from falling down them. That will take several days, before I will let you risk going down into that hole again."

She surveyed the scene in silence for several minutes. Then she said, "Well, I suppose I'll have to accept that. When will Albert and Gaston be available to help?"

"I'll collect Jean-Luc from hospital on Wednesday. That means with a bit of luck they should be free on Thursday – that is, if you help with the painting and cleaning up in the cottage. Will you do that?"

"All right."

He took a breath. "OK then. That's all we can do for now. Let's go."

And, with her still hanging on to his arm, he led the way back to her car.

21

It all worked out well. On the Sunday morning, after spending half an hour with Hubert the plumber and Jeanette, and satisfying himself that they both understood just where he wanted everything to be put, he went out to where Candice was sitting primly in the passenger seat of her little Peugeot. She was wearing a cardigan over whatever was underneath, presumably in case she felt cold. They set off and joined the autoroute near Carcassonne and headed east.

Candice gazed out at the passing countryside. She really seemed to be enjoying herself. She suddenly said, "This is almost like having a day out with my lover."

"Oh God!" said Philip. "Don't start talking like that. My personal life is already far too complicated."

"Well," she pointed out, "you've already felt more parts of my body than most lovers would expect to feel."

Phillip grinned at her. "I don't expect you were any more excited by the contact than I was."

"Oh." She wagged a finger at him. "I felt certain parts of you as well, and I would say you were enjoying warming me up quite a lot."

"I'm sure I don't know what you mean."

"Do you want me to spell it out for you?"

"No, thank you."

He decided to end such a personal discussion at that point, but he was aware of Candice grinning broadly at him as they continued the journey.

Otherwise, the drive to Béziers was uneventful. After stopping for a coffee on the outskirts of the city, they pulled up outside the block of flats where Jackie had her residence at about half past eleven.

"Do you want to come in?" he asked the girl.

"You bet I do. I wouldn't want to miss seeing the place where the archaeological star, Jacqueline Blontard, goes in her quiet time."

"What quiet time?"

Candice laughed and took hold of his elbow. "Ah, there speaks the spurned lover again."

"You find it funny?"

"Of course I do. She obviously doesn't know anything about the ladies queuing up to take her place."

Philip ignored her comment as he led the way into the hall and pressed the button for the lift. The doors opened straight away to admit them, and he selected the second floor. Once there, they crossed the corridor to the front door to Flat 6. His key fitted the lock perfectly and they entered the flat. Philip was pleased they hadn't met anyone in the public areas of the block. He didn't want to have to answer any embarrassing questions.

Candice followed silently behind him as he looked quickly into the kitchen and the living room to check whether anyone else had been there. After all, Charlotte might have arranged for a cleaner to come in while she was on holiday. But everything was neat and tidy and there was no sign of anybody else having been in the place. He couldn't detect any sign of the musty smell that often seems to invade properties which are unoccupied. So he led her into Jackie's office.

"Oh my goodness," Candice exclaimed as they entered. She was immediately drawn across the room to gaze out of the big picture window in front of the desk. "What a view!"

Philip stopped briefly beside her. "Beautiful, isn't it. What a lovely place to work. The only trouble is, that if I worked in this room, I think I'd be looking at the panorama all the time, instead of getting on with my work."

The window looked down on the river winding through the wooded countryside. In the distance one could see the sea with a scattering of tiny white triangles of yachts drifting in the light breeze. Through the middle of them a coastal vessel ploughed along, perhaps taking fuel from the refineries in Marseilles to Perpignan.

He tore his eyes away from the view and looked round the room. He immediately espied the stack of clothes and several bags which Charlotte had presumably piled on and around one of the two armchairs in the room. When he searched through the stuff, he soon found the bag with the double-headed eagle crest on the side. He picked it up and put it on the desk, the better to search through the contents.

Somebody had closed the zip on the top of the bag, but he had no trouble in opening it. Despite the warning not to look inside which he had received from Vauclus, he intended to search the contents of the bag to see if he could find the list of Cathar treasures, which Jackie had asked him to hold back for her. However, in this he was unsuccessful. He pulled out all Alain Hébert's clothes, now somewhat disarranged by having been sorted through several times, but he could find no papers in the bag whatsoever. He lifted the flap in the bottom which, César had discovered, concealed Hébert's diary and the list which Professor Ramise had been desperate to get hold of until he found out it was worthless. However, that void was also empty.

"Vauclus isn't going to be happy about this," he said to himself.

"What?"

He realised he had spoken aloud. "This is the bag we came here to collect," he explained to her. "You saw the guy with one arm, didn't you? He was expecting to find a letter in here which he had been given the job of recovering." He shook his head. "Well, he's going to be unlucky."

Philip started to stuff the clothes back into the bag. Then he had a sudden thought that perhaps Hébert might have folded it up and stuffed it into one of his pockets, but a search of the jacket and two pairs of trousers was fruitless. He finished putting the things away and zipped up the bag. He decided to check whether the list had already been taken out and perhaps left on Jackie's desk. So he dropped the bag on the floor and searched through the papers lying there. Most of them were unopened envelopes which Charlotte must have tossed there to await Jackie's next visit. There was no sign of the list she wanted.

He thought, "I'll send a message to her hotel to tell her I've picked up the bag but there's nothing in it and I can't find the list. She'll have to make what she can of that. Perhaps she's already stashed it away in another of her bags. I'm not going to search through them all to try to find it. That'll be something she'll have to do for herself when she has the time."

"OK," he told Candice, "I'm afraid it's been a bit of a wasted trip. Still, it will have been a restful day for you."

There was no reply and, before he bent down to pick up the bag, he looked up at his companion. She had taken off her cardigan, revealing that she was wearing a green summer dress, the top half of which seemed to consist of no more than a couple of small triangles of fabric. They were held in place by colourless, thin shoulder-straps. He hadn't noticed before when they got out of the car, that the skirt was quite short, flaring out to display a lot of leg. She was regarding him with her mouth slightly open and the ghost of a smile on her lips.

"My goodness, Candice." He was taken aback.

"Do you like it?"

"Er – well – yes, of course I do."

"All you have to do is slip the shoulder-straps off my shoulders and I will be bare to the waist." She moved towards him. "Would you like to do that?"

"Candice! What are you saying?"

"I could feel yesterday, when you were rubbing my body to warm me up, that you would like to have done more than that, even though I was dirty and smelly. Now I am clean, and I smell nice, so now you can do what you wanted to do yesterday. I see that Jackie has a very comfortable sofa in front of the bookshelves. You can have me there if you wish and I will then believe that I have said thank you for saving me."

Philip shook his head violently to rid it of the urge which had threatened to overwhelm him. "Thank you, Candice, but I am not looking for payment. If I make love to a woman, I don't want to regard it as some sort of a reward for services rendered."

"Oh, I am sure I would enjoy it as well." She smiled. "I can't think of anyone I would rather say thank you to."

But he had recovered his good sense by now

"Drop it, Candice. We're finished here," he said, picking up the bag, "Let's start back, shall we? We can stop for a drink on the way and be home in time for an early night. We've got a busy day ahead of us tomorrow. However, I think you should put your cardigan back on for the return trip. I wouldn't want anybody else to think you were on offer."

"Especially not Jeanette," she said as she reluctantly followed him.

So they let themselves out of the flat and returned to the car, once again seeing nobody as they went.

That night his lovemaking was more violent than usual, much to the pleasure of Jeanette. Of course, she wasn't aware that the image in his mind was of Candice's beautiful, slim body in the green dress with only two triangles of fabric covering her breasts, rather than the soft, voluptuous sensation beneath him.

22

Philip collected Jean-Luc Lerenard from the hospital on Wednesday morning. Before he went to the hospital, he sent off the message to Jackie, telling her about finding the bag, but that it didn't contain the list or any other papers. He didn't know whether she was really bothered about it. After all, she could surely get a copy of the list from her former professor, Hector Ramise. But he felt he had done his best to discharge the task she had set him, and now he passed the matter back to her.

For the last two days Candice had dutifully helped with the painting and the cleaning of the house to provide accommodation for the big man. Philip had avoided being alone with her, resolutely putting behind him the memories of her wearing the revealing green dress in Jackie's flat. Now everything was ready for Jean-Luc with the bed, wardrobe and chest of drawers temporarily moved from the back bedroom of the rented cottage until Philip bought new stuff. So at least he would enjoy the basic comforts in this warm time of year.

He also gave Candice permission to go back to her digging in the chateau courtyard. Avoiding direct contact with the girl, now dressed in her thin clinging overalls. He told her, "The first job for you is to dig a trench along here about one and a half metres from the wall." He indicated the suggested line with a sweep of his hand. "Get right down to the floor slab. Then, you see that stack of planks over there? There are already five planks leaning against the wall which we put up on Friday night before we dug you out. Use those to extend the protective planking along above the staircase. Do you understand what I mean?"

"Yes."

"It's important that you do not start digging the rubble out of the stairs until I have looked at what you have done up here and confirmed that it's safe to do that. Is that clear to you?"

She nodded.

"Because if you disobey me and, as a result, you get buried again," he told her, "I will personally do nothing to get you out. I will inform the local police that I gave you a warning. They may, or they may not, try to rescue you. If they get you out alive, I expect they will charge you with wasting police time. It you die down there under the piles of rubble, I will tell the examining magistrate that you committed suicide by not doing what I instructed you to do. And on your gravestone, which will have to be set up outside the churchyard, I will have the words carved – She died because she wouldn't obey instructions – in French of course. Do you understand that?"

"Yes." She looked carefully at him, not quite sure whether he was pulling her leg or whether he was serious.

"OK. You can start now. I am going to get Jean-Luc."

He went out and got into the pick-up truck he had purchased in Carcassonne late on Monday.

Lerenard was waiting for him when he got to the hospital. He was dressed in outdoor clothes and looked remarkably fit and well, although Philip had no doubt that his body would need at least a couple of months to recover its muscle strength after the near-death experience he had been through a few weeks ago.

Philip carried one of the big man's bags as they went out to the pick-up. "You see I've bought a new vehicle to take you," he informed him.

"You cheeky bugger. I'm not that big. I suppose you plan to put me in the back." It seemed Jean-Luc was developing a sense of humour after his experiences.

"The choice is yours." He gave his friend a pat on the shoulder, noticing how much weight he had lost from his once big frame.

They got back to Rennes in time for coffee which Jeanette, on her best behaviour, served to them in the yard at the back of the cottage. In the last few days, she had contrived to make the area a very pleasant place to sit out and enjoy the warmth of the mid-summer morning sun.

"We often have our evening meals out here," Philip told their guest. "Jeanette usually does them on the barbecue."

She chimed in. "I'm never quite sure what time Philip will finish his work in the evening, so I get everything prepared and have the barbecue lit. Then, when he finally turns up, I can have the food prepared and ready to eat in about a quarter of an hour."

"Just giving me time to have a shower," he agreed.

They chatted about memories and recent experiences as they drank their coffees. Then Jeanette offered a second cup which she had warmed up. Jean-Luc accepted but Philip suddenly remembered Candice working away in the heap of rubble inside the chateau.

"I'd better go and see how she's getting on," he decided. "Jeanette, can you give me a flask of coffee to take to her?"

Jeanette sniffed. "That one would rather have citron pressé laced with brandy. She'll probably need it too, if she's been putting her back into it."

"No. I'll take her some coffee."

When he got to the heap of rubble above the staircase, carrying the flask of coffee, he could see that the girl had made significant progress. At that moment she was just struggling to try and lift one of the heavy planks into place beside the others. To do this she had to lower one end into the trench then push the rest of the plank across those already in position to drop it into place beyond the last one. He put down the flask and hurried to help her. He could see she was simply not tall enough or sufficiently strong to do it on her own.

"Thank you," she gasped and stood back and stretched her back. "This is the bit I find most difficult."

It was the first time he had allowed himself to look at her directly since Sunday and he thought she presented a magnificent sight, with her back arched and the thin overalls hugging her body with the zip pulled down to her cleavage. She wiped the back of her hand across her sweating brow, leaving a grubby mark. It looked almost endearing to his eyes.

"You're doing really well," he complimented her.

"I don't mind the digging and the barrowing," she panted. "But those planks are awfully heavy and it's so awkward standing them up against the wall."

He nodded. "I can see that. Perhaps you should concentrate on the digging and call me when you've got enough cleared to put in several planks and I can help you with those."

"The trouble with that idea, is the rubble keeps falling back into the trench as I dig it out, and I can only do it one plank at a time. It's taking such a long time doing it on my own."

"Yes," he agreed, "it must very frustrating. But you were desperate to get on with the work, before I could release any of the men to help you."

Privately, he agreed that a slim little thing like Candice shouldn't be trying to do a job on her own which would normally have required two men. But she was the one who had chosen to go ahead, rather than wait for someone to help her.

She was watching him grappling with his conscience. She gave a frustrated little smile. "It would be so much quicker if you would help me, just until we've got the protective planking up."

"OK." He took a deep breath. "Just let me get Jean-Luc settled in the house and I'll see what I can arrange."

He turned to find Lerenard was already there, observing them with a tolerant smile.

"Once again you're letting these women run your life for you." The big man laughed.

"Well, to be fair, it *is* a two-person job," said Philip. "She shouldn't have to do it on her own."

"Then she has to wait until you can spare somebody to help her."

Philip sighed. "Yes, and at present the only person is me."

He rested his hand on the big man's shoulder as he directed him towards the gates out of the chateau.

"OK." Jean-Luc shrugged. "I suppose you know what you're doing."

Philip gave a half-chuckle. "I only wish I did."

He shepherded the man he had come to think of as a friend towards his new accommodation in the house.

23

By Friday they were making noticeable progress on the house. Albert and Gaston were engaged on breaking up and digging out the existing ground floor and were barrowing the excavated material to the same spoil heap where Candice was dumping the rubble from the chateau. The heap was now becoming quite large, and Philip realised he would have to decide soon what he was going to do with it all.

Back in the house he carefully oversaw the levelling of the subsoil and the laying of the damp proof membrane and the insulation below the new ground floor. He knew it was important that there should be no leaks in this area, even though the house was near the top of the hill and the subsoil was generally quite dry. Meanwhile he was fixing the windows throughout the rest of the house, ready for the glazing. From time to time, he went back to help Candice put up another protective plank. However, her demands for his assistance became fewer. He noticed that Lerenard seemed to be taking a lot of interest in the staircase that was going down to the cellars, and he suspected the big man was giving Candice assistance when she needed it in getting the planks into position. That was amusing after his comments about Philip allowing his life to be run by women.

On one visit he asked his friend, "Are you sure you should be doing hard physical work so early in your convalescence?"

"I am taking it gently," Jean-Luc replied. "I've got to do something to start building up my muscle strength."

"OK. Obviously, you know best. Just make sure you give me a call if you think any part of the work is becoming too much." He turned to Candice. "Three more planks and I think it might be safe for you to go back down the steps and start digging out the rubble again. But you must come and ask me to check, before I let you go down into the hole."

Then, having received her promise, he went back to the house. Parked in front of the building was the big black car of Gérard Vauclus. With all his other activities, Philip had actually forgotten about the one-armed man's arrangement to come back to collect the bag. There was no sign of Vauclus himself. He was presumably in the house, talking to Albert. Philip wanted to get rid of the guy as soon as possible in order to continue with his work. So he diverted immediately to the rented cottage where he had left the bag in the back bedroom. He came back a few minutes later, carrying it, just as Vauclus emerged from the house.

"Well," Philip told him, "I've collected the bag, but I don't think you're going to be very happy about it, because there's nothing in it except a bundle of Alain Hébert's clothes."

He handed the bag over and the man observed him suspiciously. "So you have looked inside the bag?"

"Yes."

Vauclus scowled. "I specifically told you not to look in the bag."

"I know you did. However, the lady in whose custody the bag had been placed, thought that a list belonging to her might have been left in the bag, and she asked me to remove it before I handed the thing over to you." He smiled weakly. "I think she might have refused to let me have it, if I'd told her I couldn't take it out for her."

"And did you take it out?"

"No. I couldn't find any papers in the bag at all – only the clothes I told you about."

"How do I know you didn't remove anything?"

"You have to take my word for it."

Vauclus advanced as though he was about to attack him, and Philip steeled himself to receive a blow.

Then – "You'd better take his word for it, Jordie."

Vauclus spun round to look at where the sound came from. "Good God! Luke?"

"That's right," said Lerenard. "And I know this man well enough to tell you, that if he says he didn't remove anything from the bag, then that is the truth."

"What the hell are you doing here?" asked Vauclus. "The last time I saw you, it looked as though you were going to be wiped out by the Muslim terrorists."

"They didn't wipe me out."

"So what the hell happened?"

"Some other time," said Jean-Luc. "I want to know why you're so interested in this bag and its contents?"

115

"I am carrying out an assignment for a client."

"Who is this client?"

Vauclus put his head on one side. "You know better than to ask me that, Luke. You know none of us gives away confidential information."

"Then may I suggest," said Lerenard acidly, "that you carry out your assignment somewhere else. Clearly you are wasting your time here."

"If you don't mind I'll just check that there's nothing of interest to my client in this bag."

"Is that all right, Philip?"

"Oh, yes. The bag is his as far as I'm concerned."

"Then you can go ahead."

"Thank you." Vauclus took the bag across to his car and rested it on the bonnet. He took out the piles of clothing and scraped around inside the bag to check that there was nothing left behind. He found the flap disguising the secret compartment in the bottom, and lifted it and peered into the void beneath, but obviously found nothing. He meticulously picked up every item of clothing, shook it and checked the pockets, if it had any. To Philip's surprise the man found two small flaps that *he* had missed, but there was nothing beneath either of them. Then Vauclus carefully folded each item and returned it to the bag, so that the clothes were tidier now than before he had taken them out. Then he zipped the bag up and handed it back.

"Don't you want to keep it?" asked Philip.

"It's no use to me any longer. Obviously, somebody has removed the letter before the bag reached me."

"And before it reached Monsieur Sinclair," interceded Jean-Luc.

"Maybe." He glared at Philip. "But let me tell you, sonny, that it will go ill with you if I find out later that it was you who removed the letter, because I know that it was in this bag in the past."

"How do you know that?"

"It was information I had extracted from a certain person."

Jean-Luc intervened again. "How long ago were you told of this?"

Vauclus paused for a moment before saying, "Thirty-seven days."

"And who was it?" Lerenard asked.

"That doesn't matter. He is no longer alive."

There was a chilling silence for a full minute.

"I would still like to know," said Lerenard.

"Come off it, Luke. I'm surprised you asked."

That seemed to be the end of the conversation. Vauclus turned his back on them, returned to his car and got in. He started the engine and reversed out of the yard. Then he drove away without a backward glance. Philip found himself standing with a bag full of somebody else's clothes. He took a deep breath and turned to the big man.

"Do you know that bloke?"

Jean-Luc hesitated before replying. "I have come across him in the past."

"So who is he?"

"I think you would call him a mercenary."

"Is that the same sort of thing that you used to do?"

Philip wondered if he'd asked too much but, after a pause, Lerenard replied, "I suppose you might have called me that, but I like to think I have been a little more selective about my clients than he is."

"So how come you met up with him in the past?"

"The last time was in Egypt six years ago. You remember the publicity about the massacre of Coptic Christians in a Cairo church? Well, the Vatican sent me to offer what help I could to the Christian community." He shook his head. "Sadly it wasn't very much."

"Why was Vauclus there?"

"I don't know why exactly." The big man gazed into the distance. "I guess he might have got his instructions indirectly from the CIA. They wouldn't want to get directly involved. But I suspect he was the guy who betrayed me to the Muslims."

"What!"

"It was to save himself of course."

"How did he lose his arm?"

"That I don't know. It was a long time ago – before Cairo. He never talked about it."

Philip was silent, wondering about this lifting of a corner of the cover to expose a little of Lerenard's former hidden life.

Jean-Luc regarded him with concern. "I hope you were telling the truth, when you said you hadn´t found whatever it was he was looking for."

"Of course I was."

Because I would strongly advise you against trying to get one across on my friend Jordie" He shook his head. "If you upset him, I´m not sure I would be able to protect you."

Philip gazed into his eyes. "I promise you, Jean-Luc, I do not intend to put one across the man, as you call it."

Lerenard nodded and the discussion ended.

24

The next day Philip agreed that sufficient protective boarding had been carried out above the staircase. So he permitted Candice to start clearing the steps again to try to get down to the basement. It was desperately slow work, because there was insufficient space beyond the apparently immovable beam to allow more than one person with a small bucket to scrape up the rubble. Once full, the bucket then had to be lifted out of the hole and carried up the steps to be deposited in one of the barrows, before the task was repeated. Lerenard volunteered to help by carrying up the small buckets of waste material, but he didn't yet have sufficient strength to push the full barrows out to the spoil heap. And he had to admit, after about two hours that he'd had enough. Philip was anxious about him and sent him to rest in the back yard and drink some of the cordial Jeanette said she had invented specially for him, revealing another of her unexpected talents.

Philip had to admit he was curious about what they would find when the steps had been cleared, and what would still need to be done in order to reach the Templar archives. He also felt it was important that Candice wasn't left on her own for too long. He had no doubt that, as soon as she could, she would start exploring the cellars, and who knew what she might find under the ruined part of the chateau? There might be other important secrets hidden away down there. He could also see that two fully-fit people would be more than twice as effective as one in clearing the area. Therefore, he decided to abandon his carpentry work in the house for a few days, until Albert and Gaston had completed the laying of the new ground floor throughout the building.

So after lunch, he went across the courtyard to the steps where the girl was still working. He was slightly startled to find she had stripped off her overalls and was now clad only in a bra and briefs in addition to her boots. He noticed the bruise on her hip had turned a deep purple, but it didn't seem to be causing her pain.

"It's so hot down here," she explained with a little smile. "In any case I'm not exposing anything to you that you haven't handled already."

"But what about Jean-Luc? What was his reaction?"

"Oh, I kept my overalls on when he was here." She scowled. "It wasn't very nice working with him. That man hardly ever talks. Sometimes when I said something to him, he wouldn't even reply."

"Yes. He doesn't possess many social skills. But I get on fine with him. In fact I consider him to be a good friend."

She glanced sideways at him. "Rather you than me."

He changed the subject. Indicating the full barrows, he said, "I hope you don't intend to push them out to the spoil heap dressed like that. I won't be able to keep Albert and Gaston working in the house if you do." Philip had to admit that seeing Candice in the near-nude did unsettle his own thoughts quite a bit.

"No, I don't like pushing barrows. Now you're here, *you* can do that."

She returned to her scraping down in the hole. However, when he got back from emptying the barrows, he told her that he would take over digging out the rubble, because he was taller and could fill the larger buckets if she balanced them on the beam, which at that time was about level with his chest. Progress was better that way and Candice had soon filled all three barrows again.

"Instead of barrowing it out to the heap outside, why don't we just pile the soil beside the barrows," she suggested. "Gaston and Albert can take it out later when they have finished whatever you have told them to do in the house."

"All right. I agree with that."

Philip was now as anxious as Candice to clear the way to the bottom of the steps. They were soon making faster progress and it was only about half an hour later, when he was digging out some rubble, that a hole about the size of a tennis ball opened up by the wall. Levering with the pickaxe, he had soon enlarged the hole to about football size and he was aided by the fact that the rubble was cascading down into the depths below. But all he could see when he peered down was blackness.

"This is where I had got to when the collapse happened last Friday."

He looked up to see that Candice was close beside him. Her sweat-covered arms were shivering with excitement. Tendrils of her hair were hanging round her dirty face. He tore his eyes away from her filthy, nearly naked body.

"We'd better be careful. With both of us perched here, our weight might collapse the heap we're standing on and we would fall down to the bottom. I'm not quite sure how we'd get out if that happened."

She ignored him. "If you made the hole a bit bigger, I think I could get down through it."

"What, dressed like that?"

"Why not? I won't have any clothes to catch on rough bits."

"Just skin."

She grinned at him. "Then you'd have to use your warm, gentle hands to rub cream on the sore places."

Philip decided to ignore her suggestive comment.

"Well," he said, "before either of us goes down, we must have a rope available to hang on to, in case we get stuck. I saw there was one in the back of the pick-up. I'll go and get it."

When he got back, he saw that Candice was already deep down the steps, digging round the hole to make it bigger and encouraging the soil to fall into the void. He could see almost nothing of her when she bent down, except her plump little bottom with the narrow strip of her briefs stretched tight across it.

"I'm going to tie the rope round the barrow legs," he said, dragging his eyes away from the prospect. "The three full-up barrows together should be enough to stand our weight one at a time if it's necessary."

She straightened up. "The trouble is, there's not enough space under the beam, and the soil is filling up lower down the stairs."

"Yes. I'm afraid there's no alternative to the slow one of filling buckets and carrying them up. Actually, that will have the added advantage, if we heap the stuff against the wheelbarrows, that the rope will be even better secured."

So they reverted to the previous system. He went down the hole and filled buckets which he lifted on to the beam, and she carried them up and piled them against the barrows. Soon he was shoulder-deep in the void, and she had to get part way down into the hole to lift the buckets onto the beam. Then another collapse occurred.

It was just as she was lifting up a bucket. The rubble she was standing on gave way and filled the hole up to above his waist. The girl tumbled into his arms and the bucket tipped over and deposited its spoil across her middle. He found himself gazing into her dark eyes from about two inches away, and gasping for breath. The next moment they were sharing a breathless kiss. Neither of them offered it or asked it of the other. It just seemed to happen, and it went on for a long time. Their mouths were half-open and the grit and dust on their faces and between their lips was unnoticed. For at least two minutes they remained in the embrace before she pulled away, panting.

"Oh, Philip."

"I'm sorry, Candice."

"Don't apologise. I liked it."

"Yes, well -" He forced his mind back to practicalities. "Now, if we push that bucket to one side and I help by pushing up your shoulders, can you get up? You can pull on the rope to help you."

"Yes, I suppose so."

It didn't take the girl long to climb out of the hole. Then she stopped and peered down at him. "What are we going to do about you?" There was a new softness in her expression that he hadn't noticed before.

"Can you get those two little buckets and the trowel we used on Friday," he asked her. "Then I think I can dig out enough of the rubble around my middle to loosen my legs and, with the help of the rope, I can pull myself out."

"OK." She went off and returned a few minutes later with the things he wanted.

It took about half an hour to dig away enough soil for him to work his legs out of the rubble that was trapping them. Then she hauled his exhausted body out of the hole by clasping her arms round his back until he stood close in front of her.

"So what now?" she asked, gazing up at him.

He averted his eyes. "So now we are going to pack up for today. It's nearly five o'clock and I'm desperate for a shower and a change of clothes." He detached himself from her embrace.

"But what about me?"

"I suggest you do the same – after you've put your overalls back on, of course."

"Will we carry on here in the morning?"

He could tell from her smile that she was aware of the innuendo in her question. But he was determined to get this relationship under control.

"*You* will. I think I'll send Gaston to work with you tomorrow and I'll help Albert in the house."

She curled her lip. "I don't like Gaston. He's old and he's dirty and he looks at me suggestively."

"Anyone would look at you suggestively, the way you're dressed at the moment."

"That's another thing. If Gaston works with me, I'll have to keep all my clothes on."

Philip couldn't help grinning. "That's up to you. I don't think Gaston will object if you ask him whether you can strip off because of the heat."

Candice was silent for a moment as she thought. "I think you owe me a meal tonight for rescuing you. I am too tired to cook for myself."

"OK. I'll ask Jeanette to do the meal for four this evening."

She sighed. "It would be better if you took me into Limoux and we could find a quiet restaurant."

"Why? Don't you like Jeanette's cooking?"

"Oh, yes. But we could talk about such a lot more if it was only we two."

Philip shook his head. "That sounds to me like a very good reason for the four of us eating together while Jeanette does one of her barbecues."

Reluctantly she seemed to accept the arrangement. She said, "All right, I will get dressed and go back to my place for a shower and to wash my hair. I don't want to wear my boots to drive back to Cuiza. Please will you get the pair of shoes I've left in the car, Philip, while I put on my clothes."

When he returned, she was once again wearing her overalls, although she was dirty and her hair was untidy. He accompanied her to the car.

"See you about seven," he told her, as he left and went to check on progress in the house and to discover how Jean-Luc was feeling.

25

Jeanette did the usual barbecue that evening in the yard behind the house, which she had now managed to make quite cosy. It had become a regular informal event in the enclosed space. Lerenard joined them for a meal on most evenings. At Philip's request, Jeanette had included food for Candice tonight, but the girl was late arriving.

"Where is the woman?" she complained. "The fire's nice and hot. I want to start cooking the food."

"That one will always make sure she is late," said Jean-Luc philosophically.

Philip sighed. "Don't worry about her. I told her to be here at seven o'clock. Start cooking now, and if she's too late she'll have to eat it dry and cold."

However, just then there was a knock at the front door, and he went to open it. What he saw took his breath away. Candice had washed and piled her beautiful silver hair up on top of her head so that it almost looked like a crown. The evening sun radiated through it, seeming to set it alight. It was the first time he had become aware of her slim neck and dainty little ears. Her face glowed with a little make-up, just a darkening of the eyelids and an accentuation of the soft lips. But then, nothing could out-paint those startling eyes. Her short black dress was made of some diaphanous, figure-hugging material that was held up by two thin shoulder straps. Matching very high-heeled, strappy sandals brought her almost up to his own height. She carried a small black purse which twinkled with artificial jewels. Her outfit was totally unsuitable for the informal meal they were expecting to eat.

"Wow," he said. "You look scrumptious."

"Thank you." She gripped his hand, and he was enveloped in some expensive perfume. "Please lead me to the food. I'm ravishing."

He chuckled. "I agree with that, but I think you mean ravenous."

"Oh, this English. It is so confusing."

"We're eating in the back yard." He led her through the kitchen and out to the rear. "Here she is," he announced, "not too late after all."

A silence greeted her arrival. Philip noted the amused grin on Jean-Luc's face. But Jeanette's expression was far from amused. Her usually sexy appearance now seemed almost frumpy by comparison with the well-groomed new arrival. His housekeeper was wearing quite a pretty, pink, draw-string blouse that just rested on her shoulders and across the top of her ample bosom. However, the exposed straps of her bra and the strip of bare stomach rather spoiled the effect. Her short frilly skirt showed off plenty of her shapely legs, but she had only flat shoes on her feet, and she seemed nearly a foot shorter than the statuesque new arrival.

Jeanette finally managed a surly, "Come and sit over here."

Philip noticed with amusement that Candice had been placed the other side of Jean-Luc, away from where he and Jeanette would sit. He poured a glass of wine and took it to her, and she sampled it without checking. Her expression was neutral. He returned to his seat, took up his own glass and raised it in a silent toast to her, to which she responded just as quietly.

The evening started badly. Jeanette, who was normally quite a chatterbox, was restrained tonight. In fact, she was virtually silent as she leaned over the barbecue, cooking the meat, and when she went into the kitchen to get the salad from the fridge. Philip was only too aware that he had caused embarrassment by inviting Candice, and then by her turning up dressed as though for an embassy reception. He was therefore unusually tongue-tied. Lerenard contributed little to the conversation as usual. The atmosphere was tense.

By contrast, Candice was the life and soul of the party. She started by toasting Jean-Luc and getting everyone to join in and congratulate him on his rapid recovery. She complimented Jeanette on the food and said how pleasant it was to be eating outside on a warm summer evening. Then she launched into a description of what it had been like, surviving the collapse the previous week. He noticed no mention was made of this afternoon's further collapse or the astonishing kiss that had followed it. In fact, he was the only one she didn't directly mention at all.

Due to Candice's lively conversation, the evening became almost jolly as the food was consumed, although Philip noticed that Jeanette was still rather restrained. He tried to make up for this by frequently topping up everybody's glasses. When the third bottle of wine had been broached, Candice finally addressed him directly.

"Philip, I'm feeling a bit cold. It was silly of me to wear this dress outside tonight. Would you mind getting my cardigan for me? It's in the car." She tossed the keys to him.

He got up obediently and winked at the amused expression on Jean-Luc's face. The big guy still seemed convinced that Philip allowed himself to be at the beck and call of the women around him.

It was virtually dark when he got outside. The little Peugeot was parked in what had become its usual place just inside the yard, round the corner from the cottage. He found it was still unlocked. He opened the driver's door and peered in, looking to see where she had left the cardigan. He could see it in the corner of the back seat but he couldn't reach it from the driver's seat. He shut the driver's door and moved to the rear passenger door.

"Have you found it?"

He looked up and saw Candice was standing just beside him.

"It's on the back seat."

"I know." She moved close. "But I told them I might have tucked it into a bag in the boot, so I ought to come and help you look for it."

He grinned. "Why did you do that?"

"You know why. I wanted a chance to talk to you alone."

"What about?"

"Do you like my dress?"

"It's – er – it's very sexy."

"Did you notice I haven't got a bra on? I don't need a bra with this dress. It has built in cups to support my boobs. If you'd taken me out to a restaurant this evening, as I asked you, I would have worn this dress. It's made of stretch material and you could have pulled the skirt over my hips and had me in it without the need to undress me – either back at my *chambre d'hôte* or on the back seat of the car, if you couldn't wait that long."

"I know," he whispered, then more loudly. "That is why I made sure we ate with the others." He took a breath. "I must make it clear to you, Candice, that my emotional life is complicated enough, without letting myself fall in love with the woman who my fiancée has employed to help her with her work on the Templar archives. You have to understand that."

She didn't respond as he reached into the car for her cardigan which he draped around her shoulders.

So he continued, "It would be very easy to fall for you, Candice, especially when you are done up like this, but I cannot allow myself to do that. I hope you will agree that we must treat this afternoon's kiss as a mistake."

"I suppose so." She nodded. "All right."

"OK. Let's go back and rejoin the others." He locked the car and rested a hand gently on her waist as they returned.

After that, the evening brightened up. Jeanette brought out the brandy and everyone chatted happily, although Philip thought that Candice was more restrained than she had been earlier. After another hour or so, Jean-Luc decided he was going back to the house and Candice accompanied him when he left.

On their own, Jeanette decided to discuss the visitor. "That woman was all dressed up to kill, as you English say. I think she is after you."

"Well," said Philip with feeling, "she is not going to get me. My personal life is too complicated already."

But that night, after another particularly passionate love-making session, as he lay beside the gently snoring Jeanette, the image of the girl with the dark, bright eyes who had no clothes on but a coating of grime, swam in his memory. Like it or not, his personal life *was* getting more complicated.

Then, the next morning, things got even worse.

26

It was Sunday and nobody was interested in working. Philip strolled across to inspect progress at the house. Of course, Jean-Luc was already up. He had obtained a chair from somewhere and had placed it in a position where the morning sun would rest on his back as he gazed out across the valley to the north. The big man seemed to be at peace with the world.

"Marvellous view," Philip commented as he came to stand beside his chair. "It feels good to be alive on a morning like this."

Lerenard didn't take his eye from the view as he replied, "Amen to that."

"We ought to have a full day today without interruptions."

Jean-Luc looked up at him but said nothing and, at that very moment, a car turned into the yard. It came right across to where Philip was standing and rolled to a halt. Out of the car stepped a person he had not been expecting.

"Good morning," said Jacqueline Blontard. "Isn't it a beautiful morning?"

"Jackie," gasped Philip, "What on earth are you doing here?"

"I received your message, so I came." She smiled. "Actually, Louis is taking his family down to stay in Provence for the summer, now that the schools have broken up. So we've been given the weekend off, and I decided to come and see how things were progressing here."

His fiancée's clothing was simple, but couldn't disguise her beauty. A white cotton blouse and dark skirt failed to hide her shapely figure. Her ankles were not spoiled by her sensible shoes. And the way her titian hair was held in a pleat at the back of her head couldn't reduce its colour. But it appeared that none of this was for him. Philip noticed that she didn't rush into his arms, so he presumed their relationship was still on ice. He thought that it would get even worse if she found Jeanette was still slumbering in his bed.

"You haven't driven all the way from Paris this morning."

"No. I stayed in Béziers last night. After I got your message, I decided I needed to have a good look round the flat yesterday."

She shook her head. "The list isn't there. I don't know what has happened to it."

"Well, I can tell you it's not in the bag. It wasn't only me who looked. Jean-Luc will confirm that his friend, Vauclus, searched the bag and its contents most thoroughly, and *he* couldn't find anything."

The big man intervened. "He is certainly not my friend."

"Anyway it's not there, so I don't know what has happened to it. Of course we could go back and ask César to check, but I'm pretty sure she hasn't got it."

"No," agreed Jackie. "We definitely had it in the Castle Hotel in Quillan, after she had given you the bag."

"Is it important? Surely you can get a copy of the original list from Hector."

"I suppose so, but I would still like to take another look in the bag, just to satisfy myself."

"OK:" Phillip shrugged. "I'll go and get it for you:"

"I'll come with you."

"That's not necessary. You stay here and chat to Jean-Luc. Or you can go and look at the progress we are making in trying to find a way down into the cellars."

Philip was aware that the bag was in the back bedroom at the cottage and that Jeanette was still asleep in the double bed in the front bedroom. It would not be a good idea to invite Jackie back to the place at this moment.

"OK. I'll wait here. I hope you won't be long."

"I think I know exactly where it is." Philip hurried back to the cottage and rushed upstairs. He shook the complaining Jeanette into wakefulness.

"Get up. Jackie has just turned up."

"What! What? Where is she?"

"She's out in the yard talking to Jean-Luc at present. I've come back to get the bag that she wants to see. I'll try to keep her away from the cottage, but you'd better get things tidied up in case she decides to come and call."

Jeanette looked at him defiantly. "If she comes upstairs, she's sure to realise that I'm not just your housekeeper. She'll see that now there's only one bed in the place."

"Well, we'll have to hope she has no reason to come upstairs. But I want you to get everything tidied up downstairs and make yourself look like a house-keeper."

"Huh. She'll guess what's going on if she comes here."

"Let's hope she doesn't, or your employment might be terminated early. Now, I've come to collect the bag, so I'll either be in the yard or in the chateau with her for the next hour or two."

He went into the back bedroom to collect the bag, which he had chucked in there after Vauclus had decided there was nothing of value in it. He supposed he would have to get rid of the thing when an opportunity arose. He saw it was lying on its side in a corner. As he picked it up, he noticed something strange. The double-headed eagle crest on the side had sprung open, as if the impact of throwing the bag down had caused a spring to open the front on a hinge. A small cavity had been revealed behind the badge and, when he peered in, he could see a little, white, square object in the hollow. It was about one and a quarter inches square and a quarter of an inch thick.

He was just going to poke into the cavity to get it out, when he thought that he ought to show it to Jackie first. She would be the right person to deal with this. So he carefully lifted the bag in his arms and carried it downstairs and out to the yard, where she was still talking to Jean-Luc. He made sure he held it flat on its side with the crest on top so that the square, white object would not fall out of the cavity. He stopped by the side of the car.

"I think you ought to see this," he called to her.

"Why? What is it?"

"Come and look."

Obediently she came over and peered at the bag where he indicated.

"When the Vauclus guy had finished looking at the contents," he told her, "he said he didn't want it. So I tossed it in a corner, planning to get rid of it in due course. However, it seems, that when I threw it down, it must have landed in such a way as to cause the front of the crest to spring open. When I picked it up just now, I noticed that there seems to be something in the cavity behind the badge. I thought I should pass it over to you to investigate in your professional way."

"My God," she breathed as she inspected the crest. "I think you're right. How exciting! Let's take it into the back seat of the car, where there's less risk of us damaging it. Keep the bag level so that the object doesn't fall out."

She opened the door for him, and he climbed in, still holding the thing level.

"Now wait a minute." She went round and opened the front passenger door and burrowed into the glove compartment. Then she came round and got in beside him. "It's lucky I carry these things in the car." She had some tweezers which she handed to him and a pair of white cotton gloves which she proceeded to put on. "Now, have you got one of your clean white handkerchiefs?"

"I think so." He ferreted in his trouser pocket and pulled out one which he shook out and she spread on her lap.

"OK. Now, if you turn the bag upside down above the handkerchief, I hope the object will fall out."

When he did that the small white object still remained in the cavity behind the crest.

"Give me the tweezers and lift the bag a bit higher. I'll see if I can loosen it."

He did as instructed, and she bent down and peered up into the cavity. Then she gently inserted the tweezers into the side and was rewarded by the thing coming loose and falling onto the handkerchief. Philip put the bag aside, making sure the crest remained open, and bent forward to look at the object which she was examining closely.

"It's actually a tightly-folded piece of paper," she informed him. "I can see the edges of the folds." She looked round. "Now where can we go to unfold it?"

"How about on Jean-Luc's bed in the house? The place is clean because it has only just been finished and he is very neat. I'm sure he won't mind and he'll have made the bed before he came out to enjoy the sun."

"Ask him if that's all right."

"Can I tell him what we're doing?"

"Just briefly."

He got out of the car and spoke to the big man, who raised no objection. So, a few minutes later, they were ready to open the paper. Philip brought up a large, clean tile from the kitchen to make a rigid base on which to work. Then Jackie opened his handkerchief on it. While he held it flat, she started to prise open the folds of the paper very carefully with the tweezers.

About twenty minutes later the sheet of paper was fully opened. It was about the size of a half-sheet of foolscap and was revealed as a letter. Jackie peered at it closely.

"It's mostly hand-written in German," she announced. "I think I understand enough of the language to read it and, my goodness - I think this could be dynamite."

"What do you mean?"

"I believe it's a private letter which was never meant to be seen by the public." She rested a gloved finger lightly on the crest at the top of the sheet of paper. "Look here."

"That's the same double-headed eagle as the badge on the side of the bag."

"Exactly. It's the family crest of the Habsbourg dynasty. And if you look at the signature at the bottom of the letter," she indicated, "you will see that it is signed by a person who calls herself the Marquise d'Hautpoul. That's a name linked with the Blanchefort family. She might possibly even have lived in this chateau in the middle of the nineteenth century."

"So what does the letter say?"

"The next significant thing is the date – 21st July, 1871."

"That's important, is it?"

"Oh, yes," She smiled. "I can see I have to give you a lesson about French history in the nineteenth century. After the French defeat in the Franco-Prussian War, Napoleon the third abdicated and a temporary republic was proclaimed with Adolphe Thiers as its chief executive. But the National Assembly had a right-wing majority, and there was a strong feeling throughout the country that the installation of a monarch subject to the will of parliament would be a good thing. The people looked across the channel at the huge success of the British constitutional monarchy and many of them wanted France to follow the same course."

She paused for a minute to order her thoughts. "The pretender to the throne was the Compte de Chambord. However, he turned down the offer of the throne, on the pretext that the assembly wouldn't agree to replace the existing tricolour national flag with the old Bourbon flag of the previous monarchy. They offered that they would be willing to add the royal standard emblem in the middle of the white central stripe of the tricolour, but he wouldn't agree even to that compromise. Everyone thought that it was a petty pretext for refusing his elevation to the throne and believed there must have been a secret reason why he decided not to accept the offer." She took a deep breath before continuing.

"This letter confirms that Adolphe Thiers offered Chambord his choice from the Cathar treasures (which must have already been found by then) if he would agree to reject the offer of the crown and to accept voluntary exile to his estates in Austria. It also confirms his agreement to the proposal. So the man disappeared with a fortune in his pocket. It seems that he declined many of the bigger items in the treasure store at le Bézu, presumably because they were too cumbersome to take away, and perhaps because of the importance of avoiding any publicity about the secret agreement. This is going to be very interesting when I get round to sorting through the treasure we found."

"What are you going to do about this?"

She bit her lip. "I don't know yet. I'll have to think very carefully about it. I think perhaps I'll discuss it first with Hector. I suspect he may already know something about the subject."

"I presume you want to take the letter with you."

"I certainly do. Can I borrow your handkerchief to keep it from further contamination?"

"Of course."

He watched while she carefully re-folded the letter and wrapped the handkerchief round it. Then she took off her gloves and led the way back downstairs. Philip carried the tile back to the kitchen.

"What about this guy Vauclus?" he asked

"What about him?"

"Well, supposing he comes back and asks about the letter?"

"Don't tell him anything. I suggest you close the front of the crest, if you can. Then the best idea would be to get rid of the bag somewhere he wouldn't be likely to find it."

"I'll chuck it in a rubbish container."

"That's a good idea, but do it somewhere well away from Rennes, like Carcassonne." She nodded to him. "Now, I'll put the letter safely in the glove box. Then you can take me to look at the progress you're making in the chateau."

He followed her back to the car.

27

When they got outside, they saw that Candice had turned up and was chatting to Jean-Luc. Jackie went round to open the front door of her car to put the handkerchief-swathed letter carefully into the glove box. So Philip went over to talk to the others.

"Don't tell them about the letter," Jackie warned him.

Today Candice was dressed for the sun. A pair of very short shorts exposed a lot of either sun-tanned or rubble-stained leg. She wore a tangerine top consisting of no more than a band of stretch material covering her boobs. Her almost white hair once again tumbled over her shoulders, and she wore low-heeled sandals. She had a guarded expression. No doubt this was caused by the arrival of her employer.

"Why is Mademoiselle Blontard here?" was her question to him.

"She's trying to find a list that has been mislaid."

"You said you weren't expecting to see her for three months."

"The director of her series took the weekend off so that left her free, and she decided to come to see if she could find a list she has lost."

"What – er – how is she?"

"She's fine, as far as I know."

The girl glowered at him. "You know what I mean."

"Nothing has changed, Candice. This weekend is merely an interval for her."

"Hmm. It seems a long way to come just for a list."

Philip nodded. "Well, she obviously has her own set of priorities."

"You can say that again."

Jackie came to join them. She was carrying the bag which she handed to him. He noticed the crest was still open. "Hello Candice. You're looking very summery."

"I've had enough of work clothes and breathing dust and dirt for the week. I want a day off to let my hair down."

"Literally," mumbled Lerenard.

"Candice," suggested Philip, "would you like to show Mademoiselle Blontard the progress you have made in digging out the staircase?"

"What's this about a staircase?"

"I'll show you." The girl turned to him. "Aren't you coming as well?"

He held out the key to her. "I'll join you in a few minutes. I want a quick word with Jean-Luc."

"Don't be too long." There was a warning note in Jackie's voice.

"No. It'll be quite brief."

As the women crossed the yard, Philip turned to the big man. "When I collected this bag from the house, you can see what had happened to it." He held it up to show him the open crest. "There's a small cavity behind the badge and there was an object in there. I promised Jackie I wouldn't tell anyone the details."

"Do you think it was the thing Jordie was looking for?"

"Probably."

"If you want my advice, I would tell you to have nothing to do with it. Forget you've ever seen it. If anyone asks, you don't know what was in the bag. You don't know anything about a secret cavity. In fact, I would advise you to close the crest and chuck the damn bag in some rubbish skip as far away from here as you can get it."

"Jackie is taking the object we found back to Paris with her."

"I would give her the same advice. Get rid of everything to do with that bag." He looked straight into Philip's eyes. "If either of you is found in possession of what Jordie is looking for, you will both be in extreme danger. He won't hesitate to eliminate anybody who he thinks might have got in the way of him carrying out the assignment he has been given to the absolute bitter end – and that includes making sure you don't have any knowledge which you might be able to pass on to others."

Philip took a deep breath. "I had a feeling you would say something like that. I'll go and tell Jackie."

He made for the gate into the chateau. In the courtyard he could see Candice explaining to her boss how they had been trying to clear the steps which they presumed led to the cellars. She turned to him as he arrived.

"I've been telling Mademoiselle Blontard how you had to dig me out when the pile of rubble collapsed and entombed me half-way down the stairs. I told her you probably saved my life."

"Apparently you had to strip her almost naked to get her out," said Jackie. "That was heroic of you." A critic might have discerned a hint of malice in the comment.

Philip snorted. "I didn't want you to lose one of your staff so soon after you'd taken her on to help you. She didn't deserve to be saved, because she had behaved foolishly and disobeyed my instructions, which resulted in her being buried alive."

"The villagers had a big celebration when he got me out," said the girl, apparently undaunted by his criticism. "Philip was the big hero, but I missed it all because the doctor said I had hypothermia and mild concussion."

"It was Albert who was the hero with the villagers," said Philip. He was quite keen that no questions should be asked about how he had helped to cure Candice's hypothermia. "He was the guy who lifted her out. I was merely helping from below." He hurried on. "After that I banned her from further digging until we'd put up the protective planking which you can see is there now."

Philip turned to the girl. "I think the next job is to dig out that beam. You can see that it is more than half blocking the steps and we won't be able to clear them until that's removed."

"You haven't any idea what's at the bottom of these steps?" Jackie asked.

"At the moment, all we can see is loads more rubble." He shook his head. "I'm afraid I haven't a clue about how long it's going to take to find a way through to your archives. In fact, we don't even know if these steps will lead to them. There may be more than one way down to the cellars, hidden under the collapsed building."

"Hmm, you've not made much progress then, have you?"

He was slightly nettled by her tone. "The only way into the archives that we know at present is the same way that I got you out of there, and I don't think either you or Candice would want to climb up that steep ladder and in through that window – certainly not on a daily basis and carrying equipment."

Jackie shuddered. "Oh no! I wouldn't ask her to do that."

"I've looked round the rest of the ground floor and there's no other possible access to the cellars that I've found yet. I don't see any alternative at present to digging our way in here."

"No," she agreed reluctantly. "I suppose not," She looked around once more. Then she said, "Well, thank you for showing me what you've done, Candice. Now, can you leave us, please. I want a private talk with Philip."

The girl gave her a little bow, and Philip a hesitant smile as she left.

As soon as she had gone, Philip said, "Before we have this private talk, Jackie, I need to tell you what Jean-Luc said."

"Did you tell him about what we'd found?"

"I didn't give him any details, but I showed him the bag which still had the open crest. He says we must get rid of it and anything we found in it, or we will be in danger of being killed by this one-armed guy called Vauclus, who I told you about."

"I *must* keep that letter, or at least a photocopy of it. Surely it will be safe in Paris."

"Not according to Jean-Luc. He obviously knows the fellow and is very wary of him. For someone like Jean-Luc to say he is worried about him, impresses me a lot,"

"OK." She shrugged. "You can get rid of the bag and then you won't have anything to worry about."

"You've got to take his warning seriously, Jackie. I certainly am. Can you take the bag back to Paris with you and dispose of it safely there?"

"Yes, if you want me to."

"Thanks." He took a breath. "Now what do you want to talk to me about?"

She was silent for a while, looking at the ground. Then she directed her gaze straight at him.

"The real reason I came here is to ask you what is going on."

"Pardon."

"Armand Séjour came to see me in Paris on Friday evening. He came to tell me that he had finished clearing the site at le Bézu as instructed, and everything there has been returned as near as possible to the way it was before we started the excavations."

"Good." Philip knew now exactly where the conversation was going.

"He also told me, that when he came down to help with preparing the site at le Bézu two or three weeks ago, he dropped Jeanette Picard off here in Rennes. Is that correct?"

"Yes it is."

"I thought you might try to deny it." She paused for a moment, then blurted out, "Are you sleeping with her?"

Philip took a deep breath. "Jackie, I'm sure you recall the conversation we had at le Bézu on that same day, when you were filming there without having told me you would be in the place. I remember exactly what you told me then. You said that I should forget you for the next three months at least, while you were recording your series about the Cathars."

"I don't recall saying I was giving permission for you to jump into bed with any woman you fancied."

"I don't see that I need your permission. What you gave me to understand, was that our relationship was on ice until the filming was finished, and that I would have to sort out any problems on my own, until you were free to meet me and discuss what we were going to do next."

"And you assume that allowed you to take up with other women whenever you fancied it."

"Look, Jackie. We aren't married. We're not even formally engaged. I don't know whether we will be able to work out a relationship in which you are apparently going to be disappearing for months on end, leaving me on my own. I also know about the sort of things that go on between people in the film and TV worlds when they're away from home."

"I've told you . . ."

"Yes. I know I'm an English prude. Well, I can't help how I am. My first wife spent a lot of her life going out and having a good time, and I let her go on her own because I found the kind of life she liked was boring for me. That relationship ended in an expensive divorce. I will have to think very carefully about whether I want possibly to repeat the same sort of mistake a second time."

"Philip," she insisted, "you are trying to avoid my question. Are you having regular nightly sex with Jeanette?"

"And my reply is, that you should mind your own business. You've made it clear you don't want to have anything to do with me for the next three months. You didn't rush into my arms when you got out of the car just now. You didn't ask my forgiveness for leaving me on my own for so long. So I think I'm free to do as I want, until you deign to find time to join me again."

Jackie was getting annoyed. "I've told you, Philip, I'm a career woman. I have the chance to rise to the top of my profession – both professions. Do you want to deny me that?"

He gave her a twisted smile. "You have to decide if that is more important to you than a complete, fulfilled personal love-life. What I want is a woman who will give me affection and physical love, and perhaps a family as well. If you're not prepared to spare enough of your life to do that, then I think I have a right to look for it elsewhere."

There were tears in her eyes as she said, "I'm also a proud woman, Philip. I gave you my love just a couple of months ago. For me that was a permanent thing. I didn't expect you to go off as soon as I'm not available and start having sex with other women."

"Well, Jackie, if your idea of permanent love is six months on and six months off, then I don't want that sort of love."

"And what about Jeanette? If I don't give you what you want, are you thinking of permanently shacking up with her?"

He shook his head. "I am not thinking of anything. I will not make any plans until I know what you are going to do."

"So you're saying I must either give up my career or give you up."

"I am saying," he tried to choose his words carefully, "that if concentrating on your career means that there will be long periods of time when I won't see you, then I don't want that kind of relationship. Am I making myself clear?"

"And what about all this?" She swept her arms round the courtyard. "What then do we do about all this?"

"When you can spare the time, we must sit down and discuss where we want to go with both our business and our personal relationships. You can see that I am carrying on doing what we agreed I would do a couple of months ago. I am continuing to prepare the house for a couple to live in and I'll try to find a way for your assistant to start cataloguing the Templar archives. I am still keen on owning the chateau, either jointly or on my own." He took a breath. "I'm here, Jackie, and I'm continuing with our agreement until I have to change my plans."

She calmed down. "All right. You're saying it's up to me to make the first move."

"As I see it, Jackie, the future is here. I'm here. You're not."

"And what about Jeanette when I come back?"

"She knows that I expect you to return here in three months. If she doesn't like that idea she can leave tomorrow. I'm not holding her here."

She took a deep breath. "OK. Maybe I'll see you in three months. Goodbye."

Jackie went out to her car and Philip followed more slowly. He noticed that both Candice and Jean-Luc had gone but the bag was lying beside the car. She picked it up and tossed it on the back seat. Then, with the briefest of waves, she drove away.

28

Jackie drove towards Carcassonne with a feeling of distressed anger. She was now certain that Philip was sleeping with Jeanette. She knew the Paris *poule* was attracted to him and had tried to get into his bed more than once before. The woman was also very sexy and very alluring in an earthy sort of way. Philip was upset that she hadn't been able to spare more time with him and, as a result, he had been a fruit ripe for the plucking by this voluptuous woman. Jackie couldn't help feeling humiliated by the ease with which Jeanette had reeled him in.

Philip didn't seem to understand that she was on the threshold of the greatest success in her career. All he was interested in was settling down and living a normal family life, albeit in the luxurious surroundings that their recently acquired wealth was going to make possible. He didn't have any particular ambitions for himself, and he seemed unenthusiastic about her own aspirations. He obviously didn't wish to be at her side when she met the important people in the world who she believed would be delighted to welcome the couple into their opulent society. She felt that, for herself, the sky was the limit. He didn't feel the same. He would rather jump into bed with some plump little woman who offered him sex and comfort.

She shook her head. There was nothing she could do about it at the moment. When she had finished this series, she would go back to Rennes and confront him. They would have to make their decisions at that time. Until then she had better forget about him.

Jackie decided she would return to Paris via her flat in Béziers where she could photocopy the letter. She pushed on, hoping she would be able to find enough in the fridge to provide her with a scratch lunch while she was copying the sheet of paper and hiding it away. To her surprise, when she arrived at the flat, she found that Charlotte and Hector had already returned from their holiday.

"Tante Charlotte," she exclaimed, "I thought you weren't due to get back for another five or six days."

"Well," said her aunt, "we decided we'd had enough of hunting round old Greek temples. After a fortnight they all seem to be the same. Even Hector agreed that he wasn't looking forward to it any longer. He wanted to get back and start his new hobby."

"Really? What's that?"

The old lady grinned at him. "Can I tell her, darling?"

He shrugged. "Why not?"

"Hector has joined the Languedoc Historical Society. He was particularly keen on joining this local group, because he's always had an interest in the history of our region. They were very pleased when he applied to join them. In fact they've asked him to give them a talk on the influence of the Habsbourgs on the area. That's a subject he knows a lot about."

"My goodness, Hector," said Jackie. "What a coincidence!"

"What do you mean?" He'd been sitting in an armchair, reading through his post, and appearing to take little interest in the women's chatter. Now he was suddenly interested.

Jackie wondered for a moment if she'd said too much. But she had to discuss it with somebody and Hector Ramise, a former archaeological professor at the Sorbonne and her one-time tutor, seemed to be the best man.

"You'll have to promise to keep this under your hat, Hector, but a letter from one of the Habsbourgs has recently come into my possession. I think it's absolutely devastating. I suspect you may even know something about it, but probably not the details."

"Please go on," said the professor.

"Well, you were aware of the bag with the Habsbourg crest on the side which César Renoir gave to us. You thought you were very interested in a list contained in the bag, but later you decided it was no longer important."

"Oh, yes – not important at all."

No doubt, thought Jackie without saying it, he wished to forget that episode in which he didn't cut a very good figure.

"Well," she said, "César has had some guy turn up, hassling her because he wanted to look in the bag, which was among my things sent back here when we finished excavations at le Bézu, and she asked Philip if he could show it to the man. He guessed it was probably here in my office, and he sent me a message about it. Of course you were away. So I let him have one of my keys, and he came over here and found the bag and took it back to show it to this guy. Apparently the man was expecting to find some letter in the bag, but it wasn't there. So he went off unsatisfied and left the bag with Philip, who chucked it in a corner in his back bedroom and forgot about it until today, when I called in to see him."

"So what happened?"

Jackie noticed that the professor had now become very interested in her story. "I was still looking for my list – which incidentally I hope you'll help me with – but that's not relevant to this. At my request Philip dug out the bag and discovered that the badge on the crest had sprung open when he chucked it in the corner. When we investigated, we found a letter had been folded up in a small cavity behind the badge."

She paused for a moment and Hector urged her. "Go on. What was in this letter?"

"It was written by the Marquise d'Hautpoul and dated 21st July 1871 and it purports to record the agreement between the Compte de Chambord and Adolphe Thiers to turn down the offer of the throne of France in return for a substantial golden hand-shake, thus torpedoing the popular desire at the time to restore the French Bourbon monarchy." Jackie paused, watching the professor closely. "Since you have contacts with the Habsbourg family, would you know anything about this Marquise d'Hautpoul, and perhaps be able to authenticate the letter?"

"How interesting," he responded. "It's certainly something I would be pleased to look into."

"I'll go and get it from the glove compartment in my car."

"While you're doing that," said Charlotte, "I'll rustle up something to eat. It won't be much because the fridge is rather empty, but I can manage some cheese and crackers and a bottle of white wine."

"OK. Thank you, aunt." Jackie went outside to get the letter.

When she returned with it, still loosely wrapped in its clean handkerchief, she said to Ramise, "Let's go into the office. I can open it out on the desk."

In there she laid the handkerchief on the desk and extracted two pairs of clean cotton gloves from a drawer, one of which she handed to the professor. Then, after putting on her own pair, she carefully unfolded the letter and stood back to let him read it. He peered down at it for some time.

"This is very interesting," he said. "I would like to show it to a friend I have in Vienna when I next go there."

"But that's not likely to be for some time?" she asked.

"Well, maybe later this year."

"OK, Hector. Let me know when you are going and we'll discuss it again."

"Can you let me have a copy?"

"Ah, no. Not just yet. For now, I want to keep it confidential. I appreciate that you'll need a copy if and when you go to Vienna, but we'll talk about that when the time comes."

The professor stood back from the desk. "All right. We'll leave it for now."

Just then Charlotte called out, "Lunch is on the table," and he turned and ambled off into the hall, leading into the dining room. Before she followed him, Jackie switched on the photocopier, laid the letter face down on the glass platen and programmed it to take two copies, then left it to do its work when it had warmed up.

Over lunch the conversation turned to more general matters. But after a while it became clear that Charlotte wanted to know about Jackie's personal life.

"How is Philip?" she asked.

"Oh. He's doing all right. He's working furiously in Rennes, improving a house where it's planned we will live for a couple of years while we're renovating the chateau."

"He seems very committed to your future," said her aunt, in a way that made Jackie want to scream. "Philip's such a nice man, Jackie. I'm so pleased you decided he was the right person for you."

Hector stood up. "If we're into personal matters, I think I'll go into the other room." He left them to their chatting.

"Is everything still fine between you?" Charlotte persisted.

"I'm not sure." Jackie didn't know just how much to open up to her aunt. "If I'm honest, he's not happy about me spending so much time in Paris, while I'm working on this new series."

"Surely you get back to Rennes-le-Chateau at the weekends, don't you? Isn't that enough for him?"

"Well, actually, I haven't been able to spare the time to go back there until today. He came to see me in Paris one weekend, but that wasn't a success, and he was upset when I did a few days site-work at le Bézu, and I didn't call in to see him while I was there."

"Goodness, I should think so. That's less than ten kilometres from Rennes, isn't it?"

"But aunt, I was *very* busy, and to be honest, I find it's a big distraction if he's hanging round when I'm working."

Charlotte shook her head. "I think you're being very foolish, my girl. Throughout your life you've been courted by dozens of characters who were only really interested in your fame and your money, and now you come across a man who loves you for yourself, and you're ready to risk losing him, because you're too busy spending all your time concentrating on your career."

"That's not fair, aunt. He's got to accept that there are times when my career comes first."

"I'm sorry, Jackie, I've never been a career woman like you. I've only been a working woman and a housewife in my life, and to me the most important thing is the love between a man and a woman."

"Can't I try to combine the two?"

"Of course you can," said Charlotte. "But do you call visiting the man you say you love for one day in three months, is giving him a fair share of your life?"

"I don't think he was pleased to see me today anyway. I think he is changing his affections to another woman who is hanging round him."

"And whose fault is that?"

Jackie looked incensed. "Are you suggesting it's mine?"

"Look, my girl, you and Philip met and fell heavily for each other, and it looked to me as though you had at last found the right guy. Then you had only a couple of weeks together before you disappeared again. He spent ages hunting for you and put his own life in danger to try to find you. Doesn't that prove how strong his love is for you? Then, after a few more weeks, you clear off to Paris and leave him on his own in a foreign country with no family near. Try to see it from his point of view. You don't seem to be very interested in returning his love, do you?"

"Oh aunt, I'm under so much pressure. Everybody is on at me in Paris to make a success of this series, and we've lost so much time because of the problems with *Vendredi Treize* and now you say I'm alienating Philip. We had a big row about it this morning. I don't know what I'm going to do." She burst into tears.

Charlotte came round the table and took the girl into her arms. "I'm sorry, my dear, I didn't mean to upset you. All I ask is that you try to think a bit more about Philip. Otherwise, I believe you risk losing him. If you do, I think you'll regret it for the rest of your life." She shook her head. "But I'll say no more now."

After a while Jackie calmed down and wiped away her tears. When she had recovered, they went into the sitting room to join Hector and have a more normal conversation. However, she soon got up to leave them.

"I need to be back in Paris before it's too late this evening," she said. "I must have a good night's sleep before we resume recording tomorrow."

She went into the office to collect the letter and the photocopies. She noticed there was only one copy in the tray.

"That's funny," she thought. "I'm sure I set it to do two. Don't tell me the machine's getting temperamental as well, because I've been neglecting it"

She shrugged and took another copy and thought no more about it. Then she said her farewells and drove back to the capital.

29

The next morning Candice turned up with her overalls done up to the neck, belted round the waist and tucked into her boots. Nevertheless, the thin fabric totally failed to disguise her attractive figure despite the modifications she made. In fact, Philip thought it made her look even more sexy like that. Her long hair had been wound up into a sort of doughnut shape pinned to the top of her head and covered by a baseball cap. Her eyes shone out of a face almost totally devoid of make-up.

He was amused to think this was all for the sake of Gaston. Albert's mate hadn't objected when he was told that he was going to be working with the girl. However, he'd only been there an hour or so when he came back to complain about the way she was treating him.

"She's just digging out the earth and throwing it up over the beam," Albert translated. "He has to fill the loose earth into the buckets and carry them to the heap beside the barrows. Sometimes, when he is filling up the buckets, Candice throws earth all over him and she just laughs when he tells her off about it."

"Oh, God!" said Philip. "She's obviously decided to be awkward."

"She's told Gaston that he is useless, and she needs to have someone working with her who knows what he is doing."

"OK. I'll go and talk to her. Tell Gaston he can come back and work with you, at least until I've sorted her out."

He went across the yard to the chateau and through the courtyard to the top of the steps. He was amused to see spadefulls of earth regularly flying out of the hole in the staircase. He couldn't actually see the girl.

"Candice," he called out. "Stop it."

"What?" Her pink face appeared beside the beam.

"You're causing trouble with Gaston."

"Has he given up?" she asked. "The man's useless. He can't keep up with me. Here am I down in the hole, having to throw the soil all the way up on to the beam and he can't even clear it away and take it to the heap." She wiped the back of her hand across her perspiring forehead.

"This is stupid, Candice."

"What is?"

"Throwing the soil up here. It's not clearing the steps. It's just moving it from one side to the other."

"Not if there's somebody up there to clear it away."

"But then they get covered with the rubble you're throwing up, because you can't see they're there. Nobody's going to clear the stuff up under those conditions."

"It's making a mess of me as well. Some of the soil falls back down the hole because he's not clearing it up fast enough. It's a good job I brought my hat, or my hair would be filthy already. And look at my overalls. They were clean when I got here this morning."

"You've got to stop this silly idea of throwing shovelfuls of earth up on to the beam. You'll get nowhere doing that."

"There isn't room to get the buckets down in the hole now. In any case they are too heavy for me to lift them all the way up on to the beam." She looked up at him defiantly. "Why don't you come down here? You're much taller than me. You can carry on filling the buckets and handing them up to me like you did on Saturday. Then I can take off these filthy overalls and loosen my hair and be much cooler."

He sniggered. "And you'd do your work in your bra and pants."

"So what! Why don't you admit it? You like me with nothing on. It gets you all worked up."

"Don't be silly." He decided to change the subject. Her comment was too near to the truth. "The hole's getting too deep now anyway. I told you yesterday that we've got to dig out the beam so that we can widen the excavation. If we get the beam out of the way, we'll have the whole width of the stairs to work in, and then we can just fill the buckets and carry them up the steps to get the rubble away."

"All right then." She held out a hand. "Can you help me out please?"

When she was up at ground level, she took off her cap and shook the soil out of it. Then she undid the zip on her overalls to her waist, slid her arms out of the sleeves and let the fabric fall round her waist.

"My goodness, it's hot down there," she said. "You can hardly breathe in that hole."

"Do you want a drink? The water is still quite cool."

He handed her the bottle. She grabbed it, tipped her head back and gulped down nearly half the contents.

"Oh, thank you," she gasped as she handed it back. "I needed that."

Philip thought about the situation. It was undoubtedly hot and breathless down in the stairwell. Although the sun, slanting down into the courtyard, didn't shine directly down the steps, the heat was stifling. He shook his head.

"I think it's too hot to work here in the middle of the day. I think you should stop now."

"But the steps won't get cleared if we keep stopping because it's too hot."

Her comment gave him an idea. "How would you feel about working late evenings and early mornings while we're doing this heavy work in mid-summer? We could start at eight in the evening and work till midnight and then start again at five in the morning and continue until nine. We can rig up lights so that we won't be working in the dark."

She considered the idea for a minute. "All right. I will if you will. But what will I do about somewhere to sleep?"

"It's only four kilometres to your *chambre d'hôte*. Do you object to doing two return trips a day?"

"It's not that. I don't think the people I'm staying with will be very happy if I come in after midnight and then have my alarm go off again at four-thirty in the morning."

He smiled. "No. You're right. I hadn't thought of that."

"Why don't we get another bed and put it in the back room for me?"

"I don't think Jeanette would go along with that suggestion."

"Why not? We could both close our bedroom doors and I could put in ear-plugs so that I wouldn't hear the noises when you are bouncing up and down on her fat body like a trampoline."

He couldn't help chuckling at the picture she painted, even though it was clearly very catty. She laughed, pleased to see his amusement, and soon they were both roaring their heads off.

When he was able to regain his composure, Philip reproved her. "You're a wicked little thing, referring to Jeanette in that way."

"But I make you laugh, don't I?" Then a shade wistfully. "I could make you laugh a lot if you gave me the chance."

He pointed a finger at her, half playfully. "That's enough of that. I had a telling-off yesterday from Jackie yesterday about my relationships with other women."

"Yes. But it wasn't about me. I'd have stood up for you if it had been about me."

"Stop it, Candice. We've got to see about your accommodation. I think we could quickly get the second bedroom ready in the house, now that we're getting the place up together. You could share the bathroom with Jean-Luc." He gestured at the overalls round her waist. "Get yourself properly dressed again and I'll take you to look at it."

When they inspected the room, Candice agreed it would be OK.

"You can see I've fixed the window and the door, and the glazing has been done. It can be painted any time. You can do that at your leisure. We need to get you a bed and a dressing table - also a chair and a bedside cupboard. I'll take you into Limoux this afternoon in the pick-up and you can choose what you would like."

"OK. I'll go back and shower and wash my hair. I'll be ready by eleven and I'll treat you to lunch."

"It's ten-thirty already."

"All right – say twelve, but I'll still treat you to lunch."

She hurried out to the car and drove away.

30

When Philip told Jeanette he was taking Candice into Limoux to buy furniture, she said she wanted to go as well.

"You can drop me off at the supermarket. My stores have been depleted by all the people you've invited round for meals." Presumably she was referring to Candice. "On Saturday night we got through three bottles of wine."

"You can get more wine from the bar up the road."

"Huh! At the price they charge we'd soon be bankrupt."

Philip reflected that this woman seemed to be trying to take over the running of his life. Nevertheless, he said, "OK. There's a bench seat in the front of the pick-up so there's room for you as well."

When they set off, he was amused to notice that Jeanette had planted herself firmly in the middle of the seat. That would mean that Candice would have to get in the other side, and she would be separated from him. He saw she had also taken extra trouble with her appearance. She was wearing a scarlet blouse with a plunging neckline. Her short skirt was pulled up to reveal her plump rounded thighs and her sandals had half-heels. Philip suspected she wouldn't be able to remain upright if she wore the sort of high heels that Candice put on. She had also applied a fair amount of perfume and he thought she deserved a compliment.

"You're looking very sexy today," he told her. "For two pins I'd suggest we abandoned the shopping expedition, and I would carry you up to bed."

Jeanette loved that kind of talk, and she smiled and rubbed against him. "That's a date for when we get back."

However, her appearance was again eclipsed by Candice when they picked her up. The girl was dressed simply but very attractively. She was wearing a colourful summer dress with a V-neck and no sleeves. It had a full skirt which stopped just above the knee and seemed to swirl when she turned. White strappy sandals completed her outfit. Her blonde hair had been brushed and shone in the sun as it cascaded over her shoulders. She wore little makeup but her eyes sparkled as she smiled at him. She made Jeanette look what she was - a Parisian *poule*.

He jumped out and helped Candice into the high seat of the pick-up and was rewarded by a squeeze of the hand and a whiff of light, summery perfume as she climbed in beside his housekeeper.

"Jeanette has come to do some food and drink shopping," he told her. "We'll drop her off at the supermarket first and then go and look for your furniture."

"OK."

When they left Jeanette at the big store on the outskirts of town, he said, "I don't know exactly how long we'll be. If we haven't returned by the time you've finished shopping, I suggest you sit and have some refreshment in the coffee bar. Then you'll see us when we drive into the car park."

A rather silent Jeanette nodded and left them. Philip thought that it was slightly unsettling, during the time they were in Limoux, that both men and women stopped to look at Candice as she walked beside him. And, as he got back into the driver's seat, he noticed the girl had moved into the centre position, and was in fact actually rubbing shoulders with him, as they made for the furniture store.

"I think perhaps we will have to be a very long time," she said playfully. "I need plenty of time to make up my mind about what I want."

"Don't be silly, Candice. If you're going to be living in the house and sharing our meals, we've got to make sure that we all get on. I don't want you and Jeanette to be sniping at each other all the time."

However, by the time they had found all the furniture to her satisfaction and bought several little extras which she said she "absolutely" needed, it was nearly two hours before they got back to the supermarket – two hours of close proximity, trying out beds and looking into chests of drawers. He saw that Jeanette was sitting by the window of the coffee house with a face like thunder.

"Sorry about the time," he said. "I didn't realise what a complicated business it is, getting furniture for a woman's bedroom. Candice offered to buy us lunch, but I think it is too late to go to a restaurant, so I suggest we eat here."

"It's only self-service."

"I can cope with that. I've parked where we can see the vehicle, so there's no risk of anything being taken by some light-fingered person." He smiled at her reassuringly. "Now, what do you want?"

They all made their choices, and he went to buy the food and drink. Candice came with him to help carry the trays back to the table. When they returned, Jeanette was looking out of the window.

"There's a man peering in the back of the pick-up," she announced.

"It's that man with only one arm," said Candice. "The guy who came to see you the other day."

Philip's heart sank. "I wonder what on earth he wants," he said. "I'd better go out and talk to him."

When he got to the vehicle he asked, "Can I help you?"

Vauclus turned to look at him. He didn't seem in the least worried about being found peering into somebody else's vehicle. "I hope so."

"What do you want?"

"I want that bag I left with you the other day."

"Oh – er – I'm afraid I got rid of it."

"What did you do with it?"

"I – er – I threw it in a rubbish tip. I thought you didn't want it, and I certainly had no further use for it."

"That's a problem. Where exactly is this rubbish tip?"

Philip was thinking fast. He remembered the industrial estate in Carcassonne which he and Jeanette had visited when they were looking for Jackie and the Cathar treasure. He recalled seeing a couple of large rubbish skips beside one of the estate roads.

"I actually threw it in a rubbish skip. I had to go to Carcassonne to visit the police there about some matter and I took the bag with me and chucked it into one of the skips on an industrial estate."

"Really? When did you do that?"

"Er – on Saturday."

"Two days ago. The chances are they won't have emptied it yet." Vauclus almost seemed to be thinking aloud. "I want you to tell me exactly where this skip is, so that I can see if it's possible to recover the bag."

Philip described, as best he could, where the rubbish skips were located. Then he asked, "Why are you so interested in getting this bag, monsieur Vauclus? You had no interest in it the other day."

"That is none of your business."

Philip shrugged. "OK. I was just pleased to be shot of the damn thing."

"I will go to Carcassonne this afternoon." He gave Philip a piercing look. "Are you telling me the truth, monsieur Sinclair?"

"Of course. What would be the point of lying to you? I hope you find what you´re looking for."

"If I don´t, you can be sure I will be back."

Philip managed a shrug. "I hope that won´t be necessary."

Vauclus gave him a nod and left. As he returned to the restaurant, Philip found himself wishing he had actually done what he told the guy, rather than giving it to Jackie. At least he wouldn´t feel guilty about lying, and his fiancée would have been in a less risky position.

As soon as they got back to Rennes and he had dropped Jeanette and her shopping off at the cottage, Philip drove straight to the house. Ignoring Candice´s request for him to help her unload the furniture and get it upstairs to her room, he went in to look for Jean-Luc. The big man wasn´t there. Where had he gone? He noticed the small pedestrian door in the gates into the chateau was open, so he decided to look in there first. Sure enough, he found Lerenard mooching round the courtyard. He hurried over to him.

"Vauclus turned up again when we were in Limoux," he told Jean-Luc. "He has decided he wants the bag now. He asked me to tell him where it was."

"What did you say to him?"

Philip grinned weakly. "Well, I was rather caught on the hop, so I made up some story about throwing it into a rubbish skip in Carcassonne."

"Did he buy that?"

"I don´t think so. He said he was going to go and look and, if he can´t find it, he would be back. What do you think I should do?"

Lerenard thought for a minute. Then he said, "Leave it with me. Can I borrow your car?"

"Of course you can." He dug the keys out of his pocket and handed them over. "There's not much fuel in the tank."

"Don't worry about that. You must contact Mademoiselle Blontard and tell her to get rid of the bag and anything else that might link her to it. Tell her it is urgent."

"OK. Thank you, Jean-Luc."

"Don't thank me yet."

Ignoring the complaining Candice, Philip went back to the cottage and got out his lap-top. He made the message as short as possible:-

Jackie – The guy I told you about, Vauclus, has come back again. Now he wants the bag. I think he must have found out about the secret compartment behind the crest. Jean-Luc says it won't take the man long to work out that you have it, and you will then be in extreme danger. Please get rid of it immediately and hide the letter away where nobody will be able to find it. This is very serious – Philip.

He sent off the email and went back to help Candice carry the furniture up to her room.

31

They started the new working arrangement that evening. Candice had gone to change, and Jean-Luc had departed early as usual. Before Philip went to get into his work clothes, they were left alone, and Jeanette expressed her disappointment with the new system.

"I seem to remember you promising to have me in this outfit," she protested.

"If you're still awake when I get back at midnight, I'll fulfil my promise after I've had a shower."

"I will be."

"There's my girl." He kissed her willing lips before he went up to change.

He met Candice as he was crossing the yard to go into the chateau. He noticed she was dressed again in her now fairly grubby white shirt and some tight trousers which terminated just below the knee. Her hair was in a pony-tail.

"What, no overalls?"

"They're too mucky. I need to wash them before I wear them again. I also need to get another set to replace the ones stuck under the beam."

"Our first job," he said as he guided her through the pedestrian gate, "Is to get that beam out. Then you can have your other overalls back."

The rest of that work session was spent trying to dig round the beam as far back into the heap of rubble as they could get. However, it was obviously a long piece of timber with only the exposed end lying diagonally nearly all the way across the steps. They had cleared at least eight feet of it by midnight and it still wasn't possible to move it out of the way.

"I'm going to have to hire a chain saw to cut off a chunk of this beam," he told her. "We'll carry on here in the morning, but somehow I don't think we're ever going to be able to move it in one piece."

Candice had worked steadily and hard under the hanging light that had been rigged up to illuminate the work area.

"Never mind," she said. "We're making progress. If you can cut off this part of the beam tomorrow, we will be in a position to start clearing the whole staircase."

So they finished, and Philip returned to where a scented and compliant Jeanette was waiting to be made love to.

The next morning, they continued the digging until about nine when Philip went off to hire the chain saw. Then, at the start of the evening session, he used the saw to cut off about ten foot of the beam. It was such a large section that he had to cut it into three short lengths, and even then, they both them struggled to lift the heavy chunks of timber out of the way. Candice was able to recover her other set of overalls which proved to be useless because Philip had cut so much of them away from her body to get her out from under the beam.

"I will get another set tomorrow," she told him.

Philip had been expecting another visit from Vauclus and was surprised the man hadn't shown up. He didn't know what he was going to say to him when he revealed the bag wasn't in the rubbish skip, as Philip knew only too well. He decided that he would just have to shrug and say he was sorry but he didn't know where it had gone.

After the projecting part of the beam had been removed, they were both inspired to dig with even more enthusiasm, now that the whole width of the stairs was available, and they were no longer restricted to digging in a hole. That evening they dug furiously, taking it in turns to fill and carry the buckets. As a consequence, they were tired out when midnight came. Candice hung on his arm as he locked the chateau door, and they crossed the yard to the cottage.

"I'm too tired to shower tonight," she said. "That'll have to wait until the morning."

"Good idea," he agreed. "Unfortunately, I don't think Jeanette would be too happy if I climbed into bed all dirty and sweaty."

"You should come to bed with me. I wouldn't complain."

"I'm sure you wouldn't, but Jeanette might."

"She might be fast asleep."

"Not a chance."

"Well, kiss me good night then."

So he did. She opened her mouth and rolled her head and rubbed her body tight against him and he had to admit it was a different experience to kissing the soft, yielding Jeanette, despite the dirt and the sweat. He broke away at last.

"I'm not going to do that again."

"Why don't you send her away. She knows she won't be here for very long once Jacqueline returns. I would be much better at sharing your bed than she is."

"Be quiet. You've come here to do a job, not to try to corrupt me."

"I know you fancy me," she said.

"I fancy all sorts of women." He turned away. "Go to bed Candice. I'll see you in the morning."

"I may be sleeping very heavily. You may have to wake me up when you come at five o'clock."

"Hmm. Good night."

He set off back to the house, thinking how correctly the girl had judged him. He admitted to himself that sharing a bed with Jeanette wasn't exciting any longer. She looked after him as well as he could expect any housekeeper to do, but she had little conversation away from the everyday experiences of her life. She was voluptuous and enjoyed sex, but for her it was just a case of lying in bed and letting him climb on top of her to bring her to a quick orgasm. He guessed that was the result of years of selling her body for the same purpose.

So he wasn't altogether surprised next morning when there was no Candice waiting for him when he turned up to start work. He had his own key to the house, and he let himself in and climbed the stairs as quietly as he could to avoid disturbing Jean-Luc. He silently entered her bedroom and closed the door for the same reason. The girl appeared to be slumbering deeply. He paused, wondering if he should let her remain that way. This new regime was undoubtedly more tiring and was leaving them both short of sleep. They couldn't keep it up for long. He had just decided not to wake her and was turning towards the door when she rolled over on to her side facing him.

"Philip, what are you doing?"

"I'm going to work. I came to wake you, but you're obviously still tired. So you don't have to join me until you're ready."

"I'm ready now. Come here."

He shook is head. "No, you're not. Come over to the chateau when you're showered and dressed."

"I showered last night. Come and help me up."

He knew what she was aiming for, and now he realised he wanted the same thing. He approached the bed.

"Look at me." She tossed back the light covering and revealed that she was completely naked. Her lips were parted invitingly, and her fair hair cascaded over the pillow.

"Please take you clothes off," she invited him.

As he did so, she watched him carefully. "My goodness," she cooed as he slid down his underpants. "I don't think I've had a better lover."

"You've had a lot, have you?"

Suddenly jealous of her having had so many past lovers at such a young age, he pushed her back onto the pillow. An arm went round his neck and her open mouth latched onto his. Their lovemaking rose rapidly to a joint climax, and they collapsed exhausted and bathed in perspiration.

After she had got her breath back, she chuckled. "You knew I wasn't going to give up until I'd had you, didn't you?"

"Candice," he murmured in her ear, "this changes nothing. You're a gorgeous woman and I've been weak enough not to resist your beauty and your charms. But we're not going to become permanent lovers. I will still fulfil my promises to Jackie when she returns – if she'll have me."

"Well, you can't stop me from trying."

And he carried that thought with him when he left her to start work half an hour later. She joined him soon after with a broad grin across her unmade-up face.

32

Soon after seven Philip told Candice he was leaving her on her own.

"I've promised the guy in the hire shop that I'd return the chain-saw to him before he opens at eight," he told her.

"Can I come with you?"

"No. None of your type of shops will be open that early."

"Now that you've done it once there's no reason why you can't do it again." She grinned at him roguishly. "We could see what it's like on the front seat of the pick-up in some quiet lay-by. There won't be anyone about this early in the morning."

He slapped her bottom good-naturedly as he left. "You should have had enough for one day."

"Do you mean I'm rationed and I'm going to have to wait until tomorrow?"

"Candice," he laughed at her, "You're impossible."

"And you like it, don't you?"

As he departed, she applied herself to digging furiously to get the urge for action out of her system. She was going to show him that she was the one who got things done. Her planned seduction of the man was going well, but she also needed to convince him that they were both aiming for the same solution. She filled another couple of buckets and struggled up the steps with them. She dropped the buckets in her astonishment when she saw who was standing at the top and one of them tipped over.

"Oh," she gasped. "Hello."

Anna Sondheim looked her most severely Germanic. She didn't waste time on greetings. "Heinrich sent me."

"Why did he do that?"

"You have been here nearly two weeks. He's disappointed that you don't seem to be making any progress."

Candice looked around. "Why does he think that? It's a slow job, Anna. Just look at it. We've got to get down into the cellars. That's where the treasure will be. And, as far as we can tell, this is the only staircase down that way." She threw her arms wide. "You can see it's full of rubble from the collapsed building. We're having to dig it out. We've done a huge amount already."

"So how long will it be until you get down to these cellars that you talk about?"

"I don't know. One week. Maybe two weeks. All I can tell you is that getting down there is our first priority. I don't know any more than that at this stage."

"Who is we?"

"Er – well, I'm actually working for Jacqueline Blontard – the archaeologist. She's employed me to catalogue the archives she has found. But she's in Paris, so her partner, Philip Sinclair – he and Jackie own the chateau – is working with me some of the time."

"What do you mean – some of the time?"

"Well, he has other things he is doing, but he helps me when I need it. In fact he helps me quite a lot."

"Is he the man I saw going out just now?"

"I expect so."

"Do you get on well with him?"

Candice thought about the slightly tender feeling between her legs. "Yes. I think so."

"Do you think he would be sympathetic to the aims of Fasces45?"

"Oh, no. He is an Englishman."

"What! You are working with the English?" Anna had a horrified look on her face.

"Of course."

"It is the English who destroyed the third Reich."

"Surely it was mainly the Americans and the Russians."

"But they were tricked into the war by the English. I am not happy that you are working with our enemies."

"Anna, he is the owner of this place. Surely the most important thing is to find the treasure. I have to work with anyone who will help me do that."

"But *will* he help you?"

She smiled and nodded, thinking about her success a couple of hours ago. "I think I can persuade him to be helpful."

"He must not know about our aims. The English must not know about our aims."

"I told you, Anna, he thinks I am working for his partner. She came to check up on our progress at the weekend and she wants him to help me as much as he can. I am sure he thinks I am only interested in the archives. That is why it is such a good cover story."

The German woman nodded somewhat doubtfully. "Yes, I see that, but the other thing Heinrich wants to know is why you are working here. He says Skorzeny thought the treasure would be in the ground between the church and the chateau. Why are you not digging there?"

"If I did that, I would immediately raise suspicion. I couldn't do it for a day without somebody noticing me. And where would I dig? It is a big area. You would have to get excavating equipment in to do most of the work, and what would the owners of the site say about that?"

Anna bit her lip and looked at the ground. Her slow Bavarian mind grappled with the question of what she should do next.

Observing the other woman's dilemma, Candice continued. "Look Anna, I believe that if the Visigoths hid their treasure underground in the fortress, which was called Rhedae at the time, they would have put it in a storeroom of some kind and made sure they had a way to get to it. That would have to have been either from the church or from this chateau. In fact, the present church wasn't established until after the Visigoths had moved south into Spain. So the most likely way in would have been from this very building which, as far as we know, has been here in some form or another since the city of Redhae was founded. Tell Heinrich that it makes sense to explore this way first."

After a long wait, the German finally seemed to agree. She nodded. "Very well, I will tell him what you said. But please try to make faster progress, Heinrich does not like to be told he has to wait."

"I'll do my best."

Anna nodded. "Goodbye," was all she said as she turned and left and Candice applied herself once more to digging out rubble.

33

Jackie had been aware for some time that Louis was showing rather more interest in her physically than he really should. His hands had a tendency to linger on parts of her body, particularly on her breasts and thighs, when he was suggesting positions she should put herself in to show the best parts of her to the cameras. He had also developed the habit of asking her to stay behind at the end of the day's recording, to discuss how things went and what they should plan for the following day. Of course this was perfectly reasonable, but she also noticed his tendency to rest a hand on her waist as they left, and give her a hug to send her on her way.

So far, she had not responded or given him any encouragement. However, her visit to Rennes had convinced her that Philip was certainly having sex with the voluptuous Jeanette, who she knew had tried to entice him into her bed on several earlier occasions. She had previously believed his assurances that he had resisted the woman's advances, but now he seemed to have decided that he was justified in having sexual relations with her. His justification seemed to be that it was because Jackie was concentrating full-time on her work on the Cathar series and was temporarily excluding him from her life. She didn't agree with his thinking, but she had begun to reason that he couldn't object if she behaved in the same way. In fact it might be a way for her to relax and not feel jealous about Philip's behaviour

Of course, she realised it would be a different situation if she took Louis as a lover. He was a married man and went home to sleep with his wife every night. He had two young children and surely should not be contemplating starting an affair with his leading lady which could easily lead to a scandal that would almost certainly damage his marriage. However, his wife and children had now been removed to Provence for the summer and presumably he would only see them at weekends until the series had been completed. And he *was* a very attractive man – a little on the small side, but an absolute bundle of energy.

So, when he told her that he didn't see the sense in travelling back to an empty house every night and would therefore be moving into a suite in the Saint Michel for the four weekday nights, she realised it was almost inevitable that their relationship could be about to take another big step forward if she permitted it. The question was, should she encourage him when he made the next approach or reject him, with the inevitable problems that would cause to their working together.

On the second night that he was staying at the hotel, they dined together in the restaurant. They chatted mainly about progress on the series, which was going along well. But at times he made mildly suggestive comments which she smiled at. After a while she checked her watch.

"Oh my goodness," she said. "It's nine o'clock. Do you mind, Louis? I'm feeling tired. I think I will go up to my room and have a bath and an early night."

"OK," he agreed. "Good night."

"Bye." She didn't say, "See you in the morning."

She was aware, as she went, that he might well regard her departure as an invitation to join her later. "Oh, hell" she thought as she went up in the lift, "Let's just see what happens."

Sure enough, soon after ten o'clock there came a knock at the door.

"Wait a minute," she called as she got out of bed and put on her long silk dressing gown over the shorty nightie she had put on in preparation. When she opened the door, Louis was there of course, dressed in his own patterned dressing gown and carrying a bottle of liqueur and two modest glasses.

"I seem to remember you like Tia Maria," he said, and stood waiting to be invited in.

Now was the moment of decision. Did she apologise that she had misled him and send him away, or did she take the irrevocable step forward in their relationship?

"Welcome," she smiled and stepped aside, "oh bearer of good spirits." And she shut the door behind him.

"You're looking gorgeous," he commented, putting an arm round her waist to pull her close and nuzzling into the side of her face. "Your hair is absolutely beautiful."

She had washed and carefully dried it and brushed it out so that it tumbled in a titian haze around her shoulders. But what she couldn't help noticing was that he was at least ten centimetres shorter than Philip and had swamped himself with too much after shave.

He released her and went to the dressing table, poured out the liqueur and brought her a glass. She took a sip of hers and the strong alcohol caught at the back of her throat. She immediately started to cough. He took a gulp of his own and put it on the bedside table, then started to rub her back gently. He slid his other hand inside her dressing gown and cupped it under her breast which hung loosely in the thin fabric of her nightie.

"Jackie, have I told you what a beautiful body you have? I have often fantasised about what it would be like to run my hands over the whole of it."

He had to stretch his neck a little to kiss her from the side, but he fastened his lips on hers and started to kiss her passionately. Unfortunately, she hadn't cleared her throat and she burst into another fit of coughing.

"Here," he said, "let me take your glass."

He let go of her and put her glass on the same bedside table as his. Then he came back. She had her hand over her mouth, trying to stifle her coughs. However, he didn't allow that to distract him. He first undid the belt of her dressing gown and pulled it wide to display that she was naked from the waist down.

"You're gorgeous," he repeated, with his head slightly on one side gazing at her. "Look what you do to me."

He shrugged off his own dressing gown to reveal that he had nothing on underneath. Her eyes fastened on his genitalia. She was still striving not to let the tickle in her throat turn into another coughing spasm.

"I can't wait any longer," he said. "I've been building up to this all night. Come on, get on the bed." He heaved her up, with her dressing gown dragging behind her and climbed on top of her. His lips fastened on hers and his tongue probed into her half-open mouth, once again causing her the foolish urge to cough."

It was then that the bedroom door opened and a man with one arm stood there. "I apologise for disturbing you," he said, "but you obviously didn't hear when I knocked."

Louis twisted round. "Get out," he shouted. "Fuck off back to wherever you came from."

The man came into the room and shut the door behind him. Then he put his left hand in his pocket.

"Did you hear me?" Louis pushed himself into an upright position. She tried to find enough of her dressing gown to pull across her body and restore some modesty. Her desire to cough seemed to have disappeared.

"I want to talk to Mademoiselle Blontard," the man said, quite quietly. "It is a confidential matter, and you can go now and come back later if you wish to avoid putting yourself in danger."

Louis was up now and searching around on the floor for his dressing gown which he had so hastily abandoned. He dragged it on and turned to face the one-arm guy. "Did you hear what I said?" he threatened. "Get out this minute."

The man said, "Do I assume you will *not* be following my instructions?"

"Get out or I'll throw you out." He advanced on the man and raised his right fist.

The fellow's hand came out of his pocket carrying something metallic and it seemed to move very quickly. It hit the side of Louis' head and he collapsed in a heap.

"What have you done to him?" cried Jackie. She was now sitting on the edge of the bed and had managed to pull most of her dressing gown round her. She stood up and bent to look at her unconscious lover.

"He will be all right," said the man. "He will come round in a few hours with a nasty headache. But he will be fine tomorrow."

She looked up at him. "What do you want?" But she already had a good idea.

"My name is Vauclus," he told her. "I have been given the assignment of recovering a certain letter which went missing many years ago, and I think you have it."

"I most certainly do not."

"I'm sorry Mademoiselle, but I don't believe you." He moved towards her, and she shrank away from him.

"Get back into your bed please. I am going to search your room. You will be quite safe as long as you do what I say."

Obediently she climbed back into the bed thinking, as she did so, how unexpectedly this evening was developing.

Vauclus went first to the wardrobe and opened the doors. He immediately saw the bag with the Habsbourg crest on it which she had so casually tossed in there. She wished now that she had treated Philip's email with the urgency he had asked.

The one-armed man pulled the bag out and brought it to the end of the bed. Jackie hunched up her knees to keep as far away from him as she could. Luckily, she had at least closed the crest back over the small cavity before she took it out of the car. However, Vauclus seemed to know more about it than she did. He fiddled around the edges of the crest, and it suddenly sprang open. He peered behind the badge, then turned and looked straight at her.

"Mademoiselle Blontard, the cavity is empty. You have taken out what was inside."

"What do you mean?"

"There was a folded-up letter in here. You have removed it. Where is it?"

"I . . ." She realised it was pointless to deny it. "It's in the top drawer of my dressing table."

He went and pulled open the drawer and extracted the original and the two photocopies she had taken of it. He came back and flourished them in front of her.

"Are these the only copies you have taken?"

"Yes. I haven't had time to hide them."

"You have read the letter?"

"Yes."

"So you know the contents." He looked at her and appeared to be chewing over what he should do next. She remained silent, aware that she was in great danger. At last, he said, "I really should kill you, so that this remains a secret. Does anyone else know about this letter?"

"No."

"I think your friend, Philip Sinclair, will know."

"Philip doesn't understand German."

"No, but you will have told him what the letter contains." He paused again, as though considering what he should do. "Very well, I will take these three pieces of paper and accept your word for now that these are the only copies. However, if another copy appears anywhere, I will know you have lied to me. I like your archaeological programmes. I have watched every one of them and I would like to see many more. So I will not kill you now. But if any word of this letter gets out into the public domain, it will mean I have failed in my assignment, and I do not allow

167

myself to fail. Therefore, I will kill you and I will also kill your friend, Philip. Do you understand me?"

She gulped and nodded. "Yes."

"You should contact your friend as soon as possible and give him this warning. Then there will not be a risk of him telling anybody else. Will you do that?"

"Yes, of course."

"Very well." He nodded to her. "You can keep the bag, but I suggest you destroy it as soon as possible."

He turned and stepped over the body on the floor as he left. The door closed softly behind him.

Jackie was left with the task of dressing, getting a couple of porters to carry Louis back to his own room and bribing them to silence.

34 .

The breakthrough came at about nine o'clock on the Monday morning. Albert and Gaston had finished pouring the concrete to the ground floor the previous week. Philip had gone back as each room was prepared, to check that the damp proof membrane and the under-floor insulation were completed and sealed, and now he decided the house could be left for a while for the slab to mature. So they had been moved to join him and Candice, who had been working since five this morning, digging out the stairs. The two locals were fresh and got stuck in with a will

Now there was additional space in the staircase as a result of removing the beam, in the next hour the four of them made good progress. They concentrated on digging and carrying the rubble to the rapidly expanding heap by the barrows. As they dug down, they discovered the stairs were hemmed in by a wall on each side. Philip said this was good news, since it should mean that only rubble which had fallen from above needed to be dug out.

It was Candice who found that the twentieth step gave access to a roughly paved stone floor, and she called Philip over to look at it. They were alone at that moment.

"Yes," he agreed. "It looks as though we've reached the cellar floor level. Well done."

"Oh, isn't this exciting," she cried and planted a firm, open-mouthed kiss on his lips. She pressed her soft frame against him, and he could feel every part of her through the thin material of the new overalls she had bought. "We've got to celebrate this. I think five o'clock tomorrow morning would be the best time."

His hand happened to be resting against her back and he was aware he could easily have undone her bra through the sheer fabric of these overalls. In a way, he felt that she was more sexy, dressed like this, than if she was naked.

"Somehow I don't think Jeanette would approve," he murmured.

"She wouldn't know. You can come to pick me up for work and I'll be ready for you, just as I was on Wednesday. In fact, we could do it every day."

He shook his head. "Candice, if it was a daily occurrence, you would become just like another Jeanette."

That silenced her and he released the girl's clinging body, not without some regret, as Albert came down the steps to find out what the celebrations were about.

"Now," said Philip after everyone had shaken hands, "We've still got a big heap of rubble to clear before we can start to explore the cellars. I think we'll try to dig a strip along beside this left-hand wall to see if we can find a doorway. That will be going in the direction of the archives and we'll just have to hope enough of the ground floor structure has remained in place to let us climb through to the room where Jackie found them."

So he left instructions to Albert and Gaston to do that, while he and Candice went to catch up on their sleep.

"I don't want to sleep after that," she told him. "I think I'll have a shower and then go for a walk through the countryside."

"OK. Make sure you don't get lost. I don't want to have to send out a search party."

"You could come with me to make sure you knew exactly where I was."

It was clear what was on her mind. "No thanks. I'm tired, even if you aren't."

She pouted at him and turned away to enter the house. Philip was feeling confused as he returned to the cottage. How was he going to handle this woman?

Jeanette wasn't there when he got back. Presumably she had gone shopping. He looked for a note but there wasn't one. He went out to the yard and checked whether the pick-up was there and it wasn't. He should have noticed that, if he hadn't been thinking about Candice. He shook his head as he went for his shower.

Refreshed, he climbed into bed and tried to sleep, but without success. He wondered what the girl was doing. Where was she walking? What was she wearing once she had taken off those oh-so-thin overalls? He turned on to his side, hoping to sleep more easily in that position.

And there she was in front of him. He hadn't heard her come in through the front door or make her way up the stairs. Her top was covered in a thin, loose, wispy blouse which seemed to float round her. It was white and he could see her body clearly through it. At first, he thought that, underneath the blouse, she was bare above the waist but then he realised she was wearing a flesh-coloured bra to cover her breasts. Otherwise, she had nothing on but a short pink skirt and sandals.

She reached out and tossed aside the sheet that covered him. He hadn't bothered to put on any clothes before he got into bed, and his body was exposed.

"Oh, you want me," she murmured. "I know you do. I can see you do."

She kicked off her sandals and raised her leg to get into bed with him and he could see she was wearing nothing under her skirt. She reached behind her and undid her bra and dropped it on the floor."

"Candice," he protested. "Jeanette may come back at any moment."

"So what!" She got in beside him. "If she does, she'll know her time is up."

"We can't do that to her, Candice."

"You want to let her down gently?"

"I've told her that her role here is not a permanent arrangement, but I want her to be able to leave in a way that protects her dignity."

"Dignity? She doesn't know what dignity is."

"Well, I don't want it to end in this way. Please get out and leave me alone."

She raised her head and looked down on him. "I will only go if you agree to come with me."

"My following you across to your place in broad daylight would be just as obvious."

"All right. I'll go and get my car and I'll drive round to your front door. You can come down and join me and we'll go out into the country somewhere."

"No." He realised she was serious. "If you leave me now and go for a walk on your own, I will promise to come and wake you up tomorrow morning before we start work."

She considered for a moment. "Very well, I will accept that. I will be ready for you. What do you want me to wear?"

"Wear your overalls – clean ones of course."

"Seeing my body inside that thin material turns you on, doesn't it?" She smiled. "I'll remember that."

"Now," said Philip, "I would be very pleased if you would go and leave me alone to sleep."

She did as he asked, but it was a long time before he slept.

35

Candice had begun to realise that her all too successful attempt to seduce Philip was resulting in her own emotional involvement with the subject of her schemes. She had always been willing to use the attractions of her face and her body to get what she wanted out of men. However, she accepted the fact that now she had really gone too far with her entrapment of this latest man. Of course, he had been easy meat because his real love had abandoned him, if only temporarily. But she was beginning to understand she would have to be careful that she didn't end up falling in love with the man herself – a totally new experience for her and one she wasn't quite sure how to cope with.

He had come to her at five that morning, as requested, and the strength of his passion had surprised and overwhelmed her. By the time they had finished they were both left gasping and exhausted by the violence of his lovemaking. She had never before felt so thoroughly dominated by a man's sexual desire, and she discovered that she liked it. After the joint second climax they both fell asleep, entwined in each other's arms, and didn't surface until after seven o'clock. By then Jean-Luc was awake.

Philip quickly dressed and straightened his hair and went out of her bedroom. She heard him say, "I overslept and was late this morning. I have only just come to wake her up."

She couldn't make out the details of the gruff reply.

As soon as she could, she took off the wet, clinging overalls which had in any case been violently half-stripped from her body and hung them up to dry out. She substituted these with the grubby ones she had been wearing yesterday. A quick peer out of the door told her the bathroom was free. She scuttled across the corridor and slowly washed her tender face and applied cream to cover her pink features. She spent a long time combing her tangled hair. She couldn't remember when it was last in such a mess. But she smiled as she looked at herself in the mirror.

"My God," she said to herself. "It was worth it."

When she got down to the cellar, she found Philip was working like a maniac, driving the pickaxe into the rubble and tossing the soil behind him.

"Are you all right," she asked.

He paused and half-turned towards her. "What about you? Did I hurt you?"

She smiled and shook her head, ignoring the sore feeling between her legs. "You could never hurt me – not physically, at least."

"I'm sorry. I seemed to lose my self-control."

"Good," she said. "I like you when you lose your English self-control."

"I promise you it won't happen again."

"And I promise *you*, Mister Sinclair, that I'm going to do everything I can to make it happen again – many times."

He took a deep breath. "Well. We won't have the opportunity any longer. I've decided to stop these strange hours of working that we've been doing for the last week or so. Now we're down in the cellars and it's not so hot, we can go back to the usual day-time hours."

"I see." She hung her head. She wasn't going to let him see that he'd upset her.

"I never again want to see the look that Jean-Luc gave me as I went out just now."

"OK. I understand."

She picked up the shovel and bent down to start filling the buckets. Philip returned to his onslaught on the heap of rubble. Just a short time later Albert and Gaston turned up. Soon it was taking all three of them filling buckets energetically to keep up with his furious excavations. He continued until eleven o'clock and refused to let any of the others take over from him. Then Jeanette turned up with a flask of coffee and they all stopped to recover their energy.

It was Albert, while they were sitting round having their drinks, who pointed out that the digging had progressed so well that he thought he could make out the corner of a door frame in the wall. Philip gulped the rest of his coffee and leapt to his feet. He headed the rush to make a closer inspection.

"We've been so busy digging, that we haven't noticed the progress we've been making," he said.

Candice snorted. "*You* have."

"Well, let's get on and clear the whole doorway." He grabbed the pickaxe and resumed his attack on the pile of rubble.

By lunch they had cleared a narrow strip in front of the door. A handle had come into view. Philip dropped the pickaxe and heaved at the thing. Remarkably, it turned and the door began to open. But it moved no more than a couple of centimetres before it jammed and would go no further. The combined assault of the three men failed to make an impression.

"The floor in the next room must have collapsed against it," gasped Philip, breathless from his efforts.

Candice smiled to herself, thinking of the last time she had experienced his gasping breathlessness. "How are we going to get through?"

"We'll have to break the door down." He looked round. "I'll get the sledge-hammer and we'll see what we can do with that."

He hurried up the stairs and soon returned with the heavy thing in his hand.

"Stand clear."

The door was made up of six panels in what appeared to be a strong frame. Philip swung it with as much strength as he could manage in the restricted space and crashed it into the nearest top panel. For the first half dozen strikes the panel stoutly resisted, but then a crack appeared.

"Let me have a go," suggested Albert, and Philip surrendered the sledge to him.

The Frenchman turned out to be more accurate than Philip in striking over and over again at the weakest corner point of the panel and, in a few more blows he had soon managed to smash the piece out of the frame. Once he had done that, it took only a few more strikes to knock out the panel completely and open up a void, perhaps thirty centimetres square. He peered through the hole and then invited Philip to take a look. Candice followed and was greeted with the prospect of an area where the floor above had collapsed under the load of masonry from the ruins of the upper storeys of the chateau.

"God, where do we go from here?" she asked.

Philip had a possible solution. "I think there may be a gap along the other side of this staircase wall that we might be able to crawl along. I don't know if there's a way through that way."

"It looks awful to me. I hate being shut into small places."

"I can't say I'm enthusiastic about it myself." He took a breath. "Well, we can't go any further anyway until the door's been completely removed." He turned to Albert. "I think I'll go for an early lunch. Can you try to break down this door and start to get some of the rubble out of the room?"

"OK, boss." He picked up the sledgehammer again and returned to the attack.

Philip wearily climbed the steps and Candice went with him.

"What you need is a rest," she told him as they crossed the courtyard. "We could go to my room. I'll change the bed."

"No, we won't. I'm hungry. I want something to eat."

"OK. I'll join you."

However, when they went into the cottage, they were greeted by Armand Séjour, who was chatting to Jeanette in the kitchen.

"Look who's arrived."

Philip wasn't sure whether she was pleased to see him or not. He had thought at one time that Jeanette was Armand's woman, but she had disabused him of that idea. Nevertheless, he was certain they were good friends.

"Hi, Armand. What are you doing here?" He shook him warmly by the hand. "You know Candice, don't you?"

The fellow gave him a broad smile. "Of course. We both work for Mademoiselle Blontard now." He put his head characteristically slightly to one side. "She has sent me to help you down here, because she hasn't anything else for me to do at the moment."

"So you'll be staying with us?"

"If you can find somewhere for me."

"You can have my room." Jean-Luc had come in from the back yard where he had been spending quite a bit of his time during the last few days.

"What do you mean?" asked Jeanette.

"I have found accommodation with a friend in the village. He has promised that his wife will look after me. I think they could do with the money." He gave one of his brief smiles. "So you will be seeing less of me in the future, but I will still be close if you need me."

Philip had been thinking fast. "Well, Candice and I have decided to stop these silly hours we've been working recently. That means she can move back to her *chambre d'hôte* in Cuiza and Jeanette can go into her room. That will give me some privacy here at night." He turned to the horrified housekeeper.

176

"Of course, I'd still like you to do the cooking and cleaning here, if you're willing."

So he had been presented with a way of solving his problem with the women in his life.

36

Hector travelled to Vienna on the overnight train from Paris, arriving on the Tuesday morning. A phone call to his contact had set up a meeting for noon at the Mozart Memorial near the Ringstrasse. He was to return the same way that evening. It was an expensive arrangement, but he had just sold the original list of Cathar treasures to Jacqueline for a very good price – she could certainly afford it – and he had high hopes that the visit would prove to be worth many times the cost involved.

He was nearly a quarter of an hour early, but he was happy to sit on a seat in the sun, facing the splendid statue in front of its backdrop of trees, and wait for the other person to arrive. It wasn't long before the man he was meeting turned up. He rose and they shook hands and briefly hugged each other.

"Rudi, it must be at least two years since I last saw you." He made sure he beamed at the plump young man who had been his nominal research colleague while he was preparing his epic history of the Holy Roman Empire, but who in reality had been doing his best to have the book rejected and to replace it with his own.

"You are looking well, Hector. I understand you are now a man of leisure."

Ramise inclined his head. "Well, to be truthful, I do not retire until the first of September, but I have much holiday entitlement owed to me. So I am enjoying some of that."

"You are a lucky man to be able to retire early." Rudi shook his head. "I do not know when I will be able to afford to hang up my gown." Ramise knew he was still a junior professor at the University of Vienna.

"I am not sure I can really afford it *myself*." He told him. "In order to make my reduced pension cover my day-to-day needs, I am having to dispose of some of my collection of valuable possessions which I have built up over the past thirty years or so. I am sorry to see them go, but one has to find the means to live in this expensive modern world."

"True. True." Rudi scratched the back of his neck. "So am I to assume that the reason for this welcome meeting is to offer us one of those possessions?"

"Indeed it is. I think I made it clear on the telephone that I have discovered a copy of a letter written by a certain Marquise d'Hautpoul in July 1871 in my collection and I thought it likely that your principals might be interested in acquiring it, in order to avoid any risk of it falling into the wrong hands."

A steely glint had come into Rudi's eyes as he nodded. "Yes. I have been in touch with my principals and your assumption is correct. They would certainly be interested in hearing any proposal you may wish to make, subject of course to the normal validation and the undertakings you would be expected to sign. Have you brought the piece of paper with you?"

Hector guffawed. "Come now, Rudi, you wouldn't expect me to be so indiscreet as to travel with such an important document in my baggage. Your principals would, I am sure, be horrified if I were to be so foolish."

"So where would you make the - er – document available for me to look at it?"

"Once we have reached agreement on the various details, I will give you the information about how and where the handover is to be made. I presume you will be happy to accept my suggestions on this, so as to avoid any unnecessary publicity." He paused, waiting for the younger man's response.

"Yes." Rudi spoke slowly. "I think that might be acceptable to my principals." He paused for a moment. "And what are these details you are talking about? Would one of them be a price?"

Hector tried to smile engagingly. "Of course, I would expect that your principals would wish to offer a reward for my handing over such an important item to them."

"And exactly how much would you expect that reward to be?"

Ramise had been thinking about this very carefully since he had set up the meeting. Indeed, he had hardly thought about anything else. At first, he had set the figure very high – perhaps as much as a million euros – but then he had tended to a far more reasonable figure, aware that the possessor of an article valued too highly might well find himself in personal danger. However, whatever figure he asked for would surely be the highest he would stand any chance of getting. So he couldn't put the price too low. He was aware that the other man was watching him closely.

"Surely you have a - shall we say a negotiating figure?" Rudi reminded him.

"Yes," Hector agreed. "I had in mind a figure of about one hundred and twenty thousand euros."

"Indeed?" The fellow showed no sign of shock. "Of course, you will understand that I am not in a position to agree a figure with you at this time."

Ramise nodded, "I appreciate you will have to discuss it with your principals. However, I should perhaps point out to you personally that this figure is quite small in comparison with the funds they have available. If privation were to force me to offer it to other people who might be interested, it would be likely to attract a much higher price."

"I understand that." The young man's smile had become more of a grimace. "I presume you are not wishing me to regard that comment as a threat."

"Certainly not. I hadn't even considered that such a course might need to be followed."

Rudi took a deep breath. "Very well. Do you have any other – er – details you wish to mention?"

"No. That is all."

"And you would be prepared to sign an undertaking not to disclose anything at all about this item you are trading, or about any arrangements which are made between you and my principals?"

"Yes, I would."

He stepped back. "Well, Hector, I think that concludes our business for today. My principals can arrange for you to be contacted by telephone to advise you of acceptance or of any counter proposals they wish to make. Then it will only be a matter of us agreeing a handover arrangement which you will propose." He gave a brief nod, turned on his heel and departed.

Hector rose and made his leisurely way towards the restaurant he had noted at the foot of the hill. He decided he would have an early lunch and perhaps just a single glass of champagne. He felt his visit had been worth the cost.

37

By Wednesday morning, the excavations had almost completely cleared the staircase and an area of floor at the foot of the steps. Albert had demolished the door to get into the adjacent room, and Philip could see what was in there more clearly. It was quite a large room. The back wall, adjacent to the courtyard, appeared to be undamaged, presumably because it was supported from behind by the solid ground on which the courtyard was built. As far as he could tell, the beams of the floor above were still supported by this wall. It was the opposite, central wall which had mainly collapsed under the ruins of the chateau and so what remained of the floor sloped down from the back wall and was buried at the lower end in the rubble from the fallen wall and the building above.

Philip thought there was a good chance, that if they could clear a passage to get to the back wall, it should be possible to find a way under the floor beams at least to the far end of this room. The doorway they had opened up was located in the corner of the room at one end of the collapsed wall, so a lot of work was involved in reaching the back wall opposite. As a consequence, he set the guys the task of opening up a narrow access corridor to the back of the room alongside the staircase wall. He acknowledged that this was not going to be easy for them. The rubble they had been digging out up to this stage had been mainly loose material with occasional bits of stone and timber in it, but now much of the material was made up of large lumps of masonry and brick wall and chunks of floor made up of some sort of concrete. Many of these were too big for two men to lift, and consequently they had to be broken up into smaller pieces before they could be removed. Now Albert and his sledgehammer became vital to the progress.

"Can't we get a compressor and a pneumatic drill in," asked Armand when Philip called in to see him. He had taken over the supervision of the workforce in the cellar, thus releasing Philip to go back and concentrate on completing preparation of the house for occupation by himself and Jackie in a couple of months' time.

"I think that would be too big and cumbersome to get down here," said Philip, "But you could hire a couple of those large electric hammer-drills which would probably do just as good a job."

So Armand went off to do that and Philip explained what was planned to the other three.

Albert was clearly a traditionalist. "We don't need those electric hammer things," he said. "By the time he gets back with them, I will have finished breaking the big chunks up with my sledge."

Philip grinned. "OK, Albert. You do that and I'll pat you on the shoulder." He turned to Candice who seemed to have been keeping quiet for the last couple of days. "Are you settled back in to your *chambre d'hôte*?"

"Yes, thank you," was her curt response.

He gave a little shrug and went back to the house, where he had been making good progress in the last two days. He had now finished the carpentry work upstairs and the electricity and plumbing were also completed. The rooms only needed decoration and furnishing. Now that the floor slabs had partly matured, he was planning to start on the downstairs. However, he could see Jeanette waiting for him and he knew she wasn't happy with the new arrangements.

She tackled him as soon as he reached the cottage. "I will not spend a single night longer on that bed," she informed him. "It's like sleeping on a plank."

"Jean-Luc never complained."

"Well, he's a man, and a great bull of a man at that."

"Why didn't you take Candice's room? I think she would have made sure that her bed was comfortable." He wasn't going to tell her that he had found it perfectly comfortable when he was making love to the girl.

"That room is too small for me to get all my things in. Also, you are going to need to get a double bed and a full suite of bedroom furniture and put it in my room which is the largest one." She glared at him. "You should do that now and I will get it looking right before Mademoiselle Blontard comes back to claim it."

Philip conceded privately that she was right. What was more, the stuff in the room at the moment had been borrowed from the back bedroom at the cottage and would have to be returned sooner or later.

"OK," he agreed. "I suppose that means you want to go and get the stuff in Limoux, but I don't mind. When Armand gets back, you can take the pick-up, so you'll have plenty of room to get everything in."

"I can't do it on my own. You'll have to come with me."

When he thought about it, he agreed it made sense not to send her on her own. Quite apart from the fact that she would need help to lift the furniture into the back of the pick-up, he was afraid that Jeanette might choose garish stuff which Jackie would hate when she returned.

"All right. We'll go after lunch and when I've had a shower."

He didn't notice the self-satisfied smile that crossed her features.

They set off at just after three. Jeanette had put on a pretty summer dress which rested on her shoulders and revealed only a modest amount of cleavage. It had short sleeves and a belt round the waist to accentuate her hour-glass figure. She had flat beige sandals on her feet. Philip thought how nice it was to see her dressed in something normal like this. Her make-up was restrained. Even her perfume was redolent of a warm summer day, instead of the intoxicating heavy evening scents she usually chose.

When they went round the furniture shops, she was restraint personified. She asked him to make the decisions about what they should choose. She didn't try to persuade him to go for things with frills or fancy bits as he had expected. Just once, when they were trying out the beds and they joked about a waterbed, she bounced and rolled half on top of him, possibly by mistake. By mutual consent they didn't choose that one. When they had finished their spending spree, he invited her out for an English-type tea, and she actually seemed to enjoy the British favourite.

"Oh, Philip," she said. "This afternoon has been special. You're so much fun when you relax and don't turn your nose up at me – that's what the English say, isn't it."

"Well, we don't usually turn our noses up at other people."

"In Paris we often talk about the English as the turned-up noses."

"I'm sorry if you regard me as an example."

"If you are," she smiled warmly into his face, "then I like turned-up noses."

So they were in a happy mood as they set off back to Rennes. Jeanette leaned against him and rested her head on his shoulder, and he liked the feeling.

"Philip," she said, "we were making love every night for quite a few weeks. Now it has all stopped. It was very sudden, and I miss it."

He kissed the top of her head lightly, smelling the freshness of her hair. She must have washed it before they went out. "I'm sorry, Jeanette, but I can't carry on sleeping with you while Armand is around."

"Jackie was very clever. She knew that sending Armand was the way to stop you making love to me without her having to make any effort or any commitment herself. She can still carry on inviting men into her bed without you knowing."

Her comment made Philip stop and think. Was that the case? It was certainly correct to say that she had stopped him receiving love and affection from his housekeeper. She wasn't to know that the comparison of Jeanette to Candice was also a cause of his cooling feelings. And what about Jackie herself? She was still a free agent. He didn't actually have any evidence that she was being unfaithful, but she was certainly less affectionate towards him than she had been before she went to Paris. She had never pretended that she was a virgin. In fact, he knew that she had allowed a number of other men to have sex with her in the past. Perhaps she was getting her needs satisfied elsewhere.

He had become aware that Jeanette had half turned towards him and her hand was resting on the top of his thigh.

"I would like you to try out this new bed with me," she murmured.

"You know I can't do that, Jeanette."

"I suppose not, but why can't we still make love when there's no danger of anyone finding out – like now, for instance. This front seat is wide, and I haven't got anything on under my dress except my bra and that is easily undone." She was definitely rubbing between his legs now. "I noticed when we were going that there is a big lay-by just ahead with trees overhanging part of it. You could have me there."

He realised that now he wanted to do just that. With his free hand he pulled up her skirt to her waist and saw she wasn't wearing panties. He half turned his face towards her, and she planted a large wet kiss on his lips.

"Careful." He pulled away. "You'll have us off the road and that would spoil everything."

Just then the lay-by came into sight. It was empty of other vehicles. He brought the vehicle to a shuddering halt under the trees, ripped off his seatbelt and was on top of her as she fell away from him. The next quarter of an hour was the best session of love-making that they had enjoyed together.

38

When they got back to the chateau, Armand came out to meet them. He was anxious to tell them the latest news.

"I think we've got through to the back of the room. Candice was desperate to go into the hollow part below the wall but I wouldn't let her. I thought it was too dangerous."

"Quite right. Her car's not here. What's happened to her?"

"Oh, she threw a strop when I told her that I'd put her over my shoulder if she tried to go in there." He shrugged. "She must have gone home."

"OK. Well, it's late now. We'll shut up the chateau for today. Can you help us carry in the furniture?"

Jeanette was just getting out of the pick-up. She had a smug smile on her face but didn't appear to be entirely steady on her legs. They had made love twice in quick succession in the lay-by and she claimed the second time was the best. But perhaps he had handled her too roughly.

"Armand and I will load the furniture into the house, Jeanette. Can you go and start preparing the meal?"

"All right." She smiled at him benignly and staggered off towards the cottage.

"Is she all right?" asked Armand.

Philip chuckled. "This furniture-buying is a tiring business. I reckon she must have jumped on at least twenty beds to test them out."

"You didn't jump on with her, did you?"

Philip looked at him sideways. "What – in a furniture store?" He turned back to the vehicle. "Come on, let's get this stuff inside."

First of all, they had to empty the bedroom of the items borrowed from the cottage. Then they heaved the various things they had purchased that afternoon upstairs into the large room and placed them more or less where they thought Jeanette would want them. Finally, they loaded the items of furniture, which were to be returned to the rented cottage, into the pick-up. They carried them round the corner and manoeuvred them up the narrow stairs into the back bedroom. Then, exhausted, they collapsed into a couple of chairs in the back yard, and each downed a half-litre of ice-cold lager from the fridge.

Jeanette brought them food. She seemed to have recovered her steadiness and had no problem in serving their requirements. Then she sat with a dreamy look on her face and took little part in their conversation. It was most unlike her.

That night Philip was woken by Jeanette's arrival. She was shrouded in a sort of cloak made of a dark material.

"What are you doing?" he asked her.

"I'm moving back in here. I don't want to be in that bedroom that you've prepared for Jackie when or if she returns. I want to continue to occupy this bed." She tossed off her cloak, revealing that she had nothing on underneath except the wispy negligee that she knew he liked.

"You can't do that, Jeanette. What will Armand say?"

"I will tell him that I am taking up my bedroom here again and that I have told you to move into the back bedroom now the furniture has been replaced."

"He won't believe that."

"How can he disbelieve it, except by coming in and catching us in bed together, and he would never do that? Besides, I will lock the front door from now on, and so must you."

"But the mere fact that we're sharing the cottage will mean everybody will believe we're sharing a bed again."

"I don't mind. Of course, you can send me away, and I will go back to Paris, and I will never see you again. But after what happened this afternoon, I cannot live in the same place as you unless you are regularly making love to me." She pulled back the sheet and climbed in beside his bare body. "For me today was special."

"Yes," he admitted. "Today you were sort of softer and quieter than you've ever been before." He kissed her softly and she responded in the same way. "I must say I like you more when you're like that."

"You have taught me to be like that. Always before men have expected me to be noisy and to lead the way. I have learned from you that it is better to be slow and gentle and let the feelings build up inside you."

He chuckled. "We weren't very slow this afternoon."

187

"You weren't, but I was. I think that because I was slow it made you want to go faster. And you carried me with you. I told you the second time was the best, and I think it was really the best time ever for me." She gave him a hug. "I think you have taught me some new things. I thought until today that I was the one who was teaching you. Now I want you to teach me some more."

"Oh well," he sighed. "I suppose there's no point in fighting against it." And he pushed her onto her back – gently of course – and made slow love to her.

No comment was made by Armand or anyone else about the new arrangement and their lives settled down to the same contented routine that they had enjoyed when Jeanette had first arrived to sort him out.

39

Next morning, Philip was up bright and early to inspect progress down in the cellars. Not even Armand had arrived by the time he was feeling his way towards the back of the room. It was almost dark down here, but he had the foresight to bring a torch with him. Tight against the back wall the detritus was less than a metre deep and he was able to scramble over it without too much difficulty. But when he reached the far corner, he ran into a problem. The end wall of the room seemed to have collapsed sideways under the weight of the ruined building above. A great slab of masonry had fallen at an angle on top of the rubble and the top edge was towering above him.

He stopped and surveyed it for some time, wondering whether he had finally come up against an insoluble problem. He tried scrambling up the rubble, hanging on to a beam behind him, until he was just able to reach the top of the sloping wall. Then, clinging on to the rough edge of the slab, he managed to find enough projecting timbers and lumps of masonry for his feet to push his body gradually upwards. At last he could see over the top of the sloping wall and look down into the area beyond. He realised, with a sudden sensation of triumph, that he was looking down into the room which he and Jackie had entered when they escaped along the tunnel from the crypt under the church a couple of months ago. So they had found a way through to the Templar archives. The only problem, was that it would be a major operation to clear a way for Candice to come down here every day to do her cataloguing of the archives.

In any case he still had to get into the room. To do that he had to scramble further up the rubble until he could hook a leg over the top of the sloping wall and drag his body on to the rough ridge. Then he carefully hung on, to prevent himself from sliding too rapidly down the rough surface of the brickwork. Finally, he let go, and landed on the heap of stones and dirt at the bottom. He picked himself up, dusted his clothes off and surveyed with dismay the damage he had done to his trousers.

He could now understand the layout of the basement area. It obviously consisted of two rows of rooms. One row was along the outside wall with a number of windows looking down through the woods to the north. The other was against the base of the courtyard. Of course, the inner row was windowless, being below ground level. The outer wall had remained standing at this level, probably because it was built thicker and stronger for reasons of defence. The central wall between the two rows of rooms was the one that had mainly collapsed under the load of the ruins of the chateau above. The back wall had remained standing because it was supported by the solid ground under the courtyard. So the floors above the basement had half fallen at an angle, still supported by the walls which hadn't collapsed. Unfortunately, the doors between the rooms seemed to have been located near the centre and had therefore been largely blocked by rubble and other detritus. It didn't make it easy to move around. He thought there was no way Candice would be able to make this scramble.

Nevertheless, he had found a way to the archives. Another couple of weeks of digging and clearing and breaking up lumps of masonry and possibly sawing through timber beams, should be able to give her some sort of access to start the work Jackie had sent her here to do. Then she should be able to carry out that work without frequently requiring him to do things for her. That would be one problem solved.

Now he was here, Philip decided he would have a look in the room where Jackie had found the archives. That room must have been strengthened for protection of the valuable documents and therefore it had resisted the collapse of the building above it. He guessed it was also built below ground level against the western outside wall of the chateau, and that had helped. The surprising thing was that Jackie had been able to get into the room. Perhaps the collapse of the upper floors had burst the door open. Or perhaps it had never been locked in the first place.

He went into the room. Jackie had carefully closed the door but hadn't been able to lock it, so he was able to get in quite easily. Inside the door he stopped and surveyed the pile of chests. He could see that towards the back of the room they were at least four high. There were probably more than a hundred chests all together. When she finally managed to get here, Candice was going to have a major job on her hands. He went over to the nearest chest, presumably the one Jackie had opened to look through the contents. He lifted the lid without difficulty. She must have simply closed it, when she had found out everything she needed to confirm that the contents were in fact at least part of the Templar archives, which the world believed had been destroyed centuries ago. He didn't reach in to lift any of them out. Most of the records appeared to be long lengths of paper-like material neatly rolled round wooden spindles with knobs on the ends. There were also some sheets of parchment. He peered at one and saw what appeared to be a list written in Latin with figures down the right-hand side. Without knowledge of the language, it meant little to him, as did the title at the top of the sheet. Shaking his head, he lowered the lid gently back on the chest.

As he did so, he heard a shrill shriek. Rushing out of the room, he looked up to see Candice tottering on the edge of the steeply sloping wall he had slid down.

"Careful," he shouted out. "That's very slippery."

Howeve4, even as he said it, he saw her begin to slide and then she was falling. He rushed forward, just in time to catch her before she hit the ground. To his amazement she just grinned up at him and twined her arms round his neck and planted another of her full-mouthed kisses on his lips. Her body pressed against his.

"I like it when you are there to catch hold of me," she breathed.

He was very aware of the physical sensation he was receiving through the thin covering of her overalls. "How did you get up there?"

"I followed you of course."

"What – over all that rubble and through between those beams?"

"Why not? If you can get through, so can I." She poked him in the ribs- "I'm quite a bit smaller than you, so I have fewer problems."

"Except when you fall down a steep, sloping wall."

He set her down on her feet and let go of her shapely body, but she still had her arms round his neck, so she was resting tight against him. He reached up and released them.

"Oh," she protested, "I was enjoying that. Do you realise we've got our own secret little room here and no-one can see us, whatever we want to do?"

"It may be secret," he said. "But it may also be our prison." He gestured at the slippery, sloping wall. "I don't think we'll be able to climb up there to get out."

"Didn't you tell me you had been in here before? How did you get out then?"

"I'll show you."

He pulled away from her, somewhat reluctantly, and led the way round the corner to the window, having to crouch down below the collapsed floor beams to reach it. He looked out and gestured at the large shrub below.

"I jumped into that bush down there."

"Oh, *mon dieu*! That is a long way down. Didn't you hurt yourself?"

"No. The bush broke my fall and I more or less landed on my feet."

"Did Mademoiselle Blontard do that jump too?"

"No. She wasn't willing to risk it. I had to go and get her a ladder." He shook his head. "Even with the longest ladder I could find, held as tight to the wall as we dared, it still only reached to a couple of feet – er, half a metre – below the window-sill here. You can imagine it was a bit hairy getting her out."

"Yes. I wouldn't like to do that either."

"Well." He led her back into the room. "I think I'm going to have to jump again. Then I'll get a rope, and come back to the top of the wall, and lower it to you so that we can drag you up the wall. That's going to take me some time, so you'd better spend it looking at the job Jackie has given you. Come this way."

He took her into the room where the chests of archives were located, and she stopped just inside the door and gaped at the sight. He went over and lifted the lid on the chest which he had previously opened.

"There you are. Is that sheet written in Latin?"

She joined him and bent down to look at the hand-written document closely. "I think so. It seems to have some Latin words in it, but the phraseology is strange. It's not like the Latin we use today."

"And I estimate you've got something like a hundred chests filled with this stuff." He grinned at her. "I think I'll send a search party out for you in about ten years' time and, with a bit of luck, you may be about half-way through by then. Meanwhile we may even have managed to dig a passageway through to you."

"Don't joke about it."

"Who said I was joking?" He took a breath and turned away. "Well, I'd better take my leave of you now."

He patted her arm and went out and over to the window. Bending down, he peered out at the bush far below. It did seem a hell of a lot further down than he remembered from his previous adventure. He shrugged. He'd done it before, so why not this time. With Candice watching breathlessly, he straddled the sill and began to let his body down until he was hanging at arms' length below the window. Then he pushed himself away from the wall and let go.

As he flew through the air, he realised he hadn't got it quite right this time. He almost passed over the bush, but his foot caught in the top of it and he did a head-over-heels and fell past the shrub, which had cushioned him last time, and tumbled a further fifteen feet or so to land on his left side on the steeply sloping grass bank. Then he slid approximately another ten feet before he finally came to rest. As he tried to get up, he realised there was something seriously wrong with his left leg.

40

Jean-Luc Lerenard was feeling bored with life. He had been in this village for more than two weeks, and nothing much seemed to be happening. He would have liked to go back to Rome. There was a certain lady in the Trastevere who he believed would welcome him back into her life, now that he had retired from his profession as an enforcer for the Vatican. He would like to take up once again, the lifestyle that he had been asked to let go for a short while by his employers – for a very good payment, of course.

He admitted that meanwhile he had grown quite fond of young Philip. He took the word 'fond' out in his mind and examined it, and decided it was appropriate. The only problem was that the lad seemed frequently to get himself into trouble from which it wasn't always easy to extract him. And he also had this tendency to get involved with women – too many women and often more than one at a time. However, his employers had specifically asked him to look after the guy until things settled down and the chap's fiancée returned to sort him out. That seemed to be likely to be months, rather than weeks away. He shook his head and continued his walk.

This was an activity that he forced himself to take at least twice a day while he was trying to recover the full fitness he had enjoyed before he had received the pistol bullet in the lung nearly two months ago. He was improving fast, but he was still a long way off the physical strength which had been so vital to him, when he was sorting out some of the problems that beset the Catholic Church world-wide. The alternative was to offer his services to Philip, who had been lumbered with trying to dig his way into the cellars of the chateau, where it was rumoured, there were important documents hidden.

Walking was much more pleasant than digging and the surroundings of the village of Rennes-le-Chateau had quite a few interesting walks. He had already made some useful discoveries. Today's walk was taking him round the footpath below the village and down through the woods towards Couiza. He was striding along, taking little interest in the sounds of nature around him when he suddenly saw a young man staggering towards him. He realised immediately that it was Philip.

"Oh, thank God," the lad said as he almost fell into Lerenard arms. "I need your help, Jean-Luc."

"What is the problem?"

"I jumped out of the window back there and I didn´t get my line right and I think I may have pulled a muscle in my left thigh. I can´t put any weight on it."

"Is that the window that we rescued Mademoiselle Blontard out of a couple of months ago?"

"That´s right."

"So why did you jump out of it this time?"

"Ah." A ghost of a smile crossed Philip´s features, replaced almost instantly by a grimace of pain. "It happened like this. I had been able to find a way through the rubble to the room where the archives were discovered. But that stupid girl, Candice, had followed me and we found we were shut in there with only one way out."

"Through that window – like before."

"That´s right. But this time my aim was out." He took a breath. "I was intending to get a rescue party organised for the girl, but then I discovered I had damaged my leg and I didn´t know how I was going to get up to the chateau. Your arrival is like divine intervention."

"So what do you want to do now?"

"Well, can I hang on to you to take the load off my left leg? Then I can hop up to where the guys are working and ask them to take a rope to Candice so that she can get out of the place where she is trapped."

"I can do better than that. I can put you over my shoulder and carry you up."

Philip shook his head. "You´re not fit enough to do that sort of thing yet, Jean-Luc. My right leg´s perfectly sound so I don´t need to be carried."

"I don´t agree with that," said the big man. "I can see your leg needs treatment. Until you receive it, you shouldn´t use it at all."

"Well, in that case why don´t you leave me here and you go up to the chateau by yourself and get a couple of the guys to come down to carry me up?"

"Yes, I'll do that. You lie here on the bank and I'll be back with the others in a few minutes."

He lowered Philip to the grass slope beside the path and set off back to the village. He returned less than ten minutes later with Gaston. Armand Séjour came along as well.

"Albert knows where they keep a stretcher and he's gone to get it," Armand told him. "He'll be along in a couple of minutes. Now, let's have a look at this leg."

Philip noticed that the others seemed to let young Séjour take control when he was around. Even Jean-Luc kept quiet and took a back seat when he was present, although Philip knew the big man seldom pushed himself forward under any circumstances.

In obedience to Armand's instructions, Philip rolled on to his side and let the chap explore the length of his leg. Then his jeans were undone and his hip was explored.

"You need a doctor," was the comment. "But certainly make sure you don't put any weight on it until he's seen you."

As he stood up, Albert arrived with the stretcher and the next few minutes were occupied with getting Philip strapped on to it. Then the four of them easily carried him up to the cottage, where Jeanette clucked over him and insisted on putting him to bed. Gaston went off to phone the doctor who had to come from the nearby village of Esperaza.

Philip called Armand over. "We need to get Candice out," he told the young man. "She's trapped in the area where the archives were found."

He started by explaining how he had got through to the room and, that without his realising it, Candice had followed him. They now faced the problem of getting her out.

"The sloping wall we got in by, is very slippery and there's no way she can climb it. I thought we might lower a rope to her with a loop in the bottom that she can put her foot in. Then you could pull her up."

Armand wasn't happy about that idea. "From your description, it will be very difficult to get to the top of the sloping wall. It would need at least two men to pull her up and how are you going to get them both to that place?"

There was a lot of talk among the group, most of it in French spoken too fast for Philip to keep up. Then suddenly Jean-Luc spoke for the first time.

"What about the ladder we used to get Mademoiselle Blontard out last time?"

"God, that was awful," said Philip. "Would you want to do that again?"

"Not me. But the young lad here could do it."

They explained to him that the mayor had a long three-part ladder which, when fully extended and held almost vertical, reached to just below the sill of the window into the room. Despite the difficulties being explained to him, Armand said he was willing to try it. So the group of men departed and Philip and Jeanette were left alone.

She scolded him. "You got yourself into trouble again over that girl."

"She followed *me*, Jeanette. I didn't invite her."

"You should have sent her back as soon as she arrived."

"I couldn't. She fell down the steeply sloping wall. I only just caught her before she hurt herself."

"And I expect you enjoyed that. She was probably wearing those skimpy clothes she puts on. I've noticed before how she hangs around you with next to nothing on."

"No, Jeanette – it's you who keeps on appearing in front of me with nothing on."

"That's different. You're sleeping with me."

Philip sighed. Why was life so complicated? Then just at that moment Gaston called to tell them he had brought the doctor. Jeanette went downstairs to bring the man up to inspect his damaged left leg.

The doctor prattled away in French which was too fast for Philip to follow. He quickly realised that his instructions had to be transmitted through Jeanette.

She translated, "You must take off your trousers and underpants." She bustled round him, removing all his clothing below the waist.

The doctor examined his left leg closely. He caught hold of the femur through the flesh of his thigh and pulled it experimentally. Philip gasped with the pain. Then the man chatted again to Jeanette again.

"Your femur is dislocated at the hip," she told him.

"What!"

"Do not worry. He will fix it for you. He says he has done this many times."

"What's going to happen?"

She asked the question of the doctor. "You must reach up and hold the rail on the bed-head very tightly. I must lie across your stomach to keep your body flat. Then he will twist it back into place."

Philip didn't much like the sound of that, but he assumed the man knew what he was talking about. "OK."

They took up their positions as instructed. The doctor went to the foot of the bed and caught hold of his left foot. Then he lifted it slightly and turned it towards the other foot, reached forward and gave Philip a violent slap on the side of his thigh. A sudden pain shot through him, and his body jerked in reaction.

The man beamed and stroked his hip, "*Bon. Tres bon.*" He smiled indulgently down on his young patient. Then he turned to his large bag and extracted two lengths of what appeared to be canvas strapping. With Jeanette's help these were wrapped round Philip's body, one below the repaired hip and the other just above his knees.

"You are to keep these on for three days and you must stay in bed for that time."

"Three days!"

"That is very important. If you don't do this your hip may dislocate again."

So Philip was removed from activities for three days. He thought he would die of boredom being in bed for so long. He wasn't even allowed sex. But life would actually prove to be far from boring for him.

41

Hector Ramise received the phone call just before nine o'clock on Friday morning. The man's voice said, "My principals have sent me with the settlement of your agreement. Where can we meet?"

"Oh." The professor found it momentarily difficult to breathe. "Nobody has contacted me. Does this mean that my offer has been accepted?"

"I don't know about that," said the voice. "I am carrying a bag which I have been told contains one hundred thousand euros and I am to exchange it for the copy you hold of a certain letter. Is that what you were hoping to receive in return for your offer?"

"Er – yes. Yes, it is." It was a bit less than he had asked for, but it was still a substantial amount of money.

"Then it is obvious that we should meet. Where do you wish the exchange to take place? I don't want to keep possession of this bag any longer than is necessary."

"No. I can see that."

Ramise was thinking rapidly. Of course, he had envisaged this occurring on several occasions, and he already had a good idea of how he wanted it to take place. It was important that it should be somewhere open to public view for his own protection, but at the same time, he didn't want others to be so close that they might overhear what this man and he might be talking about. He had several possibilities in mind, but there was one that he favoured above others during daytime.

"I want the meeting place to be in central Béziers."

"That is not a problem. I am near the centre of the city already."

"In Béziers? How did you know I was living in Béziers?"

"Monsieur Ramise." The voice sighed. "I am simply a delivery boy. I was told to come to Béziers to meet you."

"Oh." Hector assumed he must have mentioned to Raul, some time in the past when they worked together, either that he owned a house in the city or that he planned to retire here.

"So, if you name the place," continued the voice, "I will tell you when I can meet you there."

"OK." Hector made his decision. "If you go to the main square, you will find that the post office building takes up a large part of the south side of the square. Opposite the post office you will see a cafe with a covered balcony at the front. It is a couple of steps above the road. They serve very good coffee there. You will note that the balcony extends round the corner of the cafe, still visible from the square but very suitable for a private conversation. I will be at the first table just round the corner from the main balcony, sitting with my back to the square. We will be safe from any flapping ears. Does that suit you?"

"It sounds very suitable."

"So how soon can you get there?"

"Let us say in a half an hour."

Ramise allowed himself to smile now that his wishes seemed to have come to fruition. "Very well, I will arrive just before half past nine and order two *café solos*. One will be in front of me and the other will be two chairs away, so that there is an empty chair between us by the wall, where the bag can be placed. I will be wearing a cream linen jacket and a straw hat with a broad brim and a red ribbon tied round the crown, so that you will not be in any doubt who you are dealing with."

"It sounds as though you have thought this through very carefully, professor."

"Oh yes, I have done my best to combine privacy with security which should suit us both, I believe."

"I will arrive at nine thirty-five. You will of course bring your copy of the letter with you."

"You can be sure of that," said Hector, but the man at the other end had already disconnected.

So Professor Ramise was sitting exactly at the appointed time in the location he had described. Under his linen jacket he was wearing an open-necked white shirt and slacks. The promised straw hat with the red ribbon was on his head, pulled down over his eyes as if to shade them from the rising sun. This early in the morning, the cafe was quiet. Only one other occupied table was at the far end of the balcony, where four men were taking part in a noisy conversation and presumably enjoying their breakfast break.

The waitress brought him the two cups of *café solo* he had ordered and placed them where he indicated. Then she retreated inside the cafe to continue her half-flirtatious conversation with the bar owner. Hector leaned forward and took an exploratory sip of the dark, scalding liquid. He nodded. It was just as he liked it.

"Good morning, monsieur Ramise."

Hector looked up. He hadn't heard the tall, strongly built man arrive. The fellow was dressed in a tee-shirt and jeans, and Hector noticed that his right arm had been amputated at the shoulder. Surely there was nothing to fear from a man with only one arm.

The man sat down on the seat Ramise indicated and dropped a cheap-looking airline bag in the chair between them.

"Please look inside, professor."

Hector took a quick look round to check they were unobserved, then he leaned over and slid back the zip along the top of the bag. Although he had been preparing for this moment for several days, what he saw took his breath away. The bag was filled with neat packs of bank notes, each held together by a broad rubber band.

"There are twenty packs, each of five thousand euros in a variety of face values and from a number of different European countries. Do you wish to count them?"

The professor picked up a pack and fanned through the notes. He could tell there was a lot of money there. He was sure it was at least five thousand euros. He dropped the bundle back in the bag and took out another pack from lower down with the same result. He quickly counted the number of packs and found they were just as the one-armed man had said.

He took a breath. "No. I trust you. I don't need to count the money."

"And you have the copy of the letter to give me?"

Ramise reached inside his jacket pocket and pulled out the piece of paper which he had folded into three. He handed it across the table, without somehow being able to take his eyes off the bag full of money.

"How did you come by it?"

"It was just lying around."

"Was it with the original in the possession of Mademoiselle Jacqueline Blontard? Did she let you have it?"

"Er – yes, you might say that."

"This is the only copy you have?"

"It is."

"You understand that it would be very dangerous for you, if you were found to have been lying to me and had kept another copy for future use."

Hector dragged his eyes away from the notes and looked at the other man. "I promise you that I have given you the only copy I have."

The one-armed man leaned towards him as if to shake the professor's hand but Ramise was once again absorbed by the prospect of all that cash.

"Well, it has been an interesting meeting." The man stood up, turned away and walked down the narrow alley beside the cafe and was quickly lost from sight.

Professor Ramise continued to gaze down at the bag of notes. After a while his head dropped on to his chest, as if he had fallen asleep. Then, slowly, the whole of his upper body settled over the bag full of his newly-acquired wealth.

Twenty minutes later the waitress came round to check whether her customers wanted second cups of coffee. She discovered one had been only half drunk and the remainder had been spilled into the saucer. The other hadn't been touched at all. When she gently shook the sleeping man's shoulder, he collapsed completely across the bag which was lying on the adjacent chair. His straw hat with the red ribbon fell on to the terrace. She rushed back into the cafe.

"Quick," she shouted to the man behind the bar. "You must call an ambulance. I think the old man with the straw hat has had a heart attack."

However, when the body was examined by the pathologist later that same day, he immediately pointed to the half-inch long incision between the sixth and seventh ribs where the stiletto had pierced the professor's heart.

42

Philip called a meeting in his bedroom the next morning. Armand and Candice were there, and of course Jeanette would not allow herself to miss it.

"How did the rescue go?" he wanted to know.

Armand grinned. "OK, I guess. It was a bit hairy at times, especially when young miss here decided she didn't fancy escaping after all and tried to climb back in through the window. So I had to prise her fingers off the sill and drag her down the ladder. After that we managed all right."

"I am not ever going to do that again." Candice's face went ashen with the memory. "I would rather stay imprisoned up there and have my food lifted up to me until you could find a way to get me out over the slippery wall."

Philip laughed. "Anyway you're back with us and ready to do something useful, I hope." He changed the subject. "So what are Albert and Gaston doing?"

"At the moment they're still moving that big heap of stuff we dug out from the stairs and barrowing it to the spoil heap in the yard."

Philip didn't ask about Lerenard. Nobody organised Jean-Luc.

"Well, lying here with nothing else to do, I've had plenty of time to think about what we ought to do next. I don't think that digging our way through the cellars to the archives is a practical possibility. Away from the staircase all three floors of the ruined building have fallen into the basement and, in doing so, they've nearly demolished the central wall. The rubble is more than six metres deep and much of it is large lumps of masonry which will have to be broken up for us to be able to lift them out. That is going to be a very slow job."

"Can't we get a mechanical digger in to get the stuff out?" asked Armand.

"I don't think so, not at this stage. Remember, we don't actually own the chateau yet, and we are likely to cause a lot more damage at the start, getting the digger into the courtyard and the truckloads of rubble out. The present owners aren't likely to be very happy about that."

"When are you going to get hold of the place?"

Philip shook his head. "The last time I discussed it with Jackie she said the title deeds of such a historic building go back many generations. Before new deeds can be drawn up, the lawyers have to sort all sorts of problems. The whole thing is very complicated and, frankly, I want just leave it to the *Vendredi Treize* lawyers to sort out. So at the moment we only have permission to get access to the archives and catalogue them." He nodded at the girl. "That's Candice's job."

"That's *when* I can get in there to do it," she complained.

"That's right. The only way in is that route she and I used yesterday, and it is so difficult and dangerous that I'm convinced she can't take that way every day."

"So what will we do?"

"I think what we are going to *have* to do is get the archives out from where they are, bring them up to the part of the chateau which is not a ruin and put them in a couple of the big empty rooms up here. Then we would still be complying with the licence to keep them in the chateau while Candice is checking through them and listing the contents." He took a breath. "That means the only practical solution is for two of us to go back the way we went yesterday but carrying a long rope and a sling so that we can lower the chests of papers down to the path below the window opening. Then the other two can load them into the wheelbarrows and push them up to the chateau and we can store them in a couple of the big ground floor rooms. That will also give Candice much more room to work in."

"That sounds a good idea," agreed Armand.

"*You* are not to go," intervened Jeanette. "You've got to stay in bed for three days."

Philip ignored her. "But I think I've got to get Jackie's permission to do that. She'll probably have to go to her colleagues in *Vendredi Treize* to get their agreement because technically the archives belong to them. But I'll send her an email to explain this is the only practical option, and I think she'll authorise it."

"Do you mean I'll have to do the cataloguing up here?" Candice didn't seem very enthusiastic, even though it would enable her to start the job she had been pressing everyone to help her with, since she arrived three weeks ago.

Armand said, "So there's not much we can do for the next few days, until we hear back from Mademoiselle Blontard."

"Well, I suggest we take the rest of the weekend off. The break will do us good. Then on Monday, we can concentrate first on clearing the mess we made digging out the steps." He turned to Armand. "I'd like you to make sure the temporary shoring we put up is strong enough to stay there, and can you put some sort of barrier across the top of the steps to make sure nobody tries to go down them without us knowing?"

"OK. I'll do that before I break this morning."

"And Armand, would you be willing to be one of the guys who scrambles through with the rope to set about lowering the chests when we get Jackie's authorisation?"

"Sure. That won't be a problem."

"You'll need to take someone with you. Who do you think would be best?"

"I'll go with him," volunteered Candice, seeming to have recovered her enthusiasm for the job.

Armand had been thinking about it. "I was going to suggest Gaston because he's younger than Albert and probably fitter." He paused. "However, if she's willing to wear rougher clothes than usual, I think Candice would be suitable. After all, she's done it once before on her own, so this should be easy for her."

"And you're happy to escape afterwards using the rope?" Philip asked her.

"Of course. I am younger and fitter than you big fat men, and I am strong too. So it won't be a problem for me." She shuddered. "As long as we don't have to go down that ladder again."

"OK. I'll send off my email to Jackie in the next hour and we can all have the rest of the weekend off." He suddenly remembered. "Oh, Armand, can you go and get a good strong rope, sufficiently long to reach twice from the window down to the path. We also need a webbed sling strong enough to carry the weight of a chest full of papers. I think they will each weigh about a hundred kilos and they're old and may be fragile, so we mustn't rely on lowering them by the handles." He passed a hand over his eyes. "My God, just imagine what it would be like if one of them fell and burst open, and Jackie's priceless archives were being blown in the wind over all the countryside. I'll tell her that in my email."

Armand laughed. "Don't worry boss. I'll make sure we get them down safely."

"You can take the pick-up and here's my wallet to pay for whatever you need." He looked around. "OK. Thanks for coming. I'll see you on Monday."

Jeanette accompanied them downstairs. "It's nearly time to prepare lunch," she said.

43

The knock came at the door about half an hour later. Grumbling slightly, she went to open it and was confronted by the man with one arm whom she had seen before in Limoux. He took a step forward and his foot effectively prevented her from closing the door on him. Jeanette had a bad feeling about this man.

"I have come to see Monsieur Sinclair."

She stood squarely in front of him. "Well, you can't today. He has hurt himself and has to stay in bed."

"That isn't a problem for me." He pushed her unceremoniously aside with his good arm and mounted the stairs.

Jeanette hesitated for only a few seconds, then she rushed out through the open door and ran up the street.

The one-armed man reached the landing and selected the open door into the front bedroom. Philip was sitting up in bed supported by several pillows, having just despatched his email to Jackie explaining the situation, and asking for authority to move the archives. Vauclus moved forward to the foot of the bed.

"You are injured? You cannot move?"

Philip felt distinctly vulnerable. "I fell and dislocated my hip. It has been reset but I'm told I should stay in bed for three days with it strapped up, so that it doesn't come out again."

"That does not have to be a problem," said Vauclus. "I have only come to collect your copy of the letter. I think you know what I am talking about."

"My copy? I don't have a copy."

"Come now, Monsieur Sinclair. I am sure you saw the letter that I am talking about."

"I take it you mean the letter written by some Marquise in the 1870's."

Vauclus nodded. "That is correct."

Philip decided there was no point in trying to avoid giving this man the facts. "I haven't seen a copy of the letter. I only saw the original. You said you didn't want the bag with the double-headed eagle crest on the side. When I told Mademoiselle Blontard, she said she wanted to see it. So I went to retrieve it from the back bedroom where I had thrown it. When I picked it up, I saw that the badge on the crest on the side of the bag had sprung open. I looked in the small cavity behind the badge and I could see something in there."

"And that was the letter?"

"That's what it turned out to be. You must understand that Mademoiselle Blontard is an archaeologist, and she is always very careful about avoiding contamination of anything she investigates. So she insisted that it was carefully removed from the cavity and was opened without damage. When she read it, she was very interested in the letter, so she carefully wrapped it up and took it with her when she went back to Paris. I have not seen her or the letter since. And I certainly don't have a copy."

"All right. You may not have a copy, but she did take copies. One has been given to me by a Professor Ramise and I have taken the original and two other copies from Mademoiselle Blontard herself."

"You have been to see her? You have been to Paris? What have you done to her?"

"She is unharmed. Unfortunately, I turned up when she was in bed with a man who I believe was her producer, and who of course objected strongly to my presence. However, collection of the documents was more important to me than some affair which I might have interrupted."

So, Philip thought, Jackie had decided to take a lover just as he had. He couldn't prevent a feeling of jealousy for the man she had chosen. He admitted he had been sleeping with Jeanette, but it seemed to him that was different. What right had she to have sex with another man? It was Jackie who had absented herself from his bed – not the other way round. Although he was aware of the hypocrisy of his attitude, he felt that in a strange way he had a right to be annoyed.

The man was regarding the emotions, which must have been showing on Philip's face, without any apparent amusement. Now he said, "There seems to be a number of copies going round. How do you explain Professor Ramise having one, while you claim you haven't got one?"

"I don't know. I haven't seen Ramise for weeks and I certainly didn't know any copies had been taken until you told me."

Philip quickly realised that Jackie must have returned to Paris via Béziers. Perhaps she had met Hector there. He remembered she had a photocopier in the office in her flat in Béziers and perhaps she had given a copy to the Professor. Philip didn't entirely trust the man after the things he had confessed to when they last met. So he thought it was foolish of her to have let him have a copy. But he wasn't going to tell Vauclus that.

"It doesn't matter," said the one-armed man. "He won't be passing on his knowledge any further."

"What do you mean?"

"I mean, Monsieur Sinclair, that I cannot risk anybody who has information about the contents of the letter passing it on to others, and that includes you."

Philip's blood ran cold. "Why me? I didn't read the letter. I can't even understand German."

"Nevertheless, I am sure Mademoiselle Blontard told you what was in the letter. You have already indicated that you know who wrote it and the date on which it was written."

Vauclus' hand went to his hip pocket. When it came out, he was holding a thin flat strip of bright steel. He advanced round the bed. He must have pressed a concealed button, for suddenly a thin stiletto blade shot out of the end of the piece of steel. Philip realised it was a similar weapon to those that Lerenard carried hidden in the soles of his shoes, but that it was somewhat longer. He knew what was going to happen now. He gathered a bundle of sheet in his hands to try and wrap round the man's fist as he came at him. His one advantage was that Vauclus only had one hand to fight with. But he had little hope that he could win this struggle. Was this the end for him?

And then: "Don't do that, Jordie."

Vauclus spun round and Philip could see that Jean-Luc was standing in the doorway.

"What are you doing here, Luke? Keep out of this. You must not try to stop me from handing out justice."

"The young man says he doesn't have a copy of the letter you are seeking, and you should believe him. Nobody else will be interested in anything *he* has to say about this letter, if he doesn't have any evidence to back up his statements."

"I'm sorry, Luke, but I cannot take that risk." Vauclus shook his head, "You can't stop me. You're out of condition. By the time you reach me, I will have finished off this lad and you will be in danger yourself. I will be much too quick for you."

"But not as quick as this." Lerenard raised his right hand and there was a steel rod sticking out of it. He pointed it at Vauclus and there came soft "Phut" as the silenced pistol shot him. The one-armed man jerked upright.

"I have owed you this since you betrayed me in Cairo," murmured Lerenard as Vauclus measured his length on the floor.

Jeanette rushed in. "What have you done?"

Nobody said a word as she looked down at the body.

"Oh," she wailed. "Will he make a mess on the carpet?"

Her question relieved the tension and made Philip burst into helpless, ridiculous laughter.

"Jeanette," he accused her. "Jean-Luc has just saved my life and all you can worry about is the mess on the carpet." He looked at his friend. "Thank you. I'd have had it without you."

The big man shrugged. "I knew, when he first turned up, that it would end like this. That is why I was prepared." He patted Jeanette on the shoulder. "Don't worry. I will remove the body after dark. But you will have to get a new carpet." He fixed her with his penetrating gaze. "And you must say nothing to anybody about what has happened here."

He left, but returned with Armand a little later, and they rolled the body up in the carpet and dragged it into the back bedroom.

"Can we borrow the pick-up tonight?"

"Of course. Armand has the keys already."

So the evidence was removed some time in the night. Philip and Jeanette were in bed with the bedroom door closed, and they heard nothing.

44

On the Saturday afternoon, when the place had been cleared up, Philip sent Jackie another email;-

The one-armed man turned up yesterday to kill me because I knew about the Marquise's letter. However, we have got rid of him and you and your lover should be safe unless he has a colleague, which we doubt. I believe it is too late for Hector.

He had his reply on the Sunday evening. It was in brisk business terms:-

You may move the archives in the way you suggest, subject to each chest being numbered in the sequence they are removed from the strong room. Each chest must also be completely wrapped in plastic and sealed before it is removed and must not be re-opened until it is to be catalogued in detail. Please take photos at various stages of the move, both in the cellars and in the rooms above ground and send them to me. When the transfer has been completed, please contact me, so that I can come down and talk to you.

He smiled grimly to himself when he saw that she had not mentioned the contents of his second email although he knew she must have read it. There was no mention of Louis or the Marquise's letter. Their next meeting would be interesting.

Philip insisted he was well enough to get up on the Monday morning. He took the strapping off round his knees, but agreed to keep the one round his hips while he was starting to move again. He promised Jeanette he would be careful. When he went into the chateau, he found that Armand had assembled the team and agreed their tasks with them. He and Candice were dressed in rough clothes to enable them to scramble through the ruins to the strong room. He had the rope wrapped round his body and she was carrying the sling and a camera to take photos of the chests in the cellar. Albert and Gaston were to do the barrowing of the chests up from the path below the window and into the rooms which Philip had allocated on the ground floor of the chateau.

He told them about Jackie's additional requirements. He had already sent Jeanette off to get the plastic and sealing tape for wrapping up the chests. It was agreed that he would stay in the chateau to arrange the stacking of the chests and to photograph them when they were brought up to the ground level.

"You can get started," he told Armand. "It's going to take you at least half an hour to get through to the strong room. Then you can start getting the chests out, ready to wrap and lower down to Albert and Gaston. When Jeanette gets back, we'll send up the plastic and the tape and chalk in the sling, so that you can start the numbering and wrapping."

They set off, as did Gaston with the first barrow. Meanwhile, Albert arranged ramps through the doorway into the courtyard and cleared two of the large rooms ready to receive the chests when they were brought up.

Jeanette turned up about an hour later. She was very proud of herself. "The place I went to in Limoux had these great big heavy-duty bags which will be much better than sheet plastic," she told him. "They only had twenty in stock, but their warehouse in Carcassonne has many more, so I've ordered another hundred and they will be delivered later this morning."

"Well done," said Philip. "That should speed things up."

She winked at him. "I shall expect my reward later, now you've taken the strapping off."

Albert barrowed the bags and the other things down the footpath and Philip accompanied him slowly, to watch and photograph the first chest being lowered. Armand had already lowered the sling and it was lying on the path, ready to take up the plastic and other things. The first chest was sent down about fifteen minutes later. Once the system was working smoothly, they were able to lower one every five to ten minutes – a rate of about eight an hour. The routine continued throughout the day. Jeanette sent lunch up to Armand and Candice in a bag in the sling so that they didn't need to stop in the middle of the day. At six o'clock, when Albert and Gaston were ready to finish, he checked the number chalked on the latest chest and saw it was fifty-two.

He called up to Armand, "These two guys down here are knackered. I think we'll stop for today. How many are left in the strong room?"

"I'll try and get a rough idea," Armand replied.

He came back a few minutes later and called down, "I reckon there are between fifty and sixty. I think we can easily complete it tomorrow. Are you ready for me to send Candice down? I've checked, and I can lower her to you in the sling."

Philip laughed. "What does she say about that?"

"I don't want to shin down the rope," she called. "I've agreed to the sling as long as he lowers it slowly and I can hold myself off the wall."

"OK. Go ahead then."

"I've been thinking about security," called Armand. "If I use the rope to come down, it will be left hanging there. I don't think Mademoiselle Blontard would like that. After all, somebody could climb up during the night."

"That is a problem," agreed Philip. "What do you suggest?"

"I'm willing to sleep up here for the one night, if you send me up some cushions and a rug."

"OK. That's good of you. Thank you very much. I'll get Jeanette to do a meal for you and I'll send it all up at about seven o'clock. Will that suit you?"

"That'll be great."

So Philip went off to make the arrangements.

The next morning Candice decided she wanted to scramble back to the strong room through the cellars as she had done the previous day. "I don't want to be pulled up swinging about in the sling," she told him.

Philip agreed with her. He had taken the strapping off his hips the previous evening so as to give Jeanette some of the pleasure she had been complaining about missing, so he felt agile enough to accompany her through the rubble in the cellar and help her over the wall.

When they got there, he called to Armand, "Candice is coming over. Are you ready to catch her?"

"I wondered when I would see her next," shouted the young man. "I've already got a dozen chests wrapped up and ready to lower."

"OK. Here she comes."

Philip helped her find stepping places then pushed her shapely little bottom and finally her feet as she clambered to the top. She disappeared down the sloping wall with a yelp. He returned up the steps to oversee the placing of the rest of the chests when they were barrowed up.

With the earlier start, all the chests had been moved to their appointed locations by mid-afternoon and Candice was once again lowered in the sling before Armand let himself down on the double rope which had been loosely looped round a beam. That meant the rope could be pulled down so that there was no practical way into the cellars through the window. Philip left the rope with the plastic-wrapped chests in the ground floor rooms and made sure the chateau gates were double-locked before they left that evening.

45

That night Philip sent an email to Jackie telling her that the move of the archives had been completed and attaching a couple of photos to show her the new arrangement. He received a reply the following day, saying she would be coming to look at their progress at the weekend. He informed Candice of this. By now she was set up with a large table and her filing system, so that she could get stuck in to the job and would be able to discuss progress with Jackie when the lady came.

"These archives are very valuable," he told the others. "From now on it's essential that the gates to the chateau are kept locked when there's nobody working in the place. I'll open up for Candice every morning when she arrives and lock up every evening as soon as she leaves. Please let me know if you see anybody hanging round and make sure nobody else goes into the chateau without my agreement."

Having completed the primary objective of starting Candice on cataloguing the archives, Philip turned everyone else back on finishing the house. He wanted to be certain it was complete and ready to be occupied by the time Jackie finished her work in Paris, so that she would have no excuse for not coming back to Rennes. The next priority was the kitchen, and he took Jeanette with him when he went to get the units. He thought she might suggest things which he wouldn't think about. Then he and Armand worked together on fixing them while Albert and Gaston concentrated on the floor tiling. He intended to be able to show Jackie that they were making good progress when she came.

In fact, the lady arrived on the Saturday afternoon. She hadn't told him when she was coming but had apparently been in touch with Candice, as he discovered when the girl knocked at the door at about nine o'clock that morning and asked for the key to the chateau. He noticed she was smartly but decently dressed.

"Goodness, Candice, you didn't tell me you were working today."

"It was the request of Mademoiselle Blontard."

"Is she coming today?"

"Of course. She told me she expects to be here after lunch."

So Jackie could find time for a chat with Candice, but couldn't be bothered to contact *him* to let him know when to expect her. His face took on a grim expression as he realised there was little likelihood of there being any sort of reconciliation this weekend.

The lady drove into the yard just before three o'clock and got out of the car and looked around. She was wearing a smart white suit and high-heeled shoes. Feeling the heat after getting out of an air-conditioned car, she took off her jacket and tossed it onto the driver's seat, revealing a scarlet sleeveless blouse underneath. Philip thought, that as usual, she looked sensational.

"Are you going out to meet her?" asked Armand, who was working with him in the kitchen.

"No. You go and ask her if there's anything she wants." Philip continued fixing a wall unit above the sink.

With a sideways glance and the ghost of a smile, Armand went out as instructed. Philip watched him covertly as he spoke to Jackie and indicated the house. He guessed the young Frenchman was telling her what her fiancé was doing. Then he escorted her into the chateau to talk to Candice. He came back about ten minutes later

"Everything OK?" asked Philip.

"Yes. She thought we had done a good job of protecting the chests."

"Nothing else?"

"No." Then he grinned, taking pity on the young Englishman. "She's going to come across and see you when she's finished with Candice."

It was about an hour later when Jackie came into the kitchen where they were working. Philip straightened up and massaged his back.

"I like that," she said, taking in the full height fridge/freezer with the cold water and instant ice feature.

"Nothing but the best," he told her. "I thought we might find ourselves living here for several years while we were restoring the chateau, so it was worth having some decent equipment. The oven's a good one and there will be a built-in microwave beside the work-top."

"The garden's a mess." She was gazing through the kitchen window at the jungle outside.

216

"Hmm. It obviously hasn't been touched in years. I'm afraid that's a long way down my list of priorities at the moment." He turned away from surveying the rear of the property. "Do you want to see the rest of the house?"

"OK." She didn't seem to be very enthusiastic.

"There's going to be a shower room and toilet just inside the front door. I thought it would be useful to be able to go straight in there when we came back from working, to avoid bringing too much dirt and dust into the rest of the house."

She turned away without comment and walked into the living room.

"Albert and Gaston are just levelling up the floor and will start laying the tiles next week. They're not working today." He picked up a sample and showed it to her. "I chose a fairly neutral colour. Then you can over-lay it with rugs in the winter. Are you happy with that?"

"All right." She advanced into the centre of the room, and once more looked out through the full height glazed double doors at the tangled vegetation in the back garden. Her face was a picture of distaste.

"I thought we might put a conservatory on the back and pave a substantial part as a sitting-out area," he suggested.

She turned a pitying gaze on him. "You English like your conservatories, don't you?"

"I suppose we do." He ignored the sarcasm. "Come and have a look upstairs."

He led the way up the dog-leg staircase onto the landing. He indicated the smaller room at the back. "Armand is sleeping in there at the moment. The main bathroom is at the back over the kitchen. And this is the master bedroom."

He preceded her into the large room which they had furnished but had not yet been used by anybody. He noticed a small vase of flowers had been placed on the dressing-table. Presumably Jeanette had put that there.

"This is a big room so I'm going to build an en-suite in the corner," he said. "I thought that would be convenient."

Jackie surveyed the room and suddenly turned to him. "Have you fucked your prostitute in this bed?"

"What!"

"Have you had her in here?"

"Nobody has slept in here yet."

"Because I'll tell you, Philip, that I won't sleep in a bed or live in a house where you've had sex with that woman."

He was stirred to unaccustomed anger by her accusations although, if he was honest, he would have to admit they were partly justified.

"And let me tell you, Jackie bloody Blontard, that if you bring that bloke Louis into this place, I'll drag him to the end of the yard and chuck him down the hill."

That made her take a breath. Then she shook her head. "Oh, you don't know what you're talking about."

"Are you trying to pretend that Vauclus somehow got the wrong end of the stick?"

"Yes I am." She shook her head again. "The guy's dead now anyway." She looked straight at him for the first time. "What did you do with the body?"

There was no concern about the shattering events which had taken place a week ago, no sympathy for him, no suggestion of gratitude for having her life saved by Jean-Luc's action. He was reminded that she was a tough individual who had gazed at death from close up before.

"I haven't the least idea. You'll have to ask Armand about that. He and Lerenard removed it, rolled in a rug, in the back of the pick-up. I couldn't help because I was stuck in bed at the time with my hip strapped up."

"I'm not sure I want to know anyway." Again, there was no suggestion of sympathy.

Philip thrust his anger aside and tried to improve the atmosphere. "It's getting late to drive back to Paris tonight. If you want to stay here, we can make up the bed for the night."

"I can't. I must go to see Charlotte. She is devastated by Hector's death." Did he detect a softening in her attitude?

"Even Béziers is a long drive better taken in the morning." He felt he had to make a final effort to build a bridge between them. "I could take you for a meal at that restaurant we went to in Limoux when we were getting to know each other. We might manage to have a less vindictive conversation over some food."

She hesitated for just a second, and he had the absurd hope that she might be willing to try and start to rebuild the relationship they had enjoyed before she had rushed off to Paris.

He was very aware that her shapely body, clothed in the thin blouse, was extremely close to him. But then she shook her head.

"No, I'm sorry. I can't do that yet." She gave him a bleak smile. "I'm going now, Philip. As you say, it's a long way to Béziers." She turned her back on him and made for the stairs.

"Are you any closer to knowing when you'll be returning to Rennes?"

"It's still going to be several weeks." She spoke so quietly, now the anger had left her, that he found it difficult to hear what she said. "We've finished the main recording work, but we've got most of the editing to do, and that's bound to require some additional re-takes. Then there's the presentation and the publicity to prepare." She almost sighed. "There's still a lot to do."

"Oh well, I'll wait to hear from you."

She reached the top of the stairs and turned back to him. "Goodbye Philip."

He almost had the feeling that she wanted him to grab her and hold her back, but she firmly grasped the newel post and started to descend.

"Cheerio." He didn't follow her. He watched through the window as she crossed to her car, opened the door, picked up her jacket and tossed it onto the passenger seat. Then she actually raised her hand in farewell before she got in and drove away.

46

On Monday morning, Philip had got all the men working on finishing off the house, so he decided to check Candice's progress. He crossed the yard and went through the pedestrian door into the courtyard. He made his way to where she was doing the cataloguing. It was the first time he had checked up on her since she had been set to work on the archives.

He was surprised to find that she wasn't there. He noticed her jacket was hanging on the back of the chair and her handbag was lying on the table. But no chests had been unwrapped. There were no stacks of papers or rolls of vellum waiting to be inspected. No labelled files were waiting to receive their allocated documents. In fact, it appeared that nothing had been started this morning. He checked his watch. He realised it was only half past nine, but normally she would have been working by this time.

He had noticed, when she arrived that morning, and as he unlocked the door into the chateau for her, that she was once again wearing the thin overalls which she had used when she was digging, rather than the white shirt and fawn shorts which seemed to be her usual summer wear. His own unsatisfactory meeting on Saturday with Jackie, and the subsequent cloying attention he had received from Jeanette, made him only too aware of this girl's lithe body beneath the multi-patterned garment which seemed to cling to her body like a second skin.

So where was she, and why wasn't she enthusiastically at work after the recent visit from her boss? As he looked round the room, he also noticed the coil of rope, which had been left on top of one of the chests in the corner, had disappeared. A worm of suspicion was beginning to form in his mind.

"I bet she has gone back to the strongroom again," he thought to himself. "What the hell has she done that for? I thought the place had been completely cleared out."

He went back into the courtyard to check the barrier that had been placed across the top of the steps, to stop anybody from wandering down into the cellars. Sure enough, that had been pulled aside just far enough to allow a slim body to slip through. Philip paused. Before he went after her, he ought to lock the pedestrian door into the courtyard. The silly girl had gone off without telling anybody. That had left the place wide open to any casual intruder who chose to walk in and find the archives, and possibly remove some of them. Jackie wouldn't have liked to hear about that. He acknowledged that wasn't quite fair on Candice. It was unlikely that anybody would make off with a chest covered in plastic that needed two men to lift it, especially when there were men working across the yard on the house. Nevertheless, he thought he should lock the door before he went after the girl.

Having done that, he moved the barrier back a little further at the top of the steps and descended into the basement. He was pleased that his hip now gave him no pain as he walked down the steps and offered silent thanks to the doctor who had so effectively solved his dislocation problem. At the foot of the steps, he followed the narrow corridor they had made beside the staircase wall. He realised too late that he had forgotten to bring a torch with him. However, he rejected the idea of going back for one, and possibly having to explain to Jeanette what he was doing. He had come this way several times before, and a small amount of light was filtering through the ruins. So he thought he would be able to see enough to make his way to the far end of the large cellar.

He ducked under the beams and scrambled over the rubble along the back wall. At the far end the light actually improved, obviously coming from the window in the partly collapsed room. Peering up at the top of the sloping wall, he could see the rope had been tied to one of the beams resting on the wall. Clearly, she had come this way. He wanted to find out why she was here, so he decided not to call out to let her know he was following. Using the remembered footholds, he climbed up to the top of the sloping wall and peered over. The room below the wall was empty.

He noticed Candice had doubled the rope down the wall. That would make it simpler to climb up again and it also made it quite easy to let himself carefully down the slippery surface. When he reached the bottom there was no sign of the girl here, and the strongroom was completely empty. Looking round, he saw the door through which he and Jackie had originally entered this room when they were escaping from being locked in the crypt under the church. He could see that this had been pulled as far open as Candice could manage, before it came up against the large lump of masonry which had made it so difficult to get out. Clearly her slim figure had been able to slip through into the tunnel leading to the crypt. Why would she want to go and visit some old tombs?

Philip wasn't going to let this jammed door stop him. With his foot he cleared away the small pieces of stone and other rubble which allowed him to pull the door open another couple of inches.

"Well," he thought, "I did it before so I can do it again."

He took a deep breath then expelled all the air completely from his lungs, so that he could force his chest through the gap. The rest of his body followed without any serious problems. Now he was in the tunnel that he and Jackie had crept along, almost without light, as they escaped. He paused, trying to see what was ahead. For a while there was nothing, then he saw a sudden glow on the side of the tunnel a few yards ahead. He felt his way towards it but stopped when the glow disappeared. A minute later the light appeared again and this time he could see it came from a side tunnel which he and Jackie must have missed on the occasion that they had crept along here before, with only the last faltering light from his torch to guide them.

Although the light was immediately extinguished again, he had seen enough to enable him to reach the entrance to the side tunnel. The next time Candice switched her torch on he was able to see that she was only a few yards away and was bending down in front of a barrier of rough wood which blocked the side tunnel.

"Candice," he called, quite softly.

"Aaah!" The light jerked and spun round to shine in his face. "Philip! What are you doing here?"

"I might ask you the same question."

She almost seemed to chuckle. "Me? I'm doing a bit of exploring. Isn't it exciting?"

"Exciting? You're supposed to be sorting through the archives." His voice took on a severe note. "And you left the door to the courtyard unlocked. Anyone could have walked in."

"Like you for example." She gave a cheeky giggle.

"Like me." He advanced towards her. "I should punish you for that."

She switched off the torch but remained standing in the same place so that he had no trouble in catching hold of her body. It felt warm through the thin material.

"What did you have in mind?" she murmured seductively.

"Just this." His searching hands came up against her body. They explored it through her thin overalls and found her buttocks. He smacked her gently.

"Oh, that's nice." She moved against him and nuzzled up to him. Her free hand found his face and the next moment her lips were on his. It was very easy to respond.

She broke off and giggled. "We can do what we want down here. We aren't in any danger of being seen."

Philip tried to concentrate on something else. "So why did you come down here?" he asked her.

"I'm trying to get through this damned door. It needs two hands to move the bolt and a third one to hold the torch. You seem to have turned up at just the right time."

"Show me the bolt," he instructed.

Obediently, she pointed the light at the door, panning round until it came to rest on a large iron bolt at head height.

"Let me see if I can move it. Keep the torch beam on the bolt."

He moved around her and approached the door. She went to the other side of him and leaned against him as he tried to get his fingers behind the loop on the end of the bolt. For a while it resisted his attempts, but then it slowly gave way. Once his first two fingers had been inserted behind the loop, he was able to pull it out and work it up and down in the hasps which held it to the door.

"You didn't think to bring any oil with you?"

"Sorry. I didn't know what I would find down here. But never mind," she murmured in his ear. "I know just how strong your fingers are."

The comment made him put even more effort into jerking the loop up and down. At the same time, he was trying to pull the bolt back out of the hasp. Candice kept the torch focused steadily on his hands. Then suddenly the iron rod gave way and started to slide out of the keep, just a fraction of an inch at a time. He furiously yanked at it and eventually pulled it clear.

"Right, now for the bottom one."

He crouched down and grabbed the loop on the lower bolt. Now she was almost lying on top of him as she pointed the light at his clenched fists. Her free hand was round his waist. Her ponytail had fallen forward and was tickling his neck. Her hot breath was in his ear. He tried to ignore all this as he yanked at the bolt. In fact, this one moved more easily, and he was able to slide it back in only a couple of minutes. Then he stood up.

"Come on. Get it open," she urged.

There was no handle on the door, so he grasped the upper bolt and pulled. There was no immediate movement, so he tried to jerk the door open with repeated short tugs. Candice eased her body round him and crouched near the floor to get hold of the lower bolt.

"Let's pull together."

"All right. Are you ready? One, two, three – pull."

They both heaved together without any sign of movement.

"And again. One, two . . ."

At the fifth tug, Candice called out, "I'm sure it moved then – only a bit, but a few more pulls should do it."

So they repeated their combined efforts and after a few more heaves it had moved at least half an inch.

"I think it's rubbing on the floor," she told him. "Next time I'll try to lift at the same time as we pull."

"OK. I'll do the same." He stepped as close to the door as her crouched body would let him. "Are you ready then?"

Their combined effort paid off and this time the door opened at least three inches with a groan. One more heave and they had opened it a good foot and could both peer inside.

"Oh, *mon dieu!*" she gasped as she played the torch across the room, and they could see the gleam of gold reflected back to them from all around.

47

For just a few seconds they stood, tightly squeezed together in the doorway, as they looked at the astonishing spectacle that appeared through the gap.

Then Candice burst into action. "Come on. If we pull the door back another few centimetres, we can get in."

This time they both grasped the edge of the rough timber door and yanked together and pulled the door back. She came up out of the crouch between his legs and he pushed her through the enlarged gap into the treasure room. Her torch played back and forth on the jumble of precious objects. Just to one side was something Philip instantly recognised.

"Bloody hell! You see that seven-branched lamp standard nearly as high as a man?" He took a breath. "I think that's the famous menorah. If it is, that proves this lot is at least part of the treasures looted from the Temple by the Romans when they sacked Jerusalem – I believe it was in about AD 70. And then the Visigoths brought it from Rome when they captured the city in the beginning of fifth century." He pointed. "Look. I think there's another one over there. I didn't realise there were two of them."

"Are they worth a lot of money?"

"They're absolutely priceless. The Jewish state would be prepared to pay many millions of euros for them."

Clinging to each other, they moved slowly into the room. Everywhere there were gleaming gold and silver objects – shields from the Temple walls, cups, bowls, incense holders, crowns, jewellery, even a complete golden altar, all dumped higgledy piggledy along one side of the large room. Candice reached for the lid on one of the numerous chests. It was easy for her to lift it, and they could see it was filled with strange, contorted shapes of gold.

"Ah," said Philip, "I remember it was said that the Romans burned down the Temple, and the heat was so intense that it melted the gold sheathing on the walls and a lot of the other rich furnishings. Luckily the menorah had been removed before that and I wonder what happened to . . . Oh, my God!"

"What is it?"

For a few seconds Philip was unable to catch his breath. Then he said, "Do you see that big box over there with the two golden angels on top, bending forward so that their wing-tips almost touch?"

"The one that seems to be covered with gold sheathing that has patterns worked into it?"

"That's right." He shook his head. "I can't believe it. That more or less matches the description, handed down in history, of the Ark of the Covenant. I wonder whether it really is the Ark, and whether it still contains the stones on which the Ten Commandments are inscribed. My God, that would astonish the world if it really was the Ark."

They both felt an intense excitement at the wonders they had discovered. She put down the torch and swivelled round and embraced him. "Oh, Philip, we're rich. We're rich beyond our wildest imaginings." She threw her arms round his neck.

As they clung together, gazing round the room, Philip was beginning to realise the enormity of their discovery.

"Candice," he said, "we mustn't tell a soul about what we have found. It's not even under the land which we hope to own. I don't know who does own the area above this room, or what right they might have to enjoy the benefits of this treasure. So for God's sake don't tell anyone about it." Then he had a thought. "The only thing is, I think that I should tell Jackie. She'll know what to do about reporting it and keeping it safe from the thousands of people who will want to get a piece of it. And she's honest. She wouldn't try to cheat us of anything that we have a right to."

"What - not even after you've upset her by having Jeanette in your bed?"

"Oh, no. She's the ultimate professional. And our recent discoveries have made her wealthy enough not to be influenced by thoughts of personal gain. All she will be interested in, will be letting the world know about these wonders. That is when their ownership and whereabouts are safely ascertained."

They pulled apart and turned to look round the room more carefully. Now that the initial excitement of their discovery had been dissipated, they began to explore the place. It wasn't a large room - perhaps twenty feet square and no more than eight feet high. The door came in at one corner and along the left-hand wall were a number of large statues and other objects, including the two menorah and, in the corner was a substantial golden altar. Next to it at the back of the room was the Ark. Occupying the rest of the space on the right side, was a considerable number of chests – perhaps between thirty and forty. Several of them were open and empty, suggesting that somebody else had been here before them – perhaps the priest who had become fabulously wealthy. Some of the chests had been unlocked and, when they lifted the lids of the ones which hadn't been emptied, they could see they contained more of the misshapen clusters of gold.

"This seems to be all pure gold stuffed into these chests," he said. "I've got no idea of the value but that alone must be worth millions."

"And what's in the locked chests?" she asked.

"I've no idea, and I don't have the tools to force them open." He shook his head. "I don't know whether I ought to do that anyway. We probably should ask a professional to open them for us."

"Well, Philip," she said, suddenly serious. "Now we're both very rich. What are we going to do about it?"

"Actually," he said, "We're not really the rightful owners of this stuff. I don't know the laws about treasure trove in France, but in Britain I think most of the really old treasure belongs to the state, and the finders are only entitled to something like ten percent of the value. Mind you, that would still make us multi-millionaires."

She sighed. "I suppose I could make do with that."

"The other thing is this – these treasures will have to be moved to somewhere safe and you and I aren't going to be able to find the right place and move the stuff on our own. Jackie is president of this semi-secret organisation *Vendredi Treize*. They will be able to provide safe storage, and the facilities to move the treasure into it without risk. I promise you that you will be told what is happening to it and what rights you have to a share of it. Jackie will be able to do all that for us."

"All right." She snuggled against him. "I agree with what you say."

Philip noticed that the torch was growing dim. He leaned down and picked it up.

"I think we'd better go and leave these fantastic treasures alone for now, before your battery runs out." He put an arm round her trembling body and led her away from the fantastic collection of wealth. When they reached the door, they pushed it tight shut behind them and forced both the bolts back into their original place.

Half an hour later they got back into the chateau courtyard. He had fashioned loops in the rope which made it possible for them to climb the slippery wall. It was still well before lunch time, and nobody could have any suspicion of what incredible sights they had just seen. It didn't occur to him as being strange at the time, that Candice should be so willing to leave her new-found wealth behind.

48

That afternoon Philip emailed Jackie:-

Candice and I have discovered something sensational. I cannot let you have any details over the internet. I need you to come and view it and let me have your opinion. Can you come this weekend? I promise you that this is not just a ploy to persuade you to see me again before you are ready

He had persuaded Candice that they should both continue to work as normal until Jackie had viewed the treasure and agreed with them how it should be secured. He had pointed out to her, that if the slightest whisper got out, they would all be in serious danger from criminals and treasure hunters. So he continued to prepare the house for Jackie's arrival, and she carried on with her work classifying the Templar archives. At the end of the day's work, he went to see Candice out of the chateau and lock up behind her. She had a proposal.

"Philip, I've thought a lot about the treasure during the day and I'm worried about the chateau being left unlocked even when I am working here. I know that I am near the courtyard, but I cannot see if anybody comes in unless they shout or make a noise. Of course, I often go and check whether there is anyone snooping round and I haven't seen anyone so far. But with all that wealth down in the cellars, I think the gates should always be locked, even when I am working in here."

"OK. Candice," he agreed, "I can open up to let you into the chateau in the morning, then lock the door behind you so that there would be no risk of anyone getting in."

"But then I'd be shut in here all day. I wouldn't be able to get out if I wanted to."

"Of course I'd come and open up for you if you wanted to join us for lunch."

"But what if I wanted the toilet, or any of the other things a woman needs?"

He grinned. "Well, you've got your mobile. If you suddenly wanted to get out for any reason, you could ring me and I'd come across to let you out."

"But you might not always be there. If you were, you'd have to hang around while I went and until I came back. That seems a waste of your time and might also raise suspicions among the others."

Philip looked at her. "What are you suggesting Candice?"

"If you gave me the key after you'd opened up for me in the morning, I could lock myself in, and I would be able to get out without troubling you if I needed to. I would make sure I didn't leave the place unlocked when I wasn't there"

"I see. It would be important that you only unlocked the door each time you went through it, and you locked up behind yourself immediately Then when you finished in the evening, you'd have to let me have the key before you went home."

"Of course I would."

Philip agreed it was a good idea. He was a bit anxious himself about leaving the place open during the day, even though the risk of anybody secretly entering the chateau and finding their way to the treasure in the underground room was remote. Nevertheless, it would be sensible not even to run that slight risk.

"OK," he agreed. "We'll do that tomorrow." He smiled at her. "Now you can go home and celebrate your riches." He gave her fifty euros. "Buy yourself a really good bottle of vino to toast a very successful day."

"I wish you were coming with me." She put her head on one side. "You ought to be taking me out for a slap-up meal so that we could celebrate together."

"And what do you think Jeanette and Armand would make of that? How could we explain the reason for such a party?"

"I don't know. Surely you could think of something – perhaps because we had successfully moved the archives up to this room."

He thought about it for a moment before he shook his head. "I think it would be too dangerous, Candice. With a few drinks inside us, one of us might let something slip which we would regret. I've emailed Jackie and asked her to come down this weekend to discuss what we've found – without telling her any details, of course. Once we've sorted out something with *her*, that will be the time to celebrate."

"All right. I suppose so."

When he switched on his laptop that evening, he saw a reply from his fiancée. She actually sounded enthusiastic.

This is most intriguing, Philip. I will be with you as early as I can on Sunday morning. I was going to stay with Charlotte for the weekend anyway. The poor dear has been knocked sideways by Hector's death. I think she was really in love with him. Bye, Jackie.

The email filled him with mixed emotions. It was good that he would be seeing her again soon, and she sounded less hostile than before. On the other hand, she was making it clear that she wouldn't be spending any nights at Rennes this time. Also, he was bitterly aware that she could manage to take a weekend off to spend with her aunt, but couldn't spare the time to be with her fiancé. He guessed she wouldn't be prepared to come to join him until he had got rid of Jeanette.

Of course, he acknowledged to himself, the solution lay mainly in his own hands. He knew that Jeanette had had many lovers in the past. She was an attractive, sexy woman and she would doubtless have no problem in finding another man to share her bed. So he didn't have to feel too sorry for her. He took a deep breath as he switched off the computer and went downstairs to confront her.

"Jeanette," he said to her, "I'm afraid the time has come for me to make a decision."

She gazed at him but made no comment.

"Jackie has made it clear to me that she will not come back to Rennes while you and I are sleeping together." He took a breath as she remained silent. "So I'm going to end our affair." He hurried on. "You always knew it was only temporary, and I was very grateful to you for providing me with love and affection at a time when I really needed it. I realise you're going to think of me as a first-class shit for taking advantage of your generosity and then walking away as soon as my fiancée demands it." He paused. "But I'm afraid the time has come to end our relationship."

There was a long silence before she spoke. "So what are you going to do?" Her voice was calm. There was no anger, no tears.

"I've decided I'm going to move out of the cottage. Tomorrow I'm going to move into the bedroom we've furnished in the house. And I'm going to do it alone. You can stay here as long as you wish, but I am not going to share your bed any more after tonight. If you are willing to remain as my housekeeper, I will be very grateful, but we will not be lovers any longer."

She pouted. "When Jackie comes back, she will insist that I am kicked out all together."

"I don't know about that."

"That's *if* she comes back, Philip." She even gave a little smile. "Perhaps I'll stay around and look after you for a while. If she doesn't return, you may be pleased to start sharing your life with me again."

He looked down at the floor. "Thank you, Jeanette. It's possible you may be right."

And that night they had their final heart-rending love-making session.

49

It was already dark, when Anna Sondheim called at Candice's *chambre d'hôte* and threw a few pieces of gravel up at the window to alert the girl to her arrival, as was her practice. The old couple who rented out the room were downstairs watching the television with the sound turned up, because the husband was deaf. So they didn't hear the German's arrival. Candice had been given her own key to the front door, and went down to let Anna in.

"Please tread softly," she said. "I don't think they will hear you, but it's as well to be careful."

As soon as they were settled, seated side by side on Candice's bed, Anna asked. "Do you have news for me since Mademoiselle Blontard has been to see you?"

"Yes, I have fantastic news. I have found the Visigoth treasure."

"That is good," responded the German in her formal way. "Is this treasure valuable? Will it provide enough funds for the establishment of the party on the political scene in Germany?"

"Oh, yes. It will be enough to make the party the richest in Europe."

"So," Anna's eyes opened wide, "when can we receive this treasure?"

Candice hesitated for a moment. "I think that getting it out will be difficult. So I have made a careful plan."

"What is this plan that you have?"

"The way to the treasure is through the chateau where I work. Only two people know how to get to it."

"Who are these people?"

"One, of course, is myself. The other one is the Englishman, Philip Sinclair, who has the only key to get into the chateau."

"The way in is locked?"

"Yes." Candice smiled. "But I have found a way to get the key from him during the day. He agreed to let me have it when I suggested that I should lock myself inside the place during the day, so that nobody should come in while I was working there.

You see, the room where I work does not look directly on to the entrance gate or to the courtyard which they would pass through."

"You say you have the key during the day. Where is it in the night?"

"Ah. Philip has it with him, and he is sleeping with a Paris poule, so it would be difficult to get it from him during the night." The girl shook her head. "No, I have a better idea. I want you to walk along the footpath below the chateau at exactly half past nine on Wednesday morning. I will put the key in a bag and throw it down to you, so that you can take it and have a copy cut. Then you must return both of them to me at twelve-thirty, so that I can let myself out and give the original key back to Philip."

"How do I find this path?"

"I have made a little map for you." She handed over the piece of paper on which she had drawn a rough sketch of the village. "You should park down here where they want the tourists to stop. Then you will walk up the road to this bend, and the footpath forks off here to the right – do you see?"

Anna nodded.

"If you follow the path round the hill, you will soon see that you are below the chateau. Most of it is ruined, but at the far end you will see the wall is higher and there are two window openings. I will be at the right-hand one when you look up."

"I understand."

"Of course, you must make sure that there is no-one on the path when you are waiting for the key to dropped, but very few people go along the path. Also, it is important that you return the keys to me at precisely half past twelve because I usually meet the others at lunch time. When I see you come along the path alone, I will lower the bag to you, and you must put the keys in it for me to pull up."

Anna nodded. "I see. I will have to visit Limoux tomorrow to find a place which can cut keys, so that I can have it cut straight away on Wednesday when I take it in. I will only have three hours."

"That's plenty of time. It takes less than half an hour to drive to Limoux."

"Very well. What do you plan to do when we have got the copy of the key?"

"I've been thinking a lot about that. Most of the treasure seems to be odd shapes of gold which Philip says were melted when the Jewish temple was burned down by the Romans. I think this should be put into kitbags. You should get at least twenty small ones because the gold is very heavy. If you carry them to below the same window at eleven o'clock on Wednesday night, I will lower a rope to you, and you can loop it through the straps on the kitbags and I will pull them up. I will then have all day on Thursday and Friday to fill them up with this gold. Do you follow me so far?"

"Yes – Wednesday, Thursday, Friday. Why not tomorrow?"

"That is because I want Philip to have confidence in leaving the key with me. I think he may decide to check up on me tomorrow, and so I want to make sure that I am doing plenty of work, cataloguing the archives for Mademoiselle Blontard. After that, I think he'll leave me alone." She smiled. "There are certain clothes which I wear that he finds very sexy. So I will make sure I only wear ordinary clothes tomorrow."

"Humph!" Anna didn't seem to find this at all amusing. "So what do we do when you have filled these kit-bags on the Friday?"

"Then you should drive here in a big two-tonne van - a Mercedes Sprinter or something similar – and park it in the same tourist car park. You should do it at eleven o'clock at night and bring two strong men with you to carry the bags back to the van when I lower them from the window. I think there will be more than a tonne of gold and I believe it will be worth over forty million euros. It will also be unidentifiable."

"Forty million?" Anna suddenly found herself short of breath.

"So," asked Candice, "do you approve my plan?"

"Yes. Yes, of course I do."

"Can you get the bags and the men? You will have more than three days to get them to come here from Germany."

"That is no problem. I expect Heinrich will also want to come himself."

"Can you remember what arrangements we have made?"

Anna could remember everything. She was good at that sort of thing. She repeated all the days and the times and the items that were required so that Candice was certain she would carry out her part without a hitch.

"Then I will see you down on the footpath at nine-thirty on Wednesday morning. Now you should go before the old couple finish watching their television programme and decide to go to bed."

Having seen Anna out, Candice returned upstairs slowly, deep in thought. If things worked out as she had planned, she would probably empty at least six of the chests. Then she would have carried out the wishes of her great grandfather without spoiling her own chances of becoming gloriously rich. When Philip and Jackie came to check them and found them empty, she hoped they would assume that the gold had been removed by the priest who became wealthy in the 1890's. There would still be plenty left for her and Philip to share. Perhaps, once she was rich, she would be able to steal him away from Mademoiselle Blontard who didn't seem to be willing to put any effort into keeping her man.

50

Jeanette asked Armand to call on her next morning after Philip had moved his belongings across to the house. She had accepted his offer of remaining as his housekeeper, although she privately thought that arrangement wouldn't last long, if he managed to persuade his fiancée to return to Rennes-le-Chateau.

Armand had shared Jeanette's bed in the past so his approach to her was familiar.

"What do you want to talk to me about, sweetie?"

She smiled at his use of the name he had often called her in the past. "You know that Philip has moved into the double bedroom in the house – the room he has been preparing to share with Mademoiselle Blontard."

"You mustn't get too upset about that, sweetie. You always knew that your time with him was temporary and that his fiancée would come back sooner or later."

"Oh, yes." She shrugged. "I have accepted that he would want to drop me as soon as it seemed likely that Jackie would return."

"So what do you want me to do? Do you want to go back to Paris?"

She shook her head. "Not yet. I have agreed to stay on in this cottage and be his housekeeper until Jackie returns. She will probably throw me out when she comes back." She smiled at him. "When that happens, I would be grateful if you would see that I am all right. Oh, I'm sure that Philip would take me back himself, but I don't want to trouble him and perhaps cause another scene."

"OK. Well, as long as you give me a couple of days notice, I will be happy to take you back to the big city. When you're ready, just give me a call."

Jeanette took a breath. "But that's not the reason why I wanted to talk to you, Armand. The real reason is that I'm worried about the girl, Candice, and the influence she is having on Philip."

"What influence?"

"Well, I've been close to him emotionally for several weeks now and I can sense a change in him. I don't know any other way of explaining it."

"But what makes you think that Candice is involved? I would have thought it was much more likely to have been the row he had with Mademoiselle Blontard on Sunday that would have upset him."

"That's just the point. It's part of the reason why I'm worried about Candice. On previous occasions when he's had a problem with Jackie, he's been even more loving towards me for the next few days. It was as if he was wanting me to make up for the lack of her affection. But this time he has been different. I feel as though he has been getting his consolation elsewhere."

"What makes you think that?"

"I asked Albert, when he came in this morning, where Philip was yesterday morning and he said he didn't know. Apparently, he wasn't working in the house, and Albert assumed he'd either gone out shopping or that he was somewhere in the chateau." She pursed her lips. "Well, I know he wasn't shopping because I had taken the pick-up, with his agreement, to get the week's supplies. So where was he?"

"Oh, do you think he was consoling himself with Candice instead of you?" Armand gave a twisted grin. "I must say she's an attractive bird. I wouldn't mind trying her myself."

Jeanette ignored him. "I did wonder whether it was rather more than just being helpful to her, when they started working those strange hours, although I never actually saw any evidence of him having sex with her at that time. But that soon passed, and he didn't seem to change his attitude to me when things returned to the normal routine after a few days." She took a breath. "I would just like to know what he did yesterday morning and why he sent Mademoiselle Blontard an email later, asking her to come back next weekend. I feel there's something suspicious going on, and I think that girl is somehow involved."

"Why don't you ask him?"

"Because I don't want to make him lie to me. He has never actually done that until now."

Armand sighed. "Do you want me to ask him?"

She shook her head. "I don't think so. All I want you to do is just keep an eye on him. I want to make sure he isn't being led into danger. I can't be so close to him, now that he has moved across to the house, so I want you to help me look after him if he has any problems. Between us, perhaps we can protect him from any dangers that Candice may be leading him into."

He looked at her strangely. "Are you sure you aren't getting worried, because you won't be there for him to talk to? After all, he is a fully grown man. He ought to be able to look after himself."

"When it comes to facing up to the wiles of a cunning woman, he's still no more than a baby."

He chuckled. "You'd know about that, wouldn't you?"

"Yes, I would." She laid a hand on his arm. "I'm not asking you to hold his hand all the time. Please just keep an eye open to make sure he doesn't do anything stupid."

Ambrose took a breath. "OK, I'll see what I can do."

He went back to his work in the house, a slightly worried man. He knew Jeanette was no fool when it came to judging men.

51

A few days later Philip admitted to himself that, since he had moved across to the house, he hadn't been sleeping very well. He was perfectly satisfied with the layout of the bedroom. The bed was comfortable. He was working like a maniac every day, to make sure as much of the house as possible was ready for occupation, so as to try to impress Jackie. But somehow, he was finding it difficult to get to sleep at nights.

He was honest enough with himself to admit that a part of the problem was that he no longer had Jeanette to share his bed. He had become used to an hour's lovemaking at the start of the night and then dropping off to sleep, cuddled up to her soft, voluptuous body. Now he was left alone with nothing to take his mind off his thoughts.

Of course, the discovery of this huge new treasure in company with Candice, and decisions on what to do about it, weighed heavily on his mind. Since he had come to the Languedoc he seemed to have been experiencing one adventure after another. He was beginning to wonder whether he would ever be able to settle down to the simple hum-drum existence which he guessed would suit him best. All he wanted to do now, was to hand over the problems to someone else, and concentrate on the slow business of building his new life in this beautiful part of the world.

On the Friday evening he was feeling exhausted from lack of sleep and over-work. He ate the meal Jeanette had prepared for them without really tasting her delicious cooking and downed about three glasses of wine. Then he announced to the others that he was feeling tired out and wanted an early night. Armand, Jeanette and Jean-Luc looked at each other and agreed he needed the rest. When he got back to the house, he was feeling so weary that he dragged off his clothes and tossed them on the chair by the dressing table, climbed into bed and just crashed out.

However, he didn't get the full night's sleep which he expected. He was awake again before midnight, his immediate exhaustion alleviated, and was once again plagued by wondering what was going to happen in the next few days. After half an hour of tossing and turning, he acknowledged that he wasn't going to drop off again, and he got out of bed and wandered across to the window. It occurred to him that one of the things that was keeping him awake at night, was the fact that there was too much light coming in from the summer sky outside. He decided that tomorrow he would get some curtains to pull across the window during the night. Or perhaps Jeanette would be willing to make them for him if he asked her nicely

He looked out on the sleeping yard, now deserted except for the pick-up which was parked just outside the front door. The scenes of activity during the day were stilled. Then suddenly he came alert. There was a person walking silently along near the chateau wall. It was quite a slim person – just about the size of Candice. In fact, he was almost sure it *was* the girl, when she stopped at the pedestrian gate. She fiddled for a moment, obviously in the act of opening the door, let herself into the chateau, and gently closed it behind her.

Philip was astonished. Surely, she had given the key back to him when she finished work this afternoon. He went over and checked his trouser pockets. Sure enough, it was still there. She must have got another key from somewhere. How she had done it he didn't know, but one thing was for sure - her secret arrival in the middle of the night meant she was up to no good. Was she trying to make off with some of the treasure for herself, or was she merely going to gloat over the money she was going to get, as a result of the astonishing discovery they had made?

Whatever her aims, he decided he must follow her to check what she was doing. Hastily, he dressed and made sure the real key was in his pocket. He would need a torch and it took him several minutes to check through his bags, which were still unpacked, before he found it. He checked the batteries and they seemed to be in good condition. Then he carefully descended the stairs and gently let himself out of the house. He didn't want to wake Armand at this late hour. He noticed, once he was outside, that the night was mild, and he had no need of a sweater. He crossed the yard to the pedestrian door into the chateau. It was locked. Candice clearly wasn't intending that anyone should follow her.

Philip took out his key and unlocked the door. He locked it behind him and crossed to the rooms where she had been working. There were stacks of archives now on the table, all ready for cataloguing and filing, but of course the girl wasn't there. She had obviously gone to look at the treasure. He went to the steps down to the basement. Once again, the barrier had been pulled aside. Flashing his torch from time to time to avoid obstacles, he made his way down the stairs and through the large cellar. A further flash of his torch showed where the rope had been tied at the top of the sloping wall as before. He laboriously climbed through the rubble of the ruined building to the top of the wall and peered over. There was no sign of Candice, but he could see a faint glow coming through the door from the tunnel. That surely meant she was in the treasure room.

He slid down the wall, carefully avoiding making a noise, and crossed to the door. Without difficulty he eased himself through it and crept along until he reached the side tunnel. The door was now wide open and there was a can of oil standing beside it which she had obviously used to lubricate the bolts and hinges to make them easier to open. She had also brought a portable, battery-operated lamp which stood on one side of the room. He approached the door. When he could see inside, Candice was just using a small crow-bar to lever up the lid of one of the chests. Even as he watched, she pressed it down hard and the lid sprang open, revealing more of the melted clusters of gold. He saw she was wearing gloves and now she reached into the chest and lifted out several of the strange shapes and stuffed them into a small kitbag leaning against the chest.

Philip at last found words. "Candice," he asked, "what are you doing?"

"Ugh," she gasped and jerked round to look at him. "Oh, Philip, you scared me half to death."

"What are you doing down here in the middle of the night?" he repeated. "Just tell me what you're playing at."

"I – well I – er – I wanted to look at the treasure again, just to make sure it wasn't some ridiculous dream I had been through." She beamed at him. "Look at it, Philip. All this lovely gold is ours."

"You seem to be doing rather more than looking at it. You were breaking open one of the chests and putting the gold into that kitbag. Why are you doing that?"

She managed an extreme sort of shrug. "Well, it will have to be put in bags some time. We won't be able to get the chests through that blocked doorway, so we'll have to take it out in smaller bags."

"I don't know about that. Do you think you'll be able to get those kitbags through the doorway as it is at the moment?"

"Oh, yes. I've tried it. I've . . ." She paused, possibly thinking she'd said too much. Now she stood upright. He noticed she was wearing her gossamer-thin overalls again. She pulled the zip down to her waist. "Oh, Philip. Make love to me again. This gold makes me feel ever so sexy." She moved close to him, her back arched, her overalls pulled back to reveal her brassiere. "I want you to do it to me again, Philip, on top of one of the boxes."

That comment was a mistake. It made him look beyond her to the other chests and he saw several more of them had obviously been opened. The lids were lying back, showing they were empty, or in some cases half-closed. He counted seven of the boxes that had been pulled forward and prised open. They weren't the ones which had been opened previously by the priest all those years ago.

"How many of these chests have you emptied, and what have you done with the gold that was in them?"

"Oh – oh, it's all safe. I have moved it out to the place near the window, so that it will be easy to get it out when we're ready."

"Wait a minute, Candice. You've clearly been working on this for a while. You haven't told me anything about it. It's obvious that you've been planning to make off with some of this gold for your own benefit."

"Don't be silly, Philip." She moved up close against him and unclipped the strap of her bra and pulled it away to bare her chest. She took his hand in hers and placed it against her breast. He could feel the hardened nipple, just as though she really *was* sexually excited by the sight of the masses of gold. "Come on. Let's make love."

This time he found her much easier to resist. He shook his head. "I'm sorry, Candice. I don't like you doing this sort of thing behind my back. I want a full explanation from you."

He pushed her away and walked over to the kitbag and lifted it. It was quite small but was already heavy. He guessed it must weigh at least fifty to sixty pounds – perhaps half a hundredweight or twenty-five metric kilos. Of course, gold is very heavy. He knew it is also extremely valuable. This bag alone probably contained the equivalent of more than a million pounds.

"How many of these bags have you filled?"

He turned back to face her, and what he saw made his blood run cold. Just behind her stood a huge man.

52

"Who the hell is this?"

Candice jerked round. "Aah! How did you get up here?" Then she changed and spoke to him in what Philip guessed was German.

"Candice?" he asked, "Who the hell is this guy'"''

"I will ask how he came here." She spoke further to the man, and he responded in German. "He says he climbed up the rope:"

"What rope?" Then it finally dawned on Philip. "You've been lowering this gold out of the window in these kitbags, down to some group of Germans. That's what you've been doing. You're giving it away to Germany."

"No. Not to Germany."

"To some German set-up. It's these neo-Nazis, isn't it?" Suddenly he spat out at the huge German, "Heil Hitler!" and thrust his hand forward in the Nazi salute.

The other man instantly responded, "Heil Hitler." His arm shot out and he came to attention and clicked his heels together.

"So you're a member of this group and you're financing their extreme right wing campaign," Philip accused her.

Candice's face was ashen, as she realised she could no longer lie to him. "It is true," she admitted. "My great grandfather was a prominent member of the National Socialist Party of the Third Reich. In his last years he made me understand that modern Germany is making itself the servant of the rest of Europe. He made me swear I would continue the work of the Nazi movement which is the only way to save Germany."

"And that is why you inveigled yourself into Jackie's organisation and made yourself so sexually attractive to me?"

She hung her head. "Yes."

The great bull of a man who was standing behind her suddenly asked a question in German. It sounded as though he was swearing. But Candice's answer shut him up. It appeared to Philip that she now seemed to be the one in charge.

Philip took a deep breath. "Well, it's out in the open now. What are you planning to do – take all this gold and pour it into the neo-Nazi coffers?"

"Not all of it. Just as much as is necessary to make the party wealthy enough to fight the next election, when everyone will wake up to the way our politicians have been pulling the wool over our eyes."

"And what about the rest?"

"You can have it." She spread her arms wide. "These objects are no good to us. Only the loose gold is worth having. The rest is yours, for you to become famous when you tell the world about what you have found."

"And you think I can't stop you giving all this wealth to this group of yours?"

"That's right. It's really only my share of the treasure we found. I have chosen to give it to the Nazi party. In a few days this gold will be melted into bars and will be in the vaults of a Swiss bank and Fasces45 will be credited with millions of euros to fight its campaigns."

Once again, the big German made an unintelligible comment, but she silenced him with a wave of her hand.

Philip said, "And *you* will have disappeared with the rest of the gang."

"Yes." She looked straight at him. "I am sorry, Philip. I would have liked to have spent more time with you. At first, I thought you were just a stupid Englishman, but I have seen that you are much more than that. I think I have begun to realise why the British are the only people that Germany can't defeat."

"Candice. This gold is the property of the French state. It is so valuable that, if you make off with any part of it, they will pursue you to recover it. You will never be allowed to get away with it." Although he knew, that once it was melted down into gold bars, it would be impossible to locate the source.

"It will do them no good to try to follow me," she said. "The girl Candice, who you have come to know so well, will soon cease to exist. I will destroy her papers and once more I shall become the German woman with a name that is known only to the people in my homeland. Nobody will believe that Candice even existed."

"Jackie knows about you. Armand and Jeanette and Jean-Luc have got to know you well."

"So – they may tell the police whatever they wish. You have no photographs of me. There are no papers to prove who I am. In the new Europe without borders, I can go where I wish and simply show my German identity card if I am asked." She actually smiled. "I may have a great future in front of me. Who knows, if my party is successful in the elections, I may be the next chancellor of our great nation and then I shall make the whole of Europe perform as Germany instructs them. Only Great Britain will have escaped from us again."

Her proclamation made Philip smile. "Candice – or whatever your real name is – I think you're a little bit mad."

"No. I am *not* mad. Adolf Hitler was mad. He made war with America. He tried to invade Russia. He set out to exterminate the Jews. Those actions were mad. I have learned from his mistakes. My Germany will not make war on anybody. It will take over the whole of Europe by working harder and becoming wealthier than these other lazy nations like France and Spain and Italy and we will be cleverer than the backward nations like Poland and Romania. We are simply better than the rest of Europe and so we will dominate the continent."

Philip had to admit there was a kind of crazy logic in her comments. Germany was certainly the nation with the largest population and the biggest economy in Europe. He couldn't see France or Italy keeping up with Germany. Perhaps, he admitted to himself, he was looking at a woman who would sweep to international power over the continent. Candice was no longer the sexy, seductive little kitten he had come to think of her as. Now she was a tall, still sexy, but strident Amazon. He could well imagine that any man associated with her would soon come under her power.

Her chest was rising and falling as she gazed at him with her bright, almost manic eyes. "So, are you going to be with me?"

"I'm sorry, Candice. You must know I could never be a party to all that extremist stuff."

"Philip!" She glowered at him. "If you will not be my friend then you will become my enemy."

Was she suggesting he might be in danger? Somehow, he couldn't believe that this girl, who had offered him her body and who had encouraged him to make love to her, was so unfeeling that she was going to have him killed.

There was an explosive comment from the man behind her, but she silenced him.

"Carl, here, says we should kill you. But I have decided to save you. One day you may be useful to me, and I am not in the game of killing. That is too clumsy and leaves too many enemies behind." She swelled her chest. "No, we shall take these last two bags of gold and then we shall lock you in here. I will leave you with the light, although you would be sensible not to keep it shining all the time because I do not know how long it will take your friends to find you. As long as you are sensible, the air should last for several days, and I expect some will seep through the door from the tunnel outside."

"I´m going to get a bit hungry, aren´t I, and what about water?"

She shook her head. "I´m afraid there´s nothing I can do about that. Once the gold is safely deposited in our bank, I will telephone to Mademoiselle Blontard and tell her where you are. Or," she shrugged, "they may be clever enough to find you before then."

She gave an order, and the big German came forward and picked up the rucksack in one hand apparently without effort. As he went, he also lifted the one near the door in his other hand.

"How many of these bags have you taken."

"Just twenty-four. The rest is yours."

"So you´ll soon have twenty-four million euros in your National Socialist coffers, will you?"

"According to my careful calculations," she said," It should be closer to fifty million Enough to set a new fire alight in the political world in Germany, I think."

Philip prepared to launch himself at the girl as she turned to go. He had in mind that he might escape down the other tunnel towards the church crypt. They probably wouldn´t be bothered to follow him down there. Then he might be able to prevent them getting away with all the gold. However, she was ready for him.

"Stay where you are, Philip. My friend Carl will be back in a moment to shut and bolt the door."

Even as she spoke the big lump again appeared in the doorway.

She moved towards him and her eyes glowed. "You should join us, Philip. With you beside me, I could soon take over the leadership of the group. The present leader is a fat fool, but you and I would make Fasces45 a party to be reckoned with in politics. We would make the German people understand that our rightful place is to dominate Europe. If we took German money and support away from the European Union, it would collapse into bankruptcy. The other nations couldn't stand that. In the future they would have to do what we tell them, just to keep themselves afloat. I would become, not just Chancellor of Germany, but Chancellor of the whole of Europe." Her naked breasts rose and fell as she exposed her belief in her Aryan superiority. "You could be there by my side, Philip. You could be the one I came home to every night. You would help me plan the rise of the most powerful nation on earth. We would be much stronger than the Americans, who are riven by internal racial problems, or the Chinese, who are held back by their out-of-date political system. We would be rich. We would have all this wealth behind us. We would sire brilliant children and become the most powerful family on the face of the earth."

Philip was shocked by the megalomania radiating from her captivating eyes. It seemed to possess her exquisite figure. He thought again how like a leader of Amazons she was. He could almost believe the picture she was painting, but he wasn't in her thrall any more. He wouldn't allow her vision to impress him.

"Well, goodbye Philip." She gave a little smile. "If you would like to contact my group and maybe even join me in due course, our organisation is called Fasces45 and you will find us in Munich."

She turned and went out, and the next minute the door was closed, and he could hear the bolts being pushed home. He looked round. Now he was imprisoned with several emperor's ransoms. Much good did it do him.

53

Philip hadn't been quite as silent as he thought, when he let himself out of the house to follow Candice. Either that, or maybe Armand was a light sleeper. The young Frenchman sat up in bed and listened intently. He thought he could hear the sound of footsteps crossing the yard. He got up and went to the window. The moon was out, and the scene was remarkably light. He was just in time to see Philip letting himself into the chateau and closing the door behind him.

Armand stood there for a while wondering what he should do about Philip's midnight adventure. What on earth was the guy doing? Why should he decide to go into the place at this time of night? As far as he knew, nothing unexpected had been turned up in the last few days, since the archives had been moved up to ground level. In fact, Philip had shown little interest in the place since Candice had been established in there and had started on her job of cataloguing the archives. He sighed. Really, it was none of his business if the man should decide to go wandering round the ancient building in the middle of the night.

However, he then remembered the warning Jeanette had given him about looking after the young Englishman. Although he probably wouldn't be thanked for it, he decided he ought to go and check what the guy was doing. So he dressed and prepared to go out. As he went, he checked Philip's bedroom to make sure it wasn't a mistake in his mind, but he found the bed had been left in a jumble of bedclothes. Something had made him leave in a hurry. Now, feeling distinctly more worried, Armand went out into the yard and crossed to the chateau. The pedestrian door was locked. He shook it and called out "Philip?" a couple of times, but there was no response.

What should he do next? Then he had a bright idea. He knew that Lerenard was a very irregular sleeper. Perhaps it would be an idea to see if the big man was still awake. He set off up the village street to check. Sure enough, when he got to the house where Jean-Luc lodged, he could see a light was on in the ground floor room which he used as a sitting-room. Armand peered in through the uncurtained window and saw the guy was reclining in an armchair, reading.

He tapped on the window and Lerenard was immediately alert. Seeing the young Frenchman peering in at him, he got up and came to open the window.

"What is it?"

"I'm worried about Philip. About a quarter of an hour ago he suddenly got out of bed and went across to the chateau. He let himself in and locked the door behind him. I've been across and called out to him, but there's no reply."

"Well, that's surely his business. Perhaps he wants to explore when there's nobody around to ask what he's doing."

Armand shook his head. "No. He went out all of a sudden. His bed was in a mess It wasn't something he had planned to do."

"But what can *we* do about it?"

"I don't know exactly. Jeanette told me to keep an eye on him. She said something about him coming under the influence of Candice. I thought you might have some ideas."

Lerenard thought for a minute. "You say the entrance door is locked. Why don't you go round the footpath below the chateau? From there you can look up and see if anything seems to be happening in the cellars."

"Yes. I guess that's the only thing I *can* do."

"Wait a minute. I'll put on some shoes and join you."

He disappeared from the window and, a couple of minutes later, he came out of the front door carrying a torch and putting something in his pocket.

"I've brought a light in case we need it," he said. "Let's go down the hill to the lower end of the footpath."

They set off. It only took them a couple of minutes to reach the bend in the road, just below the point where the footpath forked up to pass beneath the chateau. As they neared the junction, Jean-Luc suddenly pulled Armand into the shelter of some bushes at the side of the road.

"Be quiet," he whispered.

The next minute a big, broad-shouldered fellow came out of the path onto the road. He was carrying a small rucksack on his back which appeared to be sagging under the weight of some heavy contents. The man set off down the road towards the tourist car park.

"What the hell's that?" breathed Armand.

Before they could move, a second stout chap came out, carrying another rucksack and following the first.

"And *where* the hell are they going?" asked Lerenard quietly.

They waited another couple of minutes, but no further men came.

"I think this is where we split up," murmured Jean-Luc. "You go up the path where these guys came from, but be ready to take cover if you see any more of them coming. I'll go down the road to see where they're going with their heavy rucksacks. We'll meet up back here in a quarter of an hour."

"OK." Armand set off up the path.

Lerenard went down the road. Where it straightened up to run down past the car park, he could see a large Mercedes van was pulled in just off the road and pointing down the hill. At this moment the back door was open, and the blokes were unshouldering the heavy rucksacks. They tossed them into the rear of the van where they landed with a thump which momentarily compressed the van springs. He could see there were a number of other similar rucksacks already in the back of the van. The situation looked extremely suspicious.

The two guys shut and locked the rear door and set off back up the road towards him. Lerenard melted into the shadow of the trees alongside the road. The two passed within a few metres, but they didn't see him. He noted that they walked quietly and there was no conversation between them, as they disappeared back up the footpath. He hoped Armand would hear them coming back and get out of their way.

As soon as the men had gone, Lerenard went down to the van, keeping to the verge to avoid leaving any footprints which might give him away. He circled the vehicle, checking the doors, and found everything was locked up tight. Although it was a two-tonner it was already well settled on its springs. When he pushed against the side, the dead weight of the van moved very little under his pressure. Lerenard went to the front of the vehicle and pulled the little package he had brought with him out of his pocket. He bent down and inspected the front tyre.

This was the sort of thing he was expert at. He opened the packet and took out a screw driver and a thin screw. He selected a point just below the tread pattern and carefully drove the screw through the depth of the tyre, then partly unscrewed it. He knew from past experience, that the pressure of air in the tyre would prevent the screw from coming out until the vehicle started moving. Then, within a few hundred metres, the tyre would rapidly deflate and go flat, making it impossible to drive any further. For extra result he decided to do the same to the other front tyre. The rear of the van had double wheels so there was no point in doing anything about those.

He started to go back up the road towards the bend but found a concealed place where the van was in sight. Then he waited to see what would happen next. About five minutes later the same two blokes came past his hiding place with two more rucksacks on their backs. There was a repeat performance of unlocking the back door, heaving the bags in and re-locking the van, before they returned up the path once more. After another ten minutes there again came the sound of people coming down the path. This time there were four of them – three big men and a smaller person struggling under the load of the rucksack he was carrying. Not very far behind them, he saw Armand was following. Lerenard hissed softly at him as he passed, and he came into the shadows to join the big man.

"They're making off with something heavy," murmured Jean-Luc. "Did you get to see what they were carrying?"

"No. I had to hide up a lot of the time because they were coming and going. As far as I could see these bags were stacked below the ruined part of the chateau, but I didn't get close enough to see what was in them."

"I think we ought to find out what they're doing, don't you?"

Jean-Luc hurried down the road with Armand following.

Meanwhile the last of the rucksacks had been loaded into the van and the rear door was closed and carefully locked. Then all four men went towards the front of the van. At that moment the small man looked back and saw Armand and Jean-Luc approaching. He made a comment to the others which resulted in them all leaping into the vehicle and slamming the doors. The engine was started up and they immediately set off. The driver accelerated down the hill.

Jean-Luc realised this sudden acceleration would stretch the tyres and expel his screws that much more quickly. He fancied he could see them going down even as the van reached the next bend in the road. It was going much too fast. The driver braked hard and swung the wheel over. But the vehicle didn't respond. The tyres completely collapsed under the additional pressure and the vehicle went straight on, bouncing over the slightly banked verge, and ploughed head-first at about fifty kilometres an hour into a large tree standing just past the bend.

There was a frightful, roaring impact. The van drove hard into the tree-trunk and the weight of the rucksacks in the back must have made them slide forward. It caused the front end of the vehicle to crumple and concertina into a fraction of what it had been before, as the ton and a half of rucksacks plunged into the passenger compartment, squashing the occupants against what was left of the inside of the front of the vehicle. With a tinkling of glass and other sundry shrapnel, the van came to a halt and settled on its chassis.

Jean-Luc and Armand found themselves running down the road towards the crash.

"Surely nobody can have survived that," gasped Armand.

"You're right. All four of them must have been killed. The driver was stupid. If he had approached the corner more gently, he would have been half-way down the next stretch of road before the tyres went flat."

Armand briefly turned his head towards Jean-Luc, not understanding what the man was talking about. But that was forgotten when they reached the wreck. Looking in through the shattered side window it was clear nobody would have survived the crash. The roof of the van had been driven down into the cab by the impact and one of the men had been cleanly decapitated. His body and that of the others had been mashed to a bloody pulp between the front of the cab and the mass of the heavy-weight rucksacks.

"Do you think Philip is one of them?" asked Armand.

"I don't know. Did you get a clear look at them?"

"No. I wasn't close enough."

Lerenard shook his head. "I think three of them were too big to have been Philip. I don't know about the fourth one. He was tall and slim, but seemed to be struggling with the weight of his rucksack."

"Because of his dislocated hip?"

"Perhaps."

He peered at what he could see of the rucksacks which had burst through the partition from the back. A couple of those had been ripped open and revealed the gleam of metal.

"My God! Gold!" uttered Lerenard.

"Philip never said anything about finding gold," said Armand.

"He wouldn't, would he."

"But to steal it away at night . . . It's not like him."

"Who knows what anybody is like when they discover a lot of gold?"

Armand pulled back. The scene made him feel as though he was about to faint. He thought he had a fairly strong stomach, but the horrifying sight made him feel he was going to be sick. He turned away from the crash to try to catch his breath. Then came the realisation of what needed to be done. He got out his mobile and started thumbing through his contacts.

"I think we need my friend Félix Martin here as soon as possible," he told Jean-Luc.

"Who is he?"

"Don't you remember? He's the detective inspector in Carcassonne who sorted things out when you were shot at le Bézu. He will need to sort this out as well."

"Very good."

Lerenard went round the front of the van, inspecting what remained of the front wheels of the vehicle while Armand was waiting to get through to the policeman. The young Frenchman wondered why the big man was so interested in the details of the wrecked vehicle. For himself he just wanted to get away from the mess, now silent except for the drip of some fluid out of the engine or perhaps the fuel system. He still felt as though he might be sick at any moment. This was one of the most awful sights he had ever witnessed, and it might be the death of a man he had come to regard as a friend.

At last, he got hold of Fèlix and told him what had happened. Although the inspector had been wakened in the middle of the night, he promised he would get there as soon as he was able to assemble a team to come and investigate the wreck. Armand passed on the information.

"You don't look very well," said Jean-Luc, coming back to him. "It's going to be a few hours before the police get here and you will clearly have a busy day tomorrow. I suggest you go and sleep for a couple of hours, and that will make you feel better. I will fetch you as soon as the detectives get here."

"Are you sure you'll be all right here on your own?"

"Oh, yes. I'll just make sure nobody tries to get too close to the wreck."

"Well, thanks."

Armand gratefully fled from the grisly scene. Nobody from the village seemed to have been awakened by the noise of the crash, but obviously somebody had to stay in the area to prevent anyone from interfering before the police arrived.

Lerenard was left on his own to search for the two little screws which had come out of the tyres somewhere in the van's career down the hill.

54

Jackie arrived soon after lunch on the Saturday. That was very prompt, considering that Armand had only phoned her at about six in the morning to tell her about the accident. The atmosphere at the crash site was funereal.

Inspector Martin had got there at about five-thirty. Since then he had gone a long way towards clearing up the scene of the crash. The area around the accident had been taped off to prevent the early visitors from getting too close to the wreck. A hole had been cut in the side of the van and twenty-four kitbags full of contorted gold shapes had been discovered. Two large police vans had been called from Carcassonne and, with the movements screened from public view, the kitbags had been transferred into them. It had been a grisly business prising some of them out from the mess of body parts and seat remains after they had been recorded by a white-faced police photographer. The bags were now safely locked away in Carcassonne police headquarters.

A breakdown truck had been brought in to pull the crumpled body of the van back from the tree trunk. That had allowed the remains of the bodies to be removed, separated so far as it was possible into four individuals, and taken to Toulouse pathology department. It was impossible to identify anyone at this stage although the pathologist seemed to think one of the dead might have been a woman, from the long blonde hair he had found.

A very quiet Jean-Luc had handed over contact with the police to Armand and had gone back to his lodgings in the village. The two small screws which he had found on the road after a long careful search were nestling in his pocket. He wasn't going to tell anybody about his contribution to the crash, but he was sick in his heart now that he realised that one of the dead might well have been young Philip.

Jackie pulled into the tourist car park, got out and went across to her young assistant.

"What on earth has happened, Armand?"

"You can still see the remains of the van which crashed into the tree. It was travelling too fast and didn't take the bend. Jean-Luc and I saw it happen."

"You said on the phone that people had been killed."

"Yes. As far as we know, there were four people in the van, and they were all killed."

"Do you know who they are?"

"Not yet. The van was carrying more than a tonne of loose gold packed into bags and these shot forward and squashed the occupants against the inside of the front of the van. The bodies are in too much of a mess to identify any of them until the pathologist has finished his job. However, he did say he thought one of them might be a girl with long blonde hair." He took a shuddering breath. "We're assuming that may be Candice."

"And Philip. Where is Philip?"

He looked at her and shook his head. "I'm sorry. We don't know."

"Oh, *mon Dieu*! Do you think he may have been one of the men in the van when it crashed?"

"Jackie – we just don't know." He shook his head again. "It was the middle of the night when it happened. We couldn't see the men clearly. We don't know whether one of them was Philip." He took another breath which was closer to a sob. "But the thing is, Jackie, he didn't sleep in his bed last night." The fact that he used her Christian name showed how upset he was.

"Oh, my God," she repeated. She turned away and gazed across the beautiful, sunny countryside without seeing any of it. As she stood with her mind silently contemplating whether she had seen the last of her fiancé, a car pulled up beside them and Félix Martin got out.

"Mademoiselle Blontard," he greeted her. "I'm afraid that tragedy seems to follow you around, not that you were here last night, of course."

"Have you got any answers for me, inspector?"

"Not yet, I'm afraid. I've just come from the pathologist in Toulouse, and he's no closer to identifying any of the deceased yet. We don't know where they came from, or what they were doing here."

"It's the gold that is most confusing," said Armand. "Nobody had said anything about any gold being found or why they were taking it away in the middle of the night? Where was it being taken?"

"The gold is all loose metal – unmarked. It's clear that these guys had found the stuff somewhere near here and were taking it to be melted down and formed into gold bars which would have been marked with their ownership. Once that was done, the gold would be theirs without dispute."

"There are many stories about gold being found in caves and holes around here," agreed Jackie. "But never in these huge quantities. You say there's more than a tonne here."

"That's right," agreed the inspector. "It's a big mystery, but . . ." he pulled his hand out of his pocket and held up a small plastic bag ". . . I think we may have one clue."

"What is it?" asked Armand, peering at the bag. "A key?"

"Exactly. The pathologist found it in the clothing that was attached to one of the bodies. We now have to find out who owned this key."

"Oh, *mon Dieu!*" Armand turned back to his boss. "I hadn't got around to telling you this, Jackie, but last night at about midnight I saw Philip let himself into the chateau and lock the door behind him. If that key fits the lock . . ." He left the rest unsaid.

"You think this is Philip's." She burst into tears

Armand put an arm round her shoulders, trying to comfort her. "It doesn't mean Philip was one of the men in the van. I certainly didn't see anything when they passed us, which would make me think he was one of them. The key may have been taken from him."

"But if it was, what has happened to him," she sniffed.

"I think we're getting ahead of ourselves," said Martin. "Before we make any more assumptions, I need to check if this key fits the lock on the door into the chateau."

However, ten minutes later, it was confirmed that the key did indeed fit the pedestrian door. The walk up to the chateau had calmed Jackie's emotions somewhat and she was able to speak normally.

"I suppose you want to retain this key as evidence, inspector."

"Indeed, ma'am, that is correct."

In that case will you please leave the door unlocked so that we can get into the place and look for my fiancé? There may be another crime for you to investigate."

"Very well."

"And are we permitted to change the lock so that we can maintain security here? There are some very valuable documents being held in here at the moment."

Martin looked at her carefully. "I will get the police photographer to take a photo of me using the key to unlock the door in case it is needed for evidence. He is down the road by the crash site. I will get him to come up here. After that, you may change the lock."

"Thank you," she said. "I will walk down with you and bring my car up here. Can you wait here until I get back, Armand?"

She returned a quarter of an hour later and was just getting out of her car when they saw Lerenard strolling across the yard towards them.

"I have recently taken a walk along the path below the chateau," he told them. "That is the path where the men carrying the rucksacks of gold came from."

"Oh, *mon Dieu*," cried Armand. "Why didn`t I think to do that?"

"Maybe because you haven´t had time," he replied. "The point is that I saw, when I got to a place just under the window, that there is a rope hanging down the castle wall."

"Is that from the window where Philip forced me to descend that nearly vertical ladder?" She shuddered at the memory.

"That´s right."

"So you think that may be how the gold was lowered to the men who were taking it to the van."

Jean-Luc nodded. "I would think it is very likely, wouldn´t you?"

"Wait a minute," said Jackie. "Philip sent me an email earlier in the week asking me to come down this weekend to look at what he called a sensational discovery. Perhaps it was a pile of gold which he´d unearthed in the cellars." She shook her head. "But why should he decide to carry it off in some van? Philip was already rich and he wasn´t a greedy man. Surely, he wouldn´t have asked me to come down and look at it, if he´d been planning to steal it."

She suddenly realised she was speaking of her fiancé as if he was no longer alive, and the realisation hit her hard. Her eyes filled with tears, and she found she couldn´t speak.

"I'm sorry," she mumbled. "I'm going to sit in my car for a while."

She hurried to the vehicle and fumbled with the door to get in. When she was sitting in the driver's seat, looking through the windscreen at nothing, she thought about the way they had parted the last time with bad feelings, largely caused by her selfish insistence that her career must come first. She had driven him into Jeanette's arms. Then she had refused his offer to try to heal the wounds, fuelled by jealousy of a woman who he assured her wasn't important to him. What had happened to the glorious love that they had discovered in each other only two or three months ago? And now it was too late to repair the fracture in their relationship. He had died before their wonderful love affair could be brought to fruition. She leaned her head on the steering wheel and sobbed her heart out.

Armand was watching her, feeling powerless to give her comfort. "As soon as Félix unlocks that door," he told Jean-Luc, "I'm going into the cellars to find what Philip discovered. If nothing else, I'll at least pull that rope up, so that there's no risk of anybody getting into the chateau by the back way."

55

Armand had to wait nearly half an hour before inspector Martin returned, bringing the photographer with him.

"Sorry, the guy was just in the middle of an important series indicating the way the front of the van had been driven in by the accident," he told his friend.

"OK, so now can you open up, please?"

As soon as the door was opened, he entered the chateau. Hearing a movement, he looked round and found Jackie was with him.

"What are you doing?"

"I'm coming with you."

"It's not an easy stroll," he warned her. "We have to drag ourselves up sliding heaps of rubble, hang on to ropes, let ourselves down slippery walls. It's tough going."

"You and Philip have done it several times."

"Yes, but we're men."

"And Candice did it as well."

"She was young and very agile."

She almost smiled at him. "Are you suggesting I'm not young and agile?"

"No, but . . ."

"I've taken my skirt and high-heeled shoes off and I'm wearing jeans and boots. I've got gloves to protect my hands. Is there anything else I need to change?"

He looked her over. Her hair was tied back in a ponytail and, with the exception of her fairly loose blouse which would expose her bra when she was reaching up to catch hold of beams and steel rods, he had to admit she was well enough prepared.

"OK," he agreed, "but I think you'll regret it when you start climbing through the ruins."

She shrugged. "Well, if it becomes too much for me, I can always turn back."

"Right. Follow me."

She kept up with him quite easily as he crossed the courtyard, descended the steps and made his way to the back wall of the central cellar. When they started crossing the rubble along the back wall, he suddenly realised he'd forgotten to bring a torch. It wasn't much of a problem for him, because there was enough light for him to remember where he had previously placed his feet, but it was more difficult for her, coming this way for the first time. He gave her his hand to hang on to, and tried to point out the best places for her to put her feet.

"Goodness," she said. "I agree it is a bit daunting, isn't it?"

"You haven't got to the tough bit yet."

That made her go silent as he led her to the place where she had to start climbing through the beams to try and reach the top of the sloping wall. He decided he should send her up first and show her where to catch hold of beams and place her feet in suitable footholds. He also gave her the occasional lift with his shoulder when she needed it. The ascent was a slow and painful business, and it wasn't helped when her loose blouse caught on a piece of projecting steel and sustained a large rip in the side.

"Oh, don't worry about it," she said when he tried to pull it across her half-exposed bra.

At last, they reached the top and she clung on and peered down into the empty room below.

"I'll go down here first," he told her. "Watch the way I do it and remember to hang on to the rope to slow down your descent."

He launched himself down the slippery slope and half-ran to the bottom, landing on the diminished heap of rubble to break his fall. He let go and turned back ready to catch her.

"OK. Do it just like I did, and I'll catch you at the bottom."

She launched herself down the slope. Unfortunately, she didn't slow herself down enough with the rope and she let go too soon. As a result, she crashed into him and sent him sprawling flat on his back with her landing on top of him. She managed a sort of a grin as she looked down at him.

"Well, you're not the softest of cushions, but thank you saving me from grazing my hands."

He was aware of her wonderful body stretched out on top of his, and thought how great it would be if they were together in bed at this moment. However, he accepted that Jackie was not for him at present. Perhaps, when she had got over the loss of Philip, she might be approachable. With a real sense of regret, he helped her get up.

"I can't see any heaps of gold," she said, looking round. "Or even any fragments which they might have missed."

Armand looked into the room where the Templar archives had been stored. That was empty. "This is just as it was after we had moved the archives out. There was certainly no gold around when we did that. There may be another secret store somewhere else. I think they must have gone through there." He indicated the partly opened door.

"I know where that leads. It's through that door that Philip and I originally found our way into this area. It opens into a tunnel which leads to the crypt under the church." She shook her head. "We explored the crypt pretty thoroughly, but there was no sign of any gold when we looked round there before."

"Where else could it have come from?"

"Perhaps it didn't come from the chateau cellars at all. Perhaps it was found in some cave or other hiding place further down the hill. It's possible that we have been reading too much into the fact that Jean-Luc has seen a rope hanging from this window."

Her comment reminded Armand that the rope should be pulled back up, and he went to do that before he forgot. While he was there, he peered under the ruins leaning against the outside wall, in case there was a route through there to another of the cellars. But that way was completely blocked by a cross wall after only a couple of metres. He was confident nobody had found any gold through there. Puzzled, he re-joined Jackie.

She was testing the door to the tunnel. "It looks as though the loose rubble has been cleared from behind this door," she said. "That big block of masonry still stops it from being opened fully, but I can pull it back more than I could before. See - I can get through the gap quite easily now, whereas before it was a real struggle. In fact," she did grin this time, "I had to take most of my clothes off before I could force my body through."

"That seems to suggest that somebody has recently cleared it with the object of searching the tunnel," he agreed. "Perhaps we ought to check it out ourselves."

"We haven't got a torch," she pointed out, "and I know from past experience that the tunnel becomes pitch black within a few metres of entering it."

"I still think we should take a look," he said. "Would you like me to go back and get a couple of torches?"

"Would you mind?"

"Of course not. I want to solve this mystery as much as you."

He went to the rope hanging down the sloping wall and fashioned a couple of loops for his feet as Philip had shown him. Using these he was soon at the top and, with a cheery wave, he disappeared back through the rubble.

Looking around after he had gone, Jackie decided to explore the tunnel as far as the light would let her. She slid through the gap in the doorway quite easily and started to feel her way along the right-hand wall. Suddenly she was startled by hearing a noise – a kind of semi-human yell. It froze her to the spot, and she felt a shiver run down her spine. Then the noise was repeated, and she could make out a kind of muffled call. She thought a person was shouting "Hey". That meant somebody was down here.

The noise made her move further forward. The light had almost completely faded now and she had to feel her way along the wall. Then suddenly she saw, away to her left, a slight gleam of light. After a moment's thought she realised that it came from a side tunnel which she and Philip must have missed in the darkness when they came along here before. She carefully moved towards the illumination. Soon she could see that it was a narrow strip of light at floor level. A few more paces and her hands came into contact with a rough timber surface. It was either a wooden screen blocking off the corridor or a closed door.

At that moment there came another call of "Hey". She was more or less certain that it was coming from behind the timber.

"Who is it?" she called back, enunciating the words clearly.

The voice replied to her from just the other side of the wood. "It's Philip. I'm shut in. Can you open the door?"

"Philip! Oh, Philip."

"Is that Candice? We've got to talk, Candice."

"No! It's Jackie."

"Jackie? Oh, my goodness. How did you come to be here?"

"You sent me an email asking me to come to look at something you had found."

"I know that. But how did you get to the other side of this door?"

"I climbed in with Armand."

"Ah. Is Armand there? He can probably slide the bolts back."

"He has gone to get a torch. But don't worry. I can do it."

"Are you sure?" There was a pause. "OK. There's one about a foot – I mean thirty centimetres – from the top and another about the same height from the bottom. I think they've been oiled because Candice had no trouble in closing them. If you grab hold of the loops at the ends you need to wriggle them up and down and pull them sideways to get them out of the hasps."

"OK. Wait a minute." She set about doing as he instructed. It was hard work, and she broke at least one fingernail, but she managed it after a struggle. She pulled at the edge of the door, but Philip pushed it open from the other side. Then she was in his arms.

"Oh, Philip! I thought you'd been killed."

"Killed?"

"There's been a dreadful accident just outside the village. A van containing a lot of gold crashed into a tree and four people have been killed. They think that one of them is Candice, but the other three were men. And we thought you were one of them."

He let go of her. "Candice has been killed?"

"The pathologist says one of the dead is a woman with long blonde hair. Why?" She looked at him suspiciously. "Is she important to you?"

He shook his head. "She was such a splendid girl. I was sure she was going to go far. Oh, what a dreadful waste!"

"Philip, why did this girl mean so much to you?" Then she looked past him for the first time. "Oh, *mon Dieu!*" She was gazing at the fantastic sight across the room.

"I think this may be the treasure of the Visigoths," he told her almost absent-mindedly. All he could think about was that the beautiful girl was dead. "How did she die?" he asked.

"What?" Jackie couldn't tear her eyes away from the treasure to look at him.

"Candice – how did she die?"

"Oh, she was in a big van full of gold which crashed into a tree. There were four occupants in the van. They were crushed by the bags of gold sliding on to them in the impact."

"Oh, my God! How awful."

She spared him a glance. "Why?" she repeated. "Was Candice important to you?"

"She had such a great future in front of her."

"Really? But she was trying to steal this treasure."

"Only a part of it." Then he suddenly remembered what was behind him. He turned to look at it with his fiancée. "Do you recognise the menorah? There are two of them. And at the end, beside the golden altar - do you think that could be the Ark of the Covenant?"

"My God!" she repeated as she advanced into the room. "What *have* you found?" She spoke more slowly. "This may be more important than the treasure we found at le Bézu. Do you believe these are the treasures taken from the Temple? If so, they are perhaps the most important things that have ever been found in the world." She paused. "Oh Philip, this is *horrifying*."

"What do you mean – horrifying?"

She turned to look at him. "Don't you see? The Jewish people will want to have these things back. They will want to re-establish themselves as God's special nation on earth. They will want to re-build the Temple on the Mount in Jerusalem to contain these awe-inspiring treasures. That will cause the most dreadful hatred among the Moslems surrounding Israel. It will further destroy any chance of peace in the Middle East. It will also profoundly affect the Christian Church." She shook her head. "The news of this discovery must *never* be allowed to get to the outside world."

"But there are many treasures here beside the Jewish relics. Look at all those chests. They are full of gold and silver and precious jewels. They are worth millions by themselves. Candice only emptied about eight of them and she reckoned the gold in those alone was worth more than forty million euros. We can't just hide it all away again."

"Why not? After the last few months, we are both wealthy people and you will be entitled to half the value of the gold found in the van. We don't need any more. For the sake of the peace of the world we must shut this door and never allow it to be opened again." She dragged at his arm. "Come on. Bring the light and close the door and get back to the room where the archives were found, before Armand returns. This must be a secret that only you and I know about. Some time in the future you will have to come back and build a wall across the entrance to this side tunnel so that nobody will ever realise that it is here."

Startled, Philip allowed himself to be shepherded out of the treasure room and, after bolting the door, back along the tunnel.

When Armand turned up, Jackie encouraged him to be delighted about her discovering Philip in the crypt of the church, where she said the lid had been forced off one of the tombs to discover the huge cache of gold.

"Because it was found in the church, under French law half the value of the gold will have to go to the Catholic Church and the other half to Philip, the surviving discoverer." She told them both. "That should be the end of the story."

Amid the general rejoicing of him being discovered alive and becoming a multi-millionaire, a dazed Philip allowed himself to be lowered after Jackie in a sling from the window by Armand who then pulled up the rope and said he would return through the ruins to the courtyard of the chateau. Climbing out of the sling, Philip found himself alone on the grassy path. Jackie had gone ahead up to the village without waiting for him. When he followed her, they met up in the yard outside the chateau. Armand got back at the same time.

"What are you planning?" Philip asked her.

"I must go back to Charlotte."

He was startled. "What – now?"

"Yes. The poor dear is still terribly upset about Hector's untimely death. I want to spend as much time as I can with her while she is so distressed." She looked at both men in turn, her eyes glazed. "There is nothing I can do here. So – goodbye."

She walked to the car and the two men looked at each other. Armand pulled a face and shrugged when he saw the misery in Philip's eyes. He thought there was nothing *he* could do about it.

Jackie drove out of the yard with just a glance in their direction, and Philip was left wondering why her brief affection for him, when she found that he was still alive, had so suddenly evaporated. His hoped-for reconciliation had got nowhere. She hadn't even looked at the house which was now nearly completed, or tried out the bed which so far only he had occupied. Despite his sudden riches, he felt a deep dissatisfaction with life.

56

For the next three weeks after Jackie had so precipitately returned to Paris, Philip bull-headedly concentrated on finishing off the house. The downstairs floors were completed and tiled throughout. The kitchen was finished, and the new granite worktops were built in. All the equipment was gleaming, but nothing was switched on. The shower room inside the front door had been completed and was in daily use. Upstairs all the rooms were finished. The en suite bathroom had been built in a corner of the large master bedroom and Philip used it to shower every evening before he went to his early, lonely bed. There were curtains up at the windows to keep out the light at night.

After a few days, Armand suggested that he should move out of the small bedroom and join Jeanette in the rented cottage where they ate their meals. Philip agreed this was a good idea for both of them. He hoped that Jeanette would be able to console herself with the young Frenchman. After all she had played the role of the man's wife for a while less than six months ago.

The whole of the house had now been decorated in fairly neutral colours. But the place was unfurnished except for the two bedrooms. Philip thought that it was the job of the woman of the house to choose the furnishings. Nothing happened in the chateau except that, after they had finished clearing the jungle at the back of the house to make way for a garden, Albert and Gaston were sent back to work on clearing rubble from the ruins. Jackie didn't send anyone to continue cataloguing the archives. So Philip put locked doors on the two rooms where they were stored and sheets of plywood were fixed over the small windows high up in the outside wall.

Following the accident, the remains of the wrecked van were cleared away. The pathologist was able to establish that the four bodies were of German origin. Anna Sondheim, who had been instructed to prepare a temporary garage in Limoux to store the van overnight, came forward and provided sufficient information about the individuals to enable the authorities to release the bodies. As a result, the remains of three large men and a slip of a girl were shipped back to a small town in Bavaria for burial.

Philip was given no details of the last resting place of the girl who he discovered bore the real name of Gretel Skorzeny.

The rucksacks of gold were shipped to Paris to be held with the nation's other reserves. Philip was given various forms to sign which acknowledged he was entitled to one half of the value when the economic department had weighed and priced it at current rates. Philip didn't inform the authorities that the treasure room actually lay beneath a piece of land beyond the boundaries of the chateau, and which might well be owned by the municipality. He decided that in due course he would make a gift of part of his own new wealth to the village. Perhaps Jackie would see to it that the Roman Catholic Church would do the same from its latest windfall. For now, the fact that he had become one of the top one per cent of the richest men in France meant nothing to him.

The transfer of ownership of the chateau had still not taken place and Philip was just wondering what he should do next, when a large silver Mercedes pulled into the yard. He recognised the man who got out as Alain Gisours, the president of TV France. Philip went out to meet him and they greeted each other warmly with hugs and kisses on cheeks, in the French manner. They had met and made friendly contact on several previous occasions.

"To what do I owe this honour, Alain?"

"Philip," said the visitor seriously, "I need your help."

"What do you mean?"

"This fiancée of yours, Jacqueline, has become quite impossible in the last few weeks. She is falling out with everyone. She is tormenting her wretched producer by finding all sorts of things wrong with the production, which she previously accepted as being perfectly satisfactory. We are having to take up valuable studio time with re-takes of silly little details which *he* assures me are unnecessary. She is starting to cause serious delays to the whole project. We are supposed to be having the launch in just over one week's time and, with progress the way it is at the moment, nothing is going to be ready."

Philip realised that Gisours was serious. For the chief executive of a national company personally to drive all this way to talk to him, obviously meant that the man needed his help.

"What do you want *me* to do?"

"I want you to come back with me and talk to her. You must make her see that her behaviour is unreasonable and damaging to everybody's future including her own."

Philip shook his head. "I don't think she will listen to me, Alain. She has been more or less avoiding me since she started work on this series. What makes you think she'll take any notice of me, if I turn up now and start laying down the law?"

Gisours looked into his eyes. "I have had many years of experience with all sorts of screen stars. I recognise her problem. She needs to be put in her place by the man she loves."

"What do you mean? I don't think she loves me, Alain. I believe she has decided I am not the man for her."

"Why do you believe that, Philip?"

"It's because I have told her, that if she can't spare time for me in her life, then I will have to make my own life without her."

"And what was her response to that?"

"She has turned her back on me. She has cleared off and left me to sort out the situation here all on my own."

Gisours looked at him speculatively. "Do you not think she is perhaps wanting you to *force* her to do what you require?" He shook his head. "Oh, she is used to having everybody fuss round her, trying to do just what she asks." He pointed a finger at the young man. "I think what she most needs is someone to tell *her* what to do, instead of waiting for her to make the decision."

Philip considered his comment. "I don't know."

"Well, my boy, you're my last hope. She won't take any notice of her producer."

"That's Louis, isn't it?"

"That's right. He has become disillusioned with her and has asked me to intervene, but this woman is so steamed up - I think that's what you English say, isn't it? – so steamed up about it all, that she wouldn't listen to what I had to say. She just kept going on about this and that little technical detail – all stuff that is way over my head - and details that can be easily solved by the various technicians we employ to sort out those things. So, after a half an hour or so, I decided the only person who would be able to sort her out was *you*." He grimaced. "What you need to do is come back with me and get hold of her and give her a jolly good fucking."

Philip's breath was taken away by the crudeness of the man's words. "Well, of course I'll try to help. I can easily break off here for a few days. There's nothing that's important for me to do here. But I can't promise I'll solve your problems for you."

"Well, if *you* can't make her see sense, then I don't know who can." He looked directly at the young man. "I may even have to cancel the series, and that would be an absolute disaster."

"My God, we've got to try to stop that."

Gisours took a breath. "Come on then. If we leave straight away, we can get back to Paris late this afternoon."

"Just let me pack a bag and I'll be with you in five minutes."

The extreme hurry that the chief executive was in, was soon clear to him. The minute they got on to the autoroute network near Carcassonne, he opened up the car's big engine and roared along at speeds of up to two hundred kilometres an hour. He had a pass which let him through the toll booths without stopping. No police appeared to halt his illegal, high-speed progress. Perhaps they had been warned to let him through. So, despite the inevitable snarl-ups as they got close to Paris, they were pulling into the forecourt of the Hotel Saint Michel at soon after five o'clock.

"What do I do about a room?" Philip asked.

"You share Jackie's, of course."

"Oh. OK. Is it the same one she had when I was last here?"

"It's been reserved exclusively for her for four months, whether she is in occupation or not."

"OK. I'd better shower and change."

"Wait a minute." Alain beckoned a chap standing nearby. They spoke for about half a minute before he came back. "They're doing a full dress rehearsal for the series launch ceremony, which will take place at six o'clock in the ballroom. Jackie's just being prepared now in all her finery. So come down at six." He gestured to the receptionist who was already holding a key card to hand to Philip.

57

Philip went down to the ballroom soon after six. Despite the fact that Alain Gisours had told him this was only a dress rehearsal, the ground floor of the hotel was in an uproar. Seductively clad ladies and gentlemen in dinner suits were milling about everywhere, chatting in groups, pushing towards the double doors that led to the ballroom, jealously eyeing each other up. He guessed that most of the people were probably staff and their families and friends, using this as an excuse to have a party at the expense of the company.

He realised immediately that he was spectacularly under-dressed in his light-weight blue suit over a white open-necked shirt, as he made his way into the large room filled with excited chatter. As he came through the doors, he immediately saw Jacqueline, standing with a group on a small stage at one side of the ballroom. She was wearing a full-length dress made from some sort of shiny gold fabric. It was sleeveless and backless and was held up at the top by a halter neck. The material was swathed across her front and was tied by a bow at the waist. The result was a display of a lot of the top half of her body. One knee projected through the waist-high slit at the front, hinting at an expanse of bare thigh. Her high-heeled shoes were of matching gold and her titian hair was piled on top of her head in some complicated concoction which revealed her long, fine neck. Her make-up was discreet, and she wore no jewellery except a pair of small diamond studs in her earlobes. In a room full of gorgeously, sexily clad women, she stood out as a star.

Philip moved towards her, easing his way gently through the crush which unwillingly allowed him passage. As he neared the stage, it was Alain who saw him first. A slight smile suffused the president's features as he tapped Jackie on the forearm and indicated her fiancé. Her mouth dropped open and the smile she had been bestowing on the crowd around her froze.

When he reached her, Philip said, "Jackie, we must talk."

"We certainly must." Her eyes were furious. "But we can't do it now. Come round tomorrow morning – but not too early."

"No. It has to be now." He moved close to her.

"I can't talk now, Philip, in front of all these people?"

"They can keep themselves amused for half an hour. This conversation can't wait." He caught hold of her wrist and suddenly the conversation seemed to die away.

"Stop it!" she hissed. "You'll embarrass me."

"It will only be embarrassing if you make a fuss."

Still holding her arm, he pulled her towards the doors to the reception area. In her astonishment she didn't try to stop him. The crowd seemed to part to let them through and nobody made any effort to obstruct them. In the entrance hall an empty lift was waiting, and he led her into it and pressed the button for the fifth floor. As the doors closed, he turned to face her.

"We must decide what is going to happen to our future."

She raised her head haughtily. "Nothing is going to happen while you are sharing your bed with that trollope."

"I moved out of the rented cottage a month ago and into our house where I sleep alone. Armand now shares the cottage with Jeanette. I did this well before the last time you came to look at the treasure, but you didn't even bother to look at the house which is now finished ready for you."

The lift halted and the doors slid open. He pulled her unwillingly across the corridor to door marked 513. He took the key card out of his pocket and opened the door. He drew her into the room and let go of her wrist as he shut the door, before he turned to face her.

"I can only give you five minutes," she insisted. "I must go back to my public. They will wonder what is happening to me."

"I think we can resolve this in five minutes."

"Very well. You can start by telling me why you were fucking Jeanette?"

"That is easily answered. She gave me the care and affection that my fiancée denied me. It was your idea that we should spend three months apart, deciding what we wanted out of our relationship. I have decided that I want love and affection and frequent periods of time together. Are you willing to give me that? If not, I will have to find it elsewhere."

She almost gasped. "Are you telling me that, if I don't let you bonk me at least once a week, you'll go back to fucking Jeanette nightly?"

"You put it crudely, but yes - that's exactly what I mean. If we're going to marry, I think I am entitled to a large slice of your time and your love. If you're not prepared to give me that, then we will have no future together."

"And what about my work? What about giving my audience the pictures and the - the entertainment they want?"

He shook his head. "I'm sorry Jackie, but you'll have to find a way to spare some time – a lot of time – for us, if our relationship is important to you."

"And then, when I came down last time, you told me that you were ever so upset by Candice's death. Were you having sex with her as well, while she was cataloguing the archives? Did you steal up on her and have her from behind over the table or something like that?"

Attack was the best form of defence. "Well, what about you having it away with Louis. As well as fondling your boobs, how many times has he been screwing you behind the scenes?"

"That is not what happened."

"So what did happen, or did Vauclus invent it?"

"Yes. It's true I was going to let Louis have sex with me, to pay you back for your infidelity. And he was more than willing, let me tell you. But before we could actually begin, the man with one arm came into the room. Louis tried to eject him and Vauclus knocked him out."

The shame of having to get the staff to remove the half-naked body washed over her again and angered her. She attacked him again. "So, not satisfied with fucking Jeanette, you admit you also had sex with young Candice."

"Only twice." He conveniently forgot the celebration in the treasure room.

"Only twice! Oh!"

Suddenly her fury burst out. She raised her fists and lunged at him. "You think you're entitled to as much sex as you want, but I'm supposed to remain a nun when you're not around."

He grabbed her wrists before she could hit him. "Jackie! It has been your decision that I'm not around."

Her furious, lovely face was just inches from his. He knew at that moment that she was the woman he desired above all others. He couldn't resist kissing the snarling lips. For a few seconds she struggled against him. Then suddenly she gave way. Her face softened, her striving arms relaxed. When he let go of her wrists, they slid round the back of his neck and the next second they were kissing voraciously. His hands ran down her back, slid inside her dress and fondled her bare buttocks. They explored her breasts through the thin, shiny fabric. He pushed her back to the edge of the bed. At last they broke the kiss.

"You're ruining my make-up," she complained.

"About time too."

His searching hand found the bow that fastened the front of her dress at the waist, and he pulled it undone. Under the dress she had nothing on but a white lace plunge bra and panties. He shoved her unceremoniously on to her back on the bed and undid his trousers and slid down his pants.

"What are you doing?"

"What do you think I'm doing?"

"But you can't do that now. I've got to go and talk to the people downstairs. They've come to see me."

"Later." He started to make love to her and she didn't protest any more.

Half an hour later she said, "Oh, why didn't you do this before, Philip? It would have saved us both so much heartache."

"When could I have done it before?"

"I wanted you to do it when you showed me round the house a couple of months ago."

He snorted. "It seemed to me that all you wanted to do was to get away to visit your aunt Charlotte. Of course I understood that she needed you at that time."

"I could easily have stayed another hour." She put a finger across his lips. "Or maybe even for the night."

"Well, from now on I want you to come to Rennes every weekend, for the whole weekend. If you do that, I won't even want to look at another woman."

"I can't come next weekend. It's the launch. It's what I was preparing for before you dragged me away and messed up my hair which took the hairdresser more than an hour to fix, and my make-up which took me nearly as long, and my dress which I expect you have creased terribly."

He didn't apologise. "In that case I will be here next weekend in my dinner suit to watch you and take care you don't let someone else run off with you. I will ask Alain for a ticket, and after the reception I will drag you up here and ruin your dress and your hair and everything else and give you something to remember."

"Have I got to wait until next week?"

"No. I'll be waiting for you when you come back after the rehearsal. But I'll undress you carefully before I start on you this evening."

"Do you mean I've got to go through this business downstairs in front of all the company staff, already embarrassed by the fact that my fiancé dragged me off to have his way with me, looking a mess and with the prospect of being raped for the second time tonight?"

"If you want to put it like that - yes."

"Oh. Well, I suppose I'll have to accept that's what you want."

"Now then, Jackie I have something else to say to you. Apparently, you've been messing everybody about terribly for the last three weeks; dreaming up unreasonable objections to all sorts of little details; making the life of your director and the rest of the staff hell. Now that's got to stop. Do you understand? You've done your part in preparing the series. You must leave it to the professionals to finish it off."

She looked at him suspiciously. "Did Alain ask you to come and do this to me?"

"He came and collected me. He asked me to try to make you see sense. He actually told me to drag you up here and force you to have sex with me."

"You're not one of his staff to order round."

"I didn't think I was going to carry out his instructions until I saw you looking so gorgeous down in the ballroom. That was when I decided I really only wanted one woman." He looked into her eyes. "And I knew I wanted her now. I didn't want to wait any longer."

She clung to him with all her strength, completely driving the breath out of his body. "Philip," she murmured, "we must never again go through what we've experienced during these last few months."

"I agree with that. In future we will never let a weekend go by without sharing at least some of it in bed together, however difficult that is to arrange." He disentangled himself from her embrace. "Now, we must repair your appearance as far as we can and send you back down to your demanding public in the ballroom." He grinned. "But don't forget I'll be waiting up here for you to return."

"OK," she said, and later as she went out, "You can be sure I won't be long, my English lover."

THE END

If you have read this book first, I suggest you try the two earlier books in the Languedoc Trilogy which should give you a more complete understanding of this mysterious and fascinating area. They are:-

The Secret of the Cathars

and

The Legacy of the Templars

A message from the author

I hope you enjoyed this book. If you did you can help me by giving it a review. Reviews are my most powerful marketing device in getting my books noticed. I am unknown to the great majority of readers. I can´t afford to pay for advertisements. But I have something more powerful, and that is a loyal group of readers.
Honest reviews of my books will help to bring them to the attention of other readers. So I would be grateful if you would spend five minutes giving **The Treasure of the Visigoths** a review on Amazon or Kobo.

Thank you very much – Michael Hillier.

The Treasure of the Visigoths is the ninth in the **Adventure, Mystery, Romance Series** of novels created by **Michael Hillier.** To date the others are:-

The Eighth Child (AMR No 1) – Alan Brading witnesses the shooting of his French-born wife in a London street. The police seem to think it is a mistaken terrorist attack. When he recovers from the mental problems caused by the shock, he travels to her home-town in the Loire Valley to try to find the murderer, whom he has seen there. However the local people in Chalons are hostile to his enquiries. Only his wife's younger sister, Jeanette, is willing to help him uncover what happened forty years ago. Together they risk their lives in their pursuit of the truth.

The Mafia Emblem – The Wolf of Hades (AMR No 2) – When Ben Cartwright discovers the decapitated body of his Italian business partner, he finds out that he is in danger of losing his carefully built-up wine importing business. He flies to Naples to try to recover the company, but becomes caught up in the ancient vendetta between two of the oldest families in Southern Italy. His partner's sister, Francesca, doesn't like him. However she joins him in their fight for their lives in the erupting volcanic area of the *Campi Flegraei.*(This one is available free from the author's website.)

Dancing with Spies (AMR No 3) – Caroline Daley is travelling down the Adriatic on a ferry which breaks down and has to limp into the port of Dubrovnik.

However the Yugoslav Civil War is in progress and the beautiful city is under siege from the Serb-led Jugoslav National Army. She becomes caught up in the seething web of violence and espionage among the ancient buildings. Her only hope of escape seems to be to put her trust the arrogant journalist, Ralph Henderson. And are they all in danger? Surely the JNA won´t open fire on the World Heritage Site, will they?

The Secret of the Cathars (AMR No 4) – Philip Sinclair is bequeathed the unusual legacy of the journal of a long-dead Cathar *parfait* by his grandmother, together with the request to go to the chateau of Le Bezu in the French Pyrenees to search for the mysterious treasure of the Cathars. There he meets famous French archaeologist Jacqueline Blontard who is carrying out researches for her next TV series. Together they start looking, unaware that their footsteps are being dogged by an agent of the Catholic Church, a mysterious powerful body in Paris and a group of criminals from Marseilles. Nobody can foresee what their search will unearth. (This is the first book in the Languedoc trilogy)

The Templar Legacy (AMR No 5) – This is the sequel to **The Secret of the Cathars**. Philip returns from a short visit to England to find that Jackie has disappeared. His searches for her lead him, despite considerable personal danger, to Paris and the fascinating little town of Rennes le Chateau, near Carcassonne. He also inadvertently discovers the first clues about the remains left by the Templars when they were wiped out by King Philip II. When Jackie appears again they follow the route started by Philip until they come across the sensational legacy left to the world by the Templars. (This is the second book in the Languedoc trilogy.)

The Discovery of Franco's Bankroll (AMR No 6) – Middle-aged former playboy Sebastian Bishop finds himself marooned on the Costa Blanca without any means of earning a living. His solution is to offer his services as an escort to rich single ladies. Of course he doesn't realise this is going to lead him into deep, deep trouble. After spending the night with a Spanish Condesa, he discovers her strangled body in the morning. He is sure to be charged with her murder. His desperate attempts to prove his innocence involve him with several groups of people trying to find the Nazi stolen hoard shipped to Spain in the last days of the war and threaten his life.

Bank-cor-Rupt (AMR No 7) - Andrew Denbury is summoned to his bank one morning and told they are calling in the overdraft on which his business runs and they will appoint a receiver. What can he do? His wealthy father-in-law hates him and won't help. His wife is only interested in leading an enjoyable social life with her upper class friends. His suppliers are furious because the bank has bounced their cheques. The only person who believes in him is his secretary, Samantha. Somehow Andrew must try to find a way to confound the destroyers of his business. He conceives a plan which may save him, with Samantha's help. But will it work when he puts it into practice?

Network Virus (AMR No 8) - Charlotte Faraday is searching for twelve-year-old girl who has gone missing. Is she the victim of a paedophile gang led by a rich, dissolute local gentleman? To complicate matters, the girl's mother has been raped a few nights earlier in the car park behind the Red Garter Nightclub by a soldier who has escaped back to his regiment which is currently training in Germany. Meanwhile Stafford Paulson, is convinced that the death of Joanne de Billiere is suspicious. They are not helped in their enquiries by creeping corruption in the Devon and Cornwall police force.

Other novels by **Michael Hillier:-**

The Gigabyte Detective

The Property People Series

Go to his website (http://mikehillier.com) for further details on all his writing.

About the author

He has completed fifteen novels to date and there are several others which are in progress. Eleven of the novels have been published and are for sale on various sites, including Amazon, Apple, Barnes and Noble (Nook) and Kobo. The most popular novel to date is **The Secret of the Cathars** which has sold substantially more than ten thousand copies.

He has split his novels into three groups – detective novels, a four-volume historical saga, and the **Adventure/Mystery/Romance** series which has been explained on his website mikehillier.com.

Michael Hillier gets the inspiration for many of his books from family holidays to various beautiful locations in the world. Exploring historic towns and buildings has brought to light a host of untold stories which get his creative juices flowing.

Printed in Great Britain
by Amazon

43929985R00162